Dragon Ops

BY MARI MANCUSI

SCHOLASTIC INC.

ISBN 978-1-338-71909-3

Text copyright © 2020 by Marianne Mancusi Beach. All rights reserved. Published by Scholastic Inc., 557 Broadway, New York, NY 10012, by arrangement with Little, Brown Books for Young Readers, a division of Hachette Book Group, Inc. SCHOLASTIC and associated logos are trademarks and/or registered trademarks of Scholastic Inc.

12 11 10 9 8 7 6 5 4 3   21 22 23 24 25 26

Printed in the U.S.A.   40

First Scholastic printing, January 2021

This book is set in Aeonis LT Pro, Garamond MT Pro, Goudy Text MT Std/Monotype; Alwyn New, Trajan Pro 3/Fontspring

Designed by Tyler Nevins

Prologue

The dragon was bigger than I remembered.

That was my first thought as we crept through the dark temple, entering the beast's inner lair. Atreus lay sleeping on a massive hoard of gold and jewels, his thick, scaly tail coiled around his body like a snake's. He was so large, in fact, he barely fit into the cramped space, and I wondered wildly how he could possibly be comfortable all squashed up like that. A totally ridiculous thought, I know.

But I wasn't exactly thinking straight. Too busy freaking out with fear.

I shot my sister a questioning look, wondering if she noticed the change, too. Had Atreus really grown bigger since we'd seen him last? Were his scales redder now—more blood-like—or was it just a trick of the light? His wings seemed longer, his tail thicker, his talons sharper.

As if evil had gotten an upgrade.

Suddenly, what seemed a totally doable plan down at the bottom of the mountain now seemed a craziness of epic proportion. What had we been thinking? We were just two kids—total noobs. And yet, here we were, hoping to take down the biggest, baddest dragon in all the land by ourselves.

This was so not going to end well.

Atreus stirred, rousing from his slumber. We dove behind a crumbling stone column, desperate to stay out of sight. My heart thudded madly in my chest as his eyes slid open, twin golden crescents shimmering in the darkness. A burst of steam shot from his snout as he yawned lazily, showing off a dark pit of razor-sharp teeth. Sweat dripped down my back. How could we ever hope to defeat such a creature?

But we had no choice. Everything came down to this.

I squeezed my hands into fists, trying to wake my inner hero. To remind myself that here, in this world, I was not Ian Rivera, twelve-year-old gamer geek from Austin, Texas, and real-life total wimp. Here, I was Lord Wildhammer, premier knight of the realm. Lord Wildhammer wouldn't be scared of some dumb old dragon. Lord Wildhammer would be chomping at the bit to slice its ugly head off and save the world.

Lord Wildhammer, it would seem, was a major idiot.

Atreus's eyes began to rove the chamber, and the walls seemed to close in on us, tighter and tighter with his every glance. When he reached our hiding spot, he stopped, his head cocked and his ears pricked.

I froze. Could he see us? Could he sense, somehow, that we were here? My heart beat so hard in my chest I was half convinced it would break a rib. What were we going to do? How were we going to survive this?

My sister reached out, squeezing my hand hard.

"Remember, it's only a game," she whispered.

But the thought wasn't as comforting as it should have been as my eyes fell to the dragon's belly, glowing a deep, dark red as it warmed with deadly fire.

Because this might be a game.

But one wrong move and it would be game over.

This time forever.

Welcome to Dragon Ops!

Dragon Ops is a new kind of theme park, set on a secluded island deep in the South Pacific. Unlike regular theme parks where you simply ride rides and watch shows, at Dragon Ops we want you to become part of the adventure!

Just slip on your AR goggles, zip up your SensSuit™ and step through our front gates—and into another world. Become a character in our story and leave real life's worries far behind. Based on the best-selling computer game *Fields of Fantasy*, Dragon Ops is a fully immersive gaming experience allowing visitors to fight deadly creatures, solve tricky puzzles, and take on epic quests.

Level up and earn valuable treasure that can be exchanged for exciting prizes to take home.

And if you're really good, you might just get a chance to face off against the island's biggest, baddest creature of them all: the dragon Atreus. (*Coming soon* . . .)

Welcome to Dragon Ops.

Just like real life . . . but a lot more fun!

Chapter One

One Day Earlier

"I can't believe we're stuck here for an entire week."

My cousin Derek paced the deck of the old ferry, his steps unsteady as the boat bobbed and swayed under his feet. He stopped at the railing, staring out over the choppy waters of Buccaneer Bay, a scowl creasing his slightly sunburned face. I was pretty sure I hadn't seen the guy crack a smile since his ninth birthday, when he threw a fake turd in Grandma's swimming pool, then sat back to watch the other kids run out screaming.

Too cool for school, my mother always said. Though in Derek's case it seemed like he was too cool for pretty much anything.

"Do you even know what a big deal this is?" I shot back.

"How long the waiting list is going to be once this place finally opens up? And we get to see it first—before anyone else!"

"Congratulations, Ian. You'll be king of the geeks now for sure."

Ugh. Why did I bother? I rolled my eyes and plopped down onto a nearby bench, my legs still jiggering with excitement. He could say what he wanted. I was not going to let him ruin what was sure to be the best week ever in my twelve years on this planet. A full week at Dragon Ops—the world's very first mixed-reality theme park—months before it opened to the public.

When they'd first announced plans to build the park, I'd completely freaked out. After all, no one loved the *Fields of Fantasy* video game—which the experience was based on— more than me. So when I heard there was going to be a mixed-reality version? Where, instead of sitting in front of a computer screen armed with a mouse, you'd actually get to walk around, wielding a sword and doing quests in real life? I seriously couldn't think of anything cooler. And if that made me king of the geeks, I'd wear the crown with pride.

"Hey, kids! We're almost there!"

I whirled around to see Uncle Jack—aka my complete and utter hero—step out onto the front deck of the ferry. Uncle Jack was my mom's younger brother and an amazing computer programmer just like her. He'd worked on all these super-secret gaming projects all over the world and was now consulting for the company that made *Fields of Fantasy*. Which, in my opinion, had to be the best job in the universe.

When I grew up? I wanted to be just like Uncle Jack.

When I first heard he was working for the new game, I'd imagined he might be able to score us some free tickets at some point down the road. I never dreamed he'd suggest to Mom that we should come with him on a last-minute trip to the park before it even opened. The company wanted him to debug a few issues, and Derek's mom was away on a business trip to China, meaning Uncle Jack had to take Derek with him. He figured Lilli and I could come along and keep Derek company while he worked.

Normally I would rather gnaw off my own arm like a wild animal escaping a trap than be stuck spending an entire week entertaining Derek the Drag. But this was Dragon Ops we were talking about here. Babysitting Derek seemed a small price to pay for such a life level-up.

I watched now as Uncle Jack strolled to the front of the boat, leaned against the white-painted bow, and pointed across the bay. "There she is," he announced, his voice rich with pride.

"There what is?" grumped Derek, his eyes narrowing as they followed his father's finger. "There's nothing out there but some deserted island with a beat-up old dock. I thought this was supposed to be a theme park. Where are the roller coasters?"

Uncle Jack snorted, then flashed me a meaningful grin. He knew I understood, even if his own son didn't.

"No roller coasters," he said. "But trust me, you're in for a much bigger thrill."

He beckoned me forward, toward the front of the boat. I took a cautious step in his direction, keeping my distance from the rail. I knew the boat was safe, obviously. But I still wasn't interested in getting too close to the edge. Let's just say it was a long way down. And . . . well, I wasn't the biggest fan of water. Not since back when I was six years old and Derek jokingly pushed me into Grandma's swimming pool, not knowing I couldn't swim. I'd never forget that horrible feeling of water shooting up my nose and down my throat—choking me as I struggled to claw my way back to the surface. Only to find Derek laughing his butt off when I finally did.

Grandma fished me out pretty quick after that. And Derek got grounded for a month. Also, Mom forced me to start swimming lessons the very next day. So it wasn't like I couldn't swim now if I needed to.

I just usually made sure I didn't need to.

But then Uncle Jack pulled out three pairs of game goggles from his bag, and I completely pushed away my fear. Dashing forward, I reached out to grab one, almost knocking over my sister in the process. Lilli was stepping out from the bathroom, looking more than a little green. The ferry, not to mention the choppy waters from the recent storm, clearly did not agree with her.

"Watch where you're going!" she snapped. "Unless you want to get puked on."

"Sorry," I said, giving her an apologetic look. I knew Lilli wasn't exactly thrilled to be here, either—though for a very different reason. While she used to be a total *Fields of Fantasy* superfan like me—and possibly a better player, even (not that I'd ever admit that to her)—she'd recently sworn off games entirely after her dumb online boyfriend, Logan, dumped her for some other girl.

After that, she'd become a total tech hater. No cell phone. No tablets. She only used the family computer when absolutely necessary for homework, and if she wanted the number to the local Chinese takeout she'd look it up in an actual phone book instead of googling it. (I didn't even know they made phone books anymore—until she called up the phone company and had one delivered.)

"Are these safe?" Lilli demanded, squinting at the goggles suspiciously. "What kind of electromagnetic radiation do they give off? I so do not need to come down with brain cancer the month before I start high school."

I sighed, exasperated. Lilli hadn't wanted to come here at all; she claimed she had homework or something and was way too busy. Which was totally ridiculous. I mean, who has homework over spring break? But Mom wasn't going to let me go without her, and so I'd begged and pleaded and begged again until I finally wore her down.

Finally, she'd given in. But, she insisted, that didn't mean she was going to have any fun.

"They're perfectly safe," Uncle Jack assured her, patting her on the shoulder before moving on to me. As he pressed the precious glasses into my hands, he gave me a sly wink. I winked back, knowing exactly what he was thinking. *I* was the only one who understood this—who knew how epic it was going to be.

With trembling fingers, I slipped the goggles over my eyes and plugged the attached earbuds into my ears. My vision blurred and, for a moment, I couldn't see a thing. Then, it all came blazing into focus . . .

. . . and I entered another world.

"Whoa!" I whispered. "No way!"

I'd tried virtual-reality games before. Even a really high-tech one at this fantasy convention I'd dragged my parents to a few years back. It had been cool, but jerky. With muddy colors and blocky textures. Not exactly realistic.

But this! This was on another level entirely.

I looked around, trying to keep my jaw off the floor. We were still on a boat, of course. But it was no longer some boring old ferry. Instead, the goggles had transformed it into an old-fashioned pirate ship, complete with billowy white sails, rotting floorboards, and creaky masts. It had the same layout of the original boat, but skinned with something so much cooler, as if a new layer of paint had been added over real life.

I turned to the island itself. The once-deserted stretch of beach was now crawling with creatures straight out of the *Fields of Fantasy* video game. With shimmering sand dragons slithering across the shoreline and deep-blue sea serpents diving in and out of the water like dolphins. A few mini wyverns flew overhead, swooping into the water to snap up rainbow-colored piranhas just like they did in the regular game. I once spent hours trying to shoot one down as part of a quest chain so I could use the piranha teeth to upgrade my weapon. I wondered if there was a similar quest here. It had been kind of a pain, but the spiked mace I scored in the end was epic.

I shook my head, trying to take it all in. The world was so well rendered, so high-resolution, it looked completely real. So real it felt almost unreal.

It was then that I noticed the people. There had to be half a dozen of them wandering the beach. Some were fighting off sand dragons. Others were fishing. One was trying to lasso a random unicorn, while another was leading a donkey with an oversize pack on its back over to a small tent.

"I thought you said this place wasn't open yet," I said.

"It's not," Uncle Jack replied. He looked strange and slightly blurry through the goggles, as if he wasn't really there. And his voice sounded odd somehow. Like an octave lower and slower than it should have been. "It doesn't open for another three months at least."

"Then who are those people on the beach? Beta testers?"

Of course. They had to have beta testers: professional gamers who combed the world, searching for bugs before the game officially launched. After all, you didn't want to have actual users experiencing too many glitches or your game would be bad-mouthed up and down the internet and die a miserable death before it had a chance to take off.

"Not beta testers," Uncle Jack corrected me. "NPCs."

I stared at him in shock, not sure I heard him right at first. NPCs? As in nonplayer characters? Computer-programmed people? But they looked so real...

"Are you sure?" I asked, squinting.

"Take your goggles off and see," Uncle Jack replied with a laugh.

He reached over to help me pull the goggles up over my head and I blinked my eyes to adjust them back to real-life mode as I looked out onto the beach. Sure enough, it was completely deserted. No dragons. No unicorns. And most importantly, no people.

"Whoa!" I gave a low whistle. "This is unreal!" Then I laughed when I realized my unintentional pun. "Well, you know what I mean."

"The technology behind this whole thing is truly revolutionary," Uncle Jack agreed. His mouth quirked. "Just like real life ... but a lot more fun," he added, quoting the official Dragon Ops slogan.

"There's nothing wrong with real life," Lilli butted in, tossing her goggles onto the bench. Had she even tried them on? She crossed her arms over her chest, and her mouth dipped to a frown.

I sighed. *And ... here we go again.*

"You're absolutely right," Uncle Jack agreed, giving her a reassuring smile. "But sometimes we need an escape from real life, don't you think? Not forever. Just ... like a time-out. A chance to leave it all behind. Have fun. Go on an adventure."

"You can go on adventures in real life."

"Not always safely," I pointed out.

"You don't know *this* is safe, either."

"Trust me, Lilli, the creators of this place see safety as their number one priority. They've taken all the precautions. It's safe. And it's fun." Uncle Jack gave Lilli, then Derek, a pointed look. "Can we at least *try* to have fun this week?"

"Yeah, come on, Lills," I begged. "Just try the goggles. They're really cool!"

"No thank you." She shook her head. "I'm sick, remember? VR will only make it worse." Then she clutched her stomach. "Oh no.... Not again!"

And with that, she ran back inside the boat.

Uncle Jack sighed. "I'll go check on her," he said. "Be

right back. You guys be careful with those, okay? And stay away from the edge of the boat."

"Uh, obviously," I said, trying to ignore the disappointment settling in my stomach. I had been so sure once we got here, away from home, Lilli would start getting excited about this whole thing. After all, she loved *Fields of Fantasy*. Even if she didn't want to admit it. We used to have so much fun playing together. And I thought maybe, if I could just get her here...

Whatever. Lilli could do what she wanted. I was going to make the most of this trip, no matter what. I slipped the goggles back over my head and blinked my eyes, waiting for my vision to clear again....

Suddenly, a shadow seemed to fall over the boat. I looked up, just in time to catch a fiery flash streaking across the sky like a giant comet.

"What—?" I started to ask.

Then I stopped. My mouth clamped shut as I realized exactly what it was. The only thing it could possibly be.

"Whoa," I breathed. "Atreus. That's, like, really Atreus!"

The dragon Atreus was nothing short of legendary in the *Fields of Fantasy* universe. A fabled ancient fire dragon who held the entire land in his evil thrall. All the other creatures in the world—including the other dragons—lived in fear of his wrath. And it was said that if a player were somehow able to defeat him, the game would end. The credits would roll.

And that player would become a video-game legend.

Of course, that never happened. In fact, in all the years since *Fields of Fantasy* had been released, only a few players had ever even leveled high enough to get to his lair, a crystal temple deep within a lava-filled mountain. And though some groups claimed they'd gone and beaten him, they never seemed to have any proof. Which was ridiculous. If you got to the end of the game and were fighting a legendary boss, the first thing you'd do was screenshot it—if not stream the entire fight on Twitch. The cred you'd get from the gaming world would be epic.

A thrill spun down my spine as I watched Atreus now, swimming through the sky, his crimson-colored scales shimmering with flecks of gold in the sunlight. He was so big. And yet, at the same time, so graceful, his massive wings moving up and down with perfectly rhythmic strokes. And when he suddenly dipped his snout and started diving toward our ship at full speed, I instinctively ducked to get out of his way.

"Dude, what is that thing?" I heard Derek ask, his voice sounding odd and far away as Uncle Jack's had earlier. I tried to look over at him, to see if he had put on his goggles and was seeing the dragon, too, but he was so blurry I couldn't really tell.

Whatever. I didn't have time to deal with Derek. Not when a literal dragon was hovering only a foot away from our boat, watching me with curious eyes. I took a step forward, mesmerized by the way his scales caught the light. Like tiny rainbows flickering up and down his sides. His wide, amber-colored eyes locked onto me, and, to my surprise, they seemed almost gentle. Kind. Which didn't make any sense, really, seeing as he was supposed to be the bad guy here. The baddest of bad guys.

Well, hello, tiny human, a low voice rumbled in my ear. *Welcome to Dragon Ops.*

Whoa! I almost fell over backward. Had he just talked? Had the legendary Atreus just talked to me? His mouth hadn't moved—but I could hear his voice as clear as if he were speaking out loud. I swallowed hard, my heart pounding in my chest. *This is crazy!* I thought.

Atreus cocked his head, giving me a questioning look. *Can you not speak?* he asked, sounding almost disappointed.

"Um, I can speak," I blurted out, my voice sounding way too loud and stammering compared to the dragon's smooth, velvety purr.

Atreus's mouth quirked. *Very good,* he said approvingly, as if praising a small child. *And what brings you to my island, tiny human who speaks?*

"Uh, just visiting?" I stammered. "To, uh, play the game?"

The second I said it, I realized how dumb it sounded. The dragon wouldn't know this was a game. For him, this was real life, right? I needed to get into character.

"We're here for an adventure," I corrected quickly.

Ah, yes. Atreus smiled. *There are many adventures to be found on my island. Many—*

His left ear twitched. The dragon frowned, dipping his head in an attempt to scratch it with his hind leg, much like a dog might do. But try as he might, he couldn't seem to reach the itchy spot. He gave a frustrated snort, smoke puffing from his nostrils, as he turned back to me.

Would you mind? he asked, stretching out his long neck in my direction.

Uh...

I stared at Atreus, heart in my throat, my mind racing with what I should do. Should I scratch his ear? But what if it was a trick? Atreus was evil, right? Though this Atreus didn't *seem* very evil...

In the end, I decided to go for it. Mostly because I was extremely curious whether I actually could. After all, he was virtual, right? So would my hand go right through him? I stretched out toward the dragon, not quite able to reach—

"Ian! Look out!"

I yelped in surprise as hands grabbed me from behind, yanking me backward. A moment later the goggles were ripped from my head, sending me crashing back to real-life mode. I whirled around to find Derek standing behind me, giving me an exasperated look.

"What are you doing?" I cried, furious at being interrupted moments before I could touch the dragon.

"Dude, you almost fell off the boat!" he exclaimed. "You were, like, hanging off the edge."

What? A jolt of horror shot through me as I realized he

was right. All this time I'd been keeping my distance from the rail; but when Atreus had shown up, I'd completely forgotten my fear. Had I really almost fallen overboard in real life? I stole a glance down at the gray, choppy water, and my stomach churned along with it.

"Thanks," I said weakly.

Derek rolled his eyes. "Yeah, whatever." He looked down at the goggles in his hands. "What did you see, anyway?" he asked, sounding curious, despite himself. "To me it just looked like some giant metal drone."

"Really?" I raised my eyebrows. "Like a robot?" And here I had assumed Atreus was simply a virtual creature—like a Pokémon you could see through your phone but wasn't actually there in real life.

"I guess." Derek shrugged. "It flew away pretty quick once I grabbed you."

I stared out over the horizon, hoping for another glimpse. But the dragon was gone.

Uncle Jack reemerged on the deck. "What's going on?" he asked, looking from me to Derek suspiciously. "I thought I heard yelling."

I waited for Derek to sell me out—to tell Uncle Jack I'd almost fallen off the boat. But, to my surprise, he just shook his head.

"Nothing," he said. "Ian was just dorking out over some dragon or whatever."

"Not just any dragon," I corrected. "The dragon Atreus. Uncle Jack! I actually saw the dragon Atreus."

My uncle chuckled. "I don't think so," he said.

"No! I swear he was right here!" I protested, pointing off the side of the boat, keeping my distance, this time, from the railing.

Uncle Jack frowned, grabbing the goggles from the bench and placing them over his eyes. He scanned the sky, a super-serious expression on his face.

"Do you see him?" I asked anxiously.

He pulled the goggles from his eyes. "No," he said. "And you couldn't have, either. You must have seen something else and thought it was Atreus."

I shook my head. "No way. I know what Atreus looks like, Uncle Jack! He's been on the cover of every *Fields of Fantasy* game since the beginning. It was him! I swear."

"I'm sorry, Ian, but it couldn't have been," he said.

"Why not?"

My uncle shrugged. "Because there is no Atreus in Dragon Ops."

Chapter Two

"**N**o Atreus?" I stared at my uncle in shock. Atreus was the whole point of *Fields of Fantasy*. The mascot. The big bad. A *Fields of Fantasy* game without Atreus was like Mario without Luigi. Link without Zelda. Pikachu without Ash.

Uncle Jack caught my expression and laughed. "Well, not yet," he corrected. "At least not on opening day."

"Why not?"

"Let's just say they had some issues with the prototype. It was fitted with some highly advanced artificial intelligence software, which was really cool, but they couldn't get it to gel with the rest of the game and they were running out of time. So they shelved the Atreus project temporarily, and will probably add him on as an expansion in a year or two."

I stole a glance at Derek. He shrugged, also looking a little confused. What Uncle Jack said made perfect sense.

Except I'd seen that giant dragon and Derek had seen the drone hovering beside the ship. If it wasn't Atreus, then who was it?

Uncle Jack clapped a hand on my shoulder. "Don't worry. There are plenty of other wonders to be found in Dragon Ops. You'll never miss him."

We got off the ferry just outside what looked like a rustic fishing village, tucked snugly into a small cove. Uncle Jack informed us that this was Dragonshire, the park's official starting zone. It would be a place where people could buy supplies, eat meals, sleep, and learn to interact with their new environment before heading out into the wilds to start their quests.

The actual entrance to the park sat on a small hill just beyond the back edge of town. Towering wooden fences roped with electrical wire met at a central gate made up of two massive iron plates. On the gate was etched the official Dragon Ops seal—a dragon chasing its tail. An *ouroboros*, according to my sister, who, when not on an online strike, liked to look these kinds of things up. Under the seal were three very familiar words, written in Latin: HIC SUNT DRACONES.

Here be dragons.

A chill tripped down my spine as my eyes took in the

words. Words I'd read a thousand times over the years in the regular game before walking through those gates. In fact, I'd seen them so many times I'd almost forgotten they were there. But gazing up at them now, here in real life, they looked bigger and cooler somehow—like the announcement of a grand adventure.

I broke out into a massive grin. This was seriously going to be the best week ever!

I ran to catch up to the others, walking past empty admission turnstiles (which were still being constructed) to enter the town itself. Soon we were walking down winding dirt streets lined with simple wooden houses and empty shops with tin signs hanging off their awnings. A blacksmith, a baker, a pub. Just like in the game, though deserted and empty. At the end of the road stood a large two-story building with a sign that read THE DRAGON'S YAWN over its front door. Uncle Jack pointed to it, saying this was where we'd be sleeping for the week.

"Cool," I said, probably for about the tenth time since we'd left the ferry. But who could blame me? Everything about this place was blowing my mind. It was like everything I'd ever dreamed of, come to life.

"What's so cool about it?" Derek demanded, turning to me with a scowl. He kicked over a small bucket of water at his feet and I had to jump back to avoid getting splashed. "It looks like some cheap movie set put up in two days." He pointed to a small magic shop. "There's not even any doors on the buildings."

"In Dragon Ops things are not always as they seem."

We turned at the sound of an unfamiliar voice, surprised to find a tall, thin Japanese man standing behind us, dressed in a simple white T-shirt and skinny jeans. He was probably in his late forties, with long bleached-blond hair tied back in a ponytail and a pair of black-rimmed glasses. I squinted at him, at first wondering why he looked so familiar. Then realization hit me like a blast of dragon fire.

Hiro Takanama? I mouthed, scarcely able to believe my eyes.

The man grinned, flashing a set of brilliant white teeth. He gave a short bow. "Children!" he exclaimed. "Welcome to Dragon Ops!"

I tried to return the bow—a traditional greeting in Japan—though I felt a little awkward, not sure if I was doing it right. The last thing I wanted to do was disrespect my hero.

Out of the corner of my eye I could see Derek and Lilli shuffling from foot to foot. Clearly they didn't recognize the legend who stood before them: Hiro Takanama, only son of Atsuo Takanama, the creator of the *Fields of Fantasy* video game back in the 1990s.

In other words, the most important man in the video-game industry.

From what I'd read online, Hiro's father, Atsuo, had died

ten years ago, just as the idea for Dragon Ops had started to take shape. Hiro had been a rising game maker himself with a master's in game design and a concentration in artificial intelligence from the University of Southern California. But he'd left the gaming world five years ago after his wife died in a tragic car accident, declaring he had "real-life" things to take care of. Then, two years ago, he made a surprise triumphant return to the company, and the project had been ramping up ever since.

"It's an . . . honor, sir," I stammered, feeling as if my mouth had been stuffed with cotton. "A true honor. Thank you for letting us come here. It's . . . it's . . . I'm so excited!"

"The honor is mine," Hiro replied with an indulgent smile. "Now, shall I show you around?"

I stared at him in disbelief. Wow! The man who made the game was going to show us the park? Best day ever had just gotten even better.

"Uh, do dragons fly?" I sputtered before I could stop myself. *Zero cool, Ian. Total zero cool.* I could hear Derek snickering behind my back.

"Great. And I'll go check in with the team," Uncle Jack proclaimed, giving us a wave. "I'll find you after your tour and get you settled into the hotel."

We said our good-byes to Uncle Jack, then followed Hiro down the street. As we walked, the game designer explained how the starting area was meant to work. Unlike in the rest of Dragon Ops, here in Dragonshire goggles were optional.

If you needed to take a break from the game you could return here and spend time in real-life mode. Grab a burger, buy a souvenir, get a good night's sleep in a real bed—basically unplug until you regained your equilibrium and were ready to go back into the game.

"Some of our beta testers found that being in the game world too long was a bit . . . unsettling," Hiro explained. "It's a very immersive system, and it can play tricks on your mind. We've found for some people it can help to take a break once in a while before going back in."

I tried not to make a face at this. *Noobs.* Once I got into Dragon Ops there would be no breaks. In fact, they'd probably have to drag me kicking and screaming back to real-life mode at the end of the week.

"For example," Hiro continued, "while the Dragon's Yawn Inn looks perfectly medieval from the outside, once you step through the front doors you'll find a modern hotel, complete with flat-screen TVs, electricity, and comfortable beds."

"What about Wi-Fi?" Derek piped up, looking interested for the first time since we'd gotten off the boat.

Hiro nodded. "High-speed Wi-Fi, streaming movies and TV shows. And all sorts of video game consoles if you feel like playing games the old-fashioned way."

Derek looked relieved. I rolled my eyes. Imagine coming to a place like this and wanting to stay in your hotel room to play *Fortnite.*

Hiro caught my look. "I can tell you're a purist," he said with an approving nod. "Do not worry. If you choose, you can wear your goggles twenty-four/seven and leave the real world behind for your entire trip. You can even sleep out in the park. We have small inns and homes with real beds scattered throughout. And we send you out with a good supply of protein bars to sustain you through your journey."

"What about bathrooms? You got bathrooms out there?" Derek asked.

"We were required to install bathrooms, yes. However, to keep with the medieval theme, only the hotel has flush toilets."

Derek slapped me on the back. "Virtual reality crappers! Sounds right up your alley, Ian!" I shoved him away, making a face.

"Just to be clear, this is not simply *virtual* reality we're talking about here at Dragon Ops," Hiro corrected politely. "More of an *augmented* reality—or mixed reality, you might call it."

Lilli gave him a blank look. "Is there a difference?" she asked, sounding curious despite herself. She liked learning about things like this, even if she didn't want to admit it.

"A rather big one, actually," Hiro replied. He tapped his finger to his chin. "Think of it this way. In virtual reality, you're entering an entirely computer-generated world—and all of real life goes away. Which means you can't physically walk around too much—you'd bump into everything. Or walk off a cliff." He snorted. "End up spending the rest of your vacation in the emergency room."

I grimaced, feeling a little sick again as I remembered almost falling off the boat earlier. That would have been a very bad game-over for our adventure before we even really began.

"But with *mixed* reality, you're still in the real world to some extent. You can interact with real objects and buildings like these. You can sleep in a real bed. Eat real food. But there's another layer built on top of reality. A new skin, if you will. Allowing you to fully immerse yourself in the world." His smile broadened. "Just like real life, only a lot more fun!"

"As fun as food poisoning, if you ask me," Derek grumbled.

"But how does the computer know where to put things?" I asked, ignoring Derek.

"The entire island is mapped out to the millimeter," Hiro informed us. "We use GPS coordinates to place our creatures and objects in appropriate spots, according to their profiles. After all, you wouldn't want to see a fish flying through the air or a butterfly swimming underwater. It would destroy the illusion."

"Though it would be kind of cool," I joked.

Hiro smiled. "Let me assure you, Dragon Ops contains plenty of wonders of its own. There is no shortage of 'cool' in this world, as you will soon see."

We reached a small electronic kiosk on the side of the

blacksmith's shop, the technology looking very out of place from the rest of the medieval village. I watched as Hiro pressed a code into the keypad and the machine whirred. A moment later it spit out three pairs of glasses.

Hiro reached down to pull them from the dispenser. They were similar to the ones Uncle Jack had let us try back on the boat, but smaller. More compact. Not much different, on the outside, than regular sunglasses with earbuds. Except for two blinking red sensors imbedded in each side.

"These glasses will serve a few purposes," Hiro explained, handing a pair to each of us. "They will allow you to see and hear the game world, of course. But more importantly, they send electronic pulses to your brain to synchronize it with the game and make everything appear real. Once you're in sync, you'll be able to interact with virtual objects, talk to virtual people, fight virtual monsters." He made a move, as if he were swinging a make-believe sword. "And your brain won't be able to tell the difference between the game and real life. Almost as if you were locked in an extended dream.

"There's even time-compression technology built in," he added. "To allow visitors to maximize their vacation, and experience more of the game in a shorter period of time. Your mind will believe you've been in the game for weeks—when you've only been out there for a few days. Again, much like time passes in a dream. This way you don't waste all your vacation on beginner quests."

"That's incredible!" I cried.

I had read about time-compression technology, but I had no idea anyone had a working version. We had a week to spend here—did that mean it would feel like a month once we were inside the game?

"That's *terrifying*," Lilli corrected. "You're telling me these things reprogram our brains?"

"Only temporarily," Hiro assured her good-naturedly. "Once the goggles are removed, everything goes back to normal—an instant reboot to reality." He grinned. "Don't worry. There have been extensive, long-term studies on both the glasses and the SensSuits. It's all perfectly safe."

"That's what they said about the *Titanic*," Lilli muttered.

"What are SensSuits?" I asked, ignoring Miss Doom and Gloom.

Hiro turned to me. "They're specially constructed bodysuits with microsensors woven into the fabric. The game interacts with these sensors and can recognize when you get hit during a battle and where. Sort of like a very advanced laser tag. The suit will then send signals to your brain, much like the sensors in your goggles, to make it believe the hit really happened."

"It doesn't hurt, does it?"

"Absolutely not," Hiro assured us. "It just feels like a little prickle. As if your foot has fallen asleep. This way the game can feel as real as possible—without actually hurting anyone."

"Wow!" I couldn't wait to get suited up. To get into the game. The more I heard about it, the better it sounded.

"So now," Hiro said, wagging his eyebrows. "Who wants to see the *real* Dragonshire?"

Not surprisingly, I was the first to volunteer.

Chapter Three

With trembling hands, I slid the goggles over my eyes, trying to appear ready for anything, even though I was a little scared. The whole thing about the sensors interacting with your brain—well, that was a bit freaky. And way beyond just wearing VR goggles like I'd done in the past. But Hiro and his team had tested it. They said it was safe. And it had to be, right? Uncle Jack wouldn't have brought us here if it wasn't.

The lenses slid over my eyes and I blinked twice, frowning at how blurry and dark everything looked. I could see shadows swimming in front of me, but I couldn't get anything to come into focus. I squinted and blinked a few more times, trying to adjust my eyes, starting to get a little frustrated.

"Why isn't this—?" I started to say.

A shadow reached toward me. I felt a slight pressure at my ears, as if someone were pushing the goggles into my head. There was a small stinging sensation, an audible beep, and then everything blinked into focus, as if someone had turned on a light switch.

And the world transformed before my eyes.

There was still a town. The pub, the inn, the blacksmith—all the things we'd already seen. But now they looked completely different. No longer props on a hastily constructed movie set, but rather essential pieces of a living, breathing medieval world, rendered to the tiniest detail.

The dirt roads had transformed into cobblestone streets. The run-down shacks were now thatched-roof cottages with wisps of smoke winding from their chimneys. The once-empty shops were packed with adventuring supplies and weapons. And the bakery on the corner overflowed with baskets of crusty breads and those yummy pink-and-purple unicorn cakes I remembered from the original game. Could I finally taste one for real? And would it taste as sweet as I had always imagined it?

But the unicorn cakes weren't the coolest thing. Not by a long shot. Instead, it was all the people who had suddenly appeared, bustling around town. Ladies in long-aproned dresses bartering with the local merchants. Men in tunics and leather breeches arguing as they stumbled out of the pub. A few grubby-faced children raced up and down the streets, yelling loudly as they chased what appeared to be a chicken-like beast covered in purple feathers. There were even a couple of knights in full armor, trotting by on snow-white unicorns in the direction of the inn. As they approached, I found myself leaping back to get out of their way, almost knocking Lilli and Derek over in the process.

"Sorry," I said quickly, holding up my hands in apology as I turned to face them. They were blurry and out of focus, as Derek and Uncle Jack had been on the boat, and it hurt my eyes to look at them. I turned away quickly, feeling a little dizzy.

"So, Ian. What do you think of our little world?"

I looked up at Hiro's voice, surprised to see him in sharp focus, unlike the rest of our group. Sharp focus and dressed completely differently than he had been before I put on the goggles. No longer in skinny jeans and a T-shirt, he was now wearing a crimson-colored robe with a braid of gold around his waist, and he carried a long wooden staff topped by a wooden knob carved into the head of a dragon. He even had a long, snow-white beard, as if he were Saruman from *Lord of the Rings*.

I glanced down at my own outfit, hoping I would be wearing something half as cool. But, it turned out, I was still wearing the SUPER MARIO BROS. 3 T-shirt—with Mario dressed in his raccoon outfit—I'd put on that morning. Weird.

"Sorry," Hiro said apologetically. "You'll have to create your character and put on your SensSuit to get the full effect."

"Oh. Right." I forced a smile to my face, trying to look casual and cool. Which was not easy, under the circumstances. Everything I was seeing, everything I was hearing, was so crazy real it was hard to wrap my head around. I half wanted to rip off the glasses—to get a quick, healthy dose of reality—but I didn't want Hiro to think I was a wimp.

Then something struck me. "There's no smell!"

Hiro nodded. "The eyes and ears are easier to trick than the nose," he said. "But that'll change once we're open to the public. We'll be piping in smells through special filters placed around the park. Everything from baking bread, to smoke from the forge. Maybe even a little horse manure to keep it real."

"That's a little too real, even for me," Lilli joked. I glanced back at her again, hoping she'd put her goggles on. But there she was, still blurry and goggle-free. Which was super boring. I mean, did she really plan to stay in real-life mode all week?

"Speaking of bread," Derek broke in. (Also super boring and goggle-free.) "I'm starving. When are we going to eat?"

"Whenever you like," Hiro replied good-naturedly. "There's a restaurant at the inn. They're not fully open, but our cooks are very good. Just tell them what you want and I'm sure they'll be able to make it."

"Even pizza?" Derek demanded. "'Cause I could really go for some pizza. Do they have pepperoni? What about sausage? Pineapple?"

I frowned, starting to get annoyed. All this reality talk was messing with my experience. I wanted to explore the town. Experience the awesomeness. I had zero time for pizza.

"Can I just look around a little more?" I pleaded. "I'm really not hungry."

At first Hiro looked as if he wanted to argue, but then he gave me an understanding smile. "Very well," he said. "You stay out here while I show your cousin and sister to the restaurant. I'll come back to collect you when I'm finished." He wagged a finger at me. "But stay in the town square. No wandering about. Some of the areas are still under construction and off-limits to guests." He patted me on the back. "But don't worry. You'll get a full tour tomorrow with one of our excellent guides, and I promise you'll get to see everything you want to see and more."

Excitement stirred in my stomach. He was going to let me keep playing! And alone, too! Without my annoying cousin whining about food. Or my sister being boring. "No problem," I declared. "I'll stay right here."

"Excellent. And let me give you these." Hiro reached into his pocket and pulled out a pair of white gloves. "I don't have time to fit you with an entire SensSuit," he apologized. "You'll get one later this afternoon. But these gloves will allow you to interact with the game more fully."

"Awesome. Thanks!" I slid them on my hands.

Hiro smiled again, then gestured for Derek and Lilli to

follow him to the inn. I watched them go, then turned back to the town, wondering where I should start.

Clang! I nearly jumped out of my skin at the sudden sound. I turned to find a large, muscular man hammering a sword into shape at the blacksmith's shop, sparks flying from the forge with each strike to the steel. No, not just a man, I realized after a second look, but an actual troll—with thick ivory tusks protruding from a bulbous red nose, and long, pointed ears with a multitude of piercings. How cool was that?

Also cool? There was a huge wall of weapons at the very back of the shop. Tons of swords, shields, axes, and maces hanging in organized rows. Fascinated, I walked over to get a better look. Would we be assigned weapons like these tomorrow morning before we headed into the game? I could really use an awesome sword for the warrior character I planned to create.

Without thinking, I reached out, pulling a long sword with a ruby-encrusted hilt from the wall, turning it over in my hands. It felt real, heavy even, as if it were actually in my grasp and not just a virtual creation. How was that possible? How was any of this possible?

My stomach twisted uncomfortably. I glanced over at the troll, then back down at the sword. Maybe I *did* need to take a little break. Just a tiny one. What was it Hiro had called it? Rebooting reality? Yeah, just for a moment. Then I could go back to the game. No one would even have to know.

I reached up, ready to pull the goggles off my eyes . . .

But there were no goggles.

Huh? I tried again, but still felt nothing there. My heart stuttered in my chest. Where were the goggles? I knew I was wearing goggles—otherwise I wouldn't be seeing any of this. Unless . . .

What if the goggles were tricking my brain into thinking there were no goggles?

Okay, this was so messed up.

I tried again, nearly poking myself in the eye. Panic rose inside me and I flailed, dropping the sword. It fell to the ground with a loud clank.

"What was that? Who's there?"

I looked up, heart now in my throat. The blacksmith troll had left his forge and was now stomping in my direction, an angry scowl slashing across his tusked face.

Uh-oh.

I shrank back in terror as he reached me. He towered over me, his eyes falling to the sword now lying on the ground. His face twisted.

"You thieving rat! You dare try to steal from me?"

I stumbled backward, holding up my hands in surrender. "Look. I'm sorry. I didn't mean to—"

"You know what we do to thieves here in Dragonshire?" he growled, ripping another sword from the wall and raising it threateningly in my direction.

"Um…" I squeaked. "You give them a fair trial and a lawyer to plead their case?"

The troll's mouth curled, revealing a nasty set of blackened teeth. "We make sure they never steal again."

Chapter Four

I cringed, my eyes locked on the sword above me; the troll, ready to strike.

"Um, don't you think that's a bit harsh?" I squeaked. "I mean, first offense and all that?"

He lunged at me, his blade singing a high-pitched whine as it bit through the air. I screamed, with barely enough time to duck as it came crashing down, slicing across the space where my head had just been. I threw myself on my hands and knees, crawling desperately toward the back door of the shop, then leapt up and ran down the street. My hands reached for my face, once again feeling for the goggles. I knew they had to be there—even if my brain refused to believe it.

It's just a game, I told my stupid brain. *It's just a silly game.*

From behind me I could hear the troll's screech of rage, followed by heavy footsteps pounding against the cobblestones. I picked up the pace, zagging left down a narrow alleyway, then crossing a wooden bridge and ducking under a low-hanging gate. My lungs burned in protest—I really wasn't much of a runner. And I was pretty sure he was gaining on me.

If only I hadn't dropped the sword in the shop! Maybe I could have tried to fight him. Of course he was probably way too powerful. Merchants like him were usually pretty high level in these types of games—to prevent players from simply massacring them and stealing their wares.

Also, I realized suddenly, I didn't actually know how to fight with a sword in real life. Or as real as this was, anyway. And I couldn't just button-mash the guy to death like you did in a regular game when you had no idea how to play.

This game was going to be a lot harder than I thought....

Totally winded, I pushed on, afraid to look behind me to see if he was still there. Rounding a corner, I dug my heels into the dirt, stopping short.

Uh-oh.

The street I had turned down dead-ended a few feet in front of me at a tall wooden fence that was too high to climb. My gaze darted from left to right as I tried to figure out a Plan B. Could I retrace my steps before the troll caught up? Hide somewhere until he gave up and went back to the shop? In desperation, I tried a few doors to nearby houses. But they were all locked.

What to do? What to do?

The troll burst into the alleyway, still brandishing his

sword. His eyes lit up as they fell upon me. "There you are, you thieving rat!" he growled, taking a menacing step forward. "You thought you'd get away from me?"

I backed up until I hit the fence. There was nowhere else to go.

"Please!" I begged, frightened tears streaming down my face. "Please don't kill me! I didn't mean to steal the sword and—"

The troll lunged at me. I screamed and ducked, instinctively putting my hands over my head.

But it did no good.

His weapon crashed down and everything went black.

Chapter Five

I stared at the golden words scrolling across my field of vision, cutting through the blackness. My heart was still in my throat and I could barely breathe, never mind understand what they were asking. I blinked a few times, trying to regain my senses.

Then I started to laugh.

Of course. I wasn't dead for real. This was just a game. I was totally fine—and had been the whole time. There was no real troll. There was no real sword. I had been running around like a *Minecraft* zombie on a chicken through an empty theme park. My *character* had died, not me.

Relief washed over me in waves, though I still felt a little faint. Reaching out, I selected REVIVE from the floating menu. The words swirled out of focus, then the blackness retreated and I found myself back in the alleyway. The troll, thankfully, was nowhere to be found. I slid down the fence until I was hugging my knees, needing to feel something solid and real.

"That was amazing," I found myself saying, though there was no one there to hear me. I clenched my hands together to try to stop them from shaking. Amazing—and yet super terrifying at the same time. I still felt a little sick to my stomach.

"Amazing, huh?"

I looked up. A girl around my own age was standing a few feet away, seeming to have come out of nowhere. She had curly fluorescent-pink hair that tumbled down her back in waves, and wore a long black robe trimmed with glowing, multifaceted jewels.

She looked me up and down, her glossy lips lifted in a small smile. "I must say, you didn't last very long," she observed. Her voice was light and teasing.

"Dude, it's my first day," I shot back, a little defensive. But still! Did she really need to call me out like that? (Even if she wasn't wrong.)

"Ah!" Her eyes were very large—like an anime character's—and sparkled as if there was glitter mixed into the pupils. "You must be one of our visitors!" She bobbed her head in a quick bow. "I heard you were coming this week. Welcome to Dragonshire," she said. "Just like real life, but a lot more . . . fun."

I raised an eyebrow. Did I detect a note of sarcasm in her voice? Who was this girl, anyway? A beta tester, maybe? An employee's kid?

"Thanks," I said, scrambling to my feet and dusting myself off. "I'm, uh, Ian."

"You can call me Ikumi," she replied. "And you really shouldn't steal from the merchants here. It never ends well."

"I noticed," I muttered, rubbing my head where the sword had crashed down on top of it. It didn't hurt, exactly. But it still felt a little weird. A slight throb at my temples. Like my brain believed it should hurt, so it almost did.

Seriously, this game was way too real for comfort.

Ikumi reached into a canvas bag she had tied to her waist, pulling out a small vial of red liquid. "Here," she said. "Drink this. It'll make you feel better."

I took the vial, trying to ignore the whole "don't take drinks from strangers" thing my mom had drilled into my head since I was a kid, and turned it over in my hands. Was it supposed to be some kind of in-game healing potion? Though, if so, how could it help a real-life hurt?

But then my brain only thought I was hurt, right? So if I drank this? It might believe I was better. Which would make me feel real-life better? I guess?

This game was super confusing.

I pulled off the stopper. "Looks like Gatorade."

She nodded. "Originally the healing potions were made of fermented teas and mushrooms, but too many of the American beta testers complained. So they changed their recipe."

I took a tentative sip of the potion. Thankfully, it did taste more like Gatorade than moldy tea. I tipped my head and chugged the rest of it. "Thanks," I said, handing the vial back to Ikumi, who slipped it into her bag.

"The pleasure is mine," she replied. "Anything for a fellow Mario fan." She pointed to my T-shirt and smiled. "*Super Mario Bros. 3* is my favorite of the originals."

"Really?" I asked, surprised. "Most people would say part two."

Ikumi wrinkled her nose in distaste. "Part two isn't even a real Mario game! Did you know they released an entirely different *Mario Two* in Japan? But Americans thought it was too hard." Her eyes danced in amusement. "So they skinned another Japanese game—*Doki Doki Panic*—with Mario characters to ship overseas for the gaijin." She grinned at the Japanese word for *foreigner*, making me wonder if she was Japanese herself. It was impossible to tell by looking at her game character, and suddenly I was really curious to know what she looked like in real life.

"Hey!" I protested holding up my hands. "I've played the original *Mario Two*, just so you know. And I beat it, too." In fact, my mom had built an emulator that ran all the old video games she used to play as a kid, and I'd spent hours—okay, maybe days—trying them all out.

"Really?" Ikumi asked, looking genuinely impressed. "Most people don't play old games anymore. They want the newest, the flashiest, the best graphics...."

"Not me," I declared. "I can appreciate a new game.... Like this one, of course," I added, looking around. I'd almost forgotten, for a moment, that I was still in a game. "But there's something about those old games. They're simple, but fun."

"Yes," she agreed, smiling at me. "*Not* like real life...but a lot *more* fun!" she quipped.

I laughed. Who was this girl, anyway? I didn't know anyone my age who liked the older games. In fact, most people, like Derek, made fun of me for playing them, even going so far as to nickname me Eight-Bit Ian.

Not that I cared. I mean, not really...

But this girl...she wasn't a dork. In fact, she seemed really cool. Though she might not really be my age, I suddenly realized with dismay. For all I knew she was an adult, playing a kid character. In fact, she might not even be a girl at all....

I suddenly really wished I could take off my goggles to find out.

Since I couldn't, I asked, "So, uh, you play this game often?"

"Oh yes," she said, her smile fading at the edges. "All the time, actually."

She didn't sound too happy about it. In fact, if anything she looked a little sad. Maybe she was one of the programmers' kids? I hadn't considered the fact that if you worked here and had kids you'd have to drag them along. And while at first, that might be cool, I bet it got boring after a while, being stuck on a practically empty island all day while your parents worked. Even if it was an island with the best video game ever on it.

"I just got here today," I told her. "My sister and cousin are here, too. But they're not really into video games. My sister used to be, but not now. Anyway, we're supposed to go out into the park tomorrow. You want to join our party?"

She raised her eyebrows. "You want me to play with you?"

"Why not? You're probably really good." I gave a small snort. "And, as you could probably tell from my troll fight? I'm pretty awful."

She laughed. And for a moment, I really thought she was going to say yes. But in the end, she shook her head. "Sorry," she said. "But I can't."

"Oh. Okay," I replied, disappointment washing over me

before I could stop it. Of course she wouldn't want to join us. She probably had way more important things to do than hang out with a bunch of noobs.

"Not that I don't want to!" she corrected quickly, seeing my face. "It's just... I'm not supposed to play with other guests."

"What? Why not?"

She opened her mouth to speak. Then her eyes seemed to catch something behind me. A look of panic crossed her face.

"There you are!" interrupted a familiar voice.

I jumped a mile as a hand clamped down on my shoulder, turning me around. I felt a burning pulse at my temples as my goggles were ripped from my head and dropped into my hands. I almost fell over as everything snapped back to real-life mode.

"Urgh," I gurgled, staggering on shaky legs. Everything suddenly looked too bright and too spinny—as if I'd just gotten off the teacup ride. Closing my eyes, I tried to reset myself.

But it was no use. I leaned over and threw up.

"Are you all right?"

I felt a warm hand at my back. I opened my eyes to find Uncle Jack peering at me with concern. I gave a weak nod, extremely embarrassed about the puking. The last thing I wanted was for him to think I couldn't hack it here.

"Totally fine," I chirped. "Just…a little dizzy."

"That's normal. Take a deep breath. You'll be okay."

I nodded, doing as he instructed. A moment later the dizziness began to fade and the landscape went back to non-spin mode. I let out a breath of relief.

It was then that I remembered Ikumi. Oh man, had she watched me puke my guts out? So embarrassing. I turned around so I could apologize for being so gross, but she wasn't there. The alleyway was empty.

"Wait, where'd she go?" I asked.

Uncle Jack cocked his head. "Where did *who* go?"

"There was a girl." I scrunched up my eyebrows. "With pink hair. She was standing right there!" How could she have gotten past us? Had she gone into one of the houses? But the doors had all been locked.…

Uncle Jack burst out laughing.

I frowned. "What?"

"First Atreus. Then a girl with pink hair." His eyes danced with amusement. "I love your imagination, kid."

"No! You don't understand," I protested, turning in a circle now. The girl had to be somewhere. "She wasn't a game character. She was real. Like, maybe a beta tester or something?"

"There are no beta testers out today," Uncle Jack said. "The last boat left this morning, and the new arrivals don't come till next week."

"Okay, maybe not a beta tester then," I corrected. "Someone's daughter? Do any of the employees have kids here?"

Uncle Jack shrugged. "I don't think so...It'd be kind of awful if they did. So much construction. No schools..."

"Yeah." I stared at the spot where Ikumi had just stood. This didn't make any sense. Unless...

A horrifying thought struck me. What if she'd never really been there at all? What if she was virtual, like the people in town and those on the beach? They'd looked real, too....

But no. I shook my head. She was different. She didn't blend into the game as they did. She didn't fit into the world. The way she talked. She was definitely not a game character.

But then who was she?

"There he is!" a deep voice broke into my troubled thoughts. "Didn't I tell you to stay in town?"

I whirled around to see Hiro, now standing behind me, back in his T-shirt and skinny jeans, his arms crossed over his chest.

"Sorry," I apologized. "I really meant to. But then I accidentally dropped this sword and the blacksmith thought I was trying to steal it. He started chasing me and—"

I broke off, realizing Hiro was laughing. "What?" I asked, a little offended.

"I'm just enjoying your reaction to my game," he replied,

plucking the glasses out of my hands and pocketing them. "You liked it then?"

"It was pretty amazing," I agreed. "But a little crazy, too. Like, I couldn't feel my goggles when I was inside, so I couldn't take them off."

Hiro nodded approvingly. "That's good," he said. "It means your brain is acclimating to the game environment. You must be a natural!"

I smiled weakly, trying to take that as a compliment. But I was still a little freaked out about the whole thing. Which was funny since I had just told Hiro, not thirty minutes ago, that I would never want to take the goggles off. Which I still didn't. But the fact that I *couldn't*...

Hiro caught my expression. "Don't worry," he said. "Your guide will be able to remove the goggles in case of an emergency. But I promise, you'll be perfectly fine. We've tested the system extensively. Every possible danger has been taken into account."

"Well, that's good..." I said, trying to shove the unease down my throat. I was being ridiculous. Of course they'd tested it! They'd never get insurance to open if they hadn't.

Uncle Jack clapped me on the back. "There's no pressure, Ian," he assured me. "If you've changed your mind about playing, that's perfectly okay. You can just hang out in the hotel, watch Netflix, explore the beach—whatever you like. It's all up to you."

I followed his gaze up, until my eyes rested on the iron gates high on the hill. To the dragon chasing its tail. My heart stuttered in my chest. The town itself had been so real. What wonders were out there, in the real game?

And how could I possibly miss finding out?

Hiro turned to me, his dark eyes piercing my own. "So what do you say, Ian?" he asked in a solemn voice. "Do you still want to play my game?"

"Are you kidding?" I asked. "Atreus himself couldn't keep me away."

Chapter Six

The next morning, we found ourselves standing outside the massive iron gates that led into the park, shivering a little in the crisp morning air. The hotel alarm had woken us bright and early, and the sun was barely peeking over the horizon. We crawled out of bed like zombies, sleepily slipping into our new SensSuits before heading over to the rendezvous point where our guide was meeting us to take us inside.

The SensSuit was cool but a little itchy, which made me squirm. Supposedly the suits had nanosensors woven into the fabric and had to be flush against our skin to work properly. Derek kept complaining about how ugly they were. And while he wasn't wrong—it was kind of like a Spider-Man costume without the cool spider on the chest—it wasn't as if we were entering a fashion show or something. Besides,

Hiro had assured us, we wouldn't be able to see them once we put on our goggles and took on our new roles.

Lilli yawned, looking around the clearing. "Where's Lady Farah?" she asked. "She was supposed to be here ten minutes ago."

We'd been introduced to our illustrious guide, Lady Farah, after dinner the night before through a short film. According to the video, Lady Farah was the first female knight in Dragonshire. She was beautiful, dashing, brave—

And also very late.

I stared down at the silent town below, wondering what it would look like if we had our goggles on. Was the troll back? "I'm sure she has a reason...."

"It's not like she could have gotten stuck in a Starbucks line," Lilli pointed out.

"Who cares?" Derek butted in. "She's not here. I'm going back to—"

"Hey, kids. Sorry I'm late."

We turned to see a short, grungy man with an unkempt beard and thick glasses huffing and puffing as he walked up the hill to join us. He was wearing ripped blue jeans and a T-shirt that read COOL STORY, BRO, NEEDS MORE DRAGONS rather than a SensSuit like the rest of us. A bunch of game goggles hung from cords around his neck and he held a tablet in his hands.

"Are you Lady Farah?" Lilli asked, narrowing her eyes. "'Cause, no offense, in the video you looked a lot more..."

"Ladylike?" Derek suggested.

"Maybe he transforms into a lady once you put on the goggles," I whispered.

But our guide shook his head. "Sorry. Farah couldn't make it. She had some bad barbeque last night and has been puking her guts out ever since. I'm Eugene. I'll be filling in."

We exchanged glances. "Poor Farah," my sister exclaimed, probably remembering her own seasickness the day before.

"Poor Farah?" Eugene sputtered. "Poor Farah gets to spend all day in bed binge-watching *The Bachelor*. Meanwhile I've got to abandon my entire day's work to take you twerps on a tour." He scowled. "Do you have any idea how much I have on my plate today? The park opens in three months. I've got fires to put out all over the place."

"So wait," I interjected. "You're not a guide?"

"A guide?" He let out a large belch, then puffed out his chest. "I'm a programmer, kid. A keyboard cowboy. Half of the stuff you'll see out here today? My creations." He rolled his eyes. "So no. I'm not a *guide*."

"But you're going to guide us . . ." Lilli concluded, giving him a doubtful once-over.

"Believe me, I don't like it any more than you do," he said. "But hey! At least you won't be subjected to all that LARP garbage the real guides make you do."

My heart sank. One of the coolest things I'd read about Dragon Ops was how the guides really got into their roles, never breaking character no matter what you asked them, except in a serious emergency. They called it LARPing, which stood for Live Action Role Playing. I'd been really looking forward to it.

I'd even come up with a cool backstory the night before, when they sat us down at the computer terminals so we could create our game characters and assign them skill points. I was going to play a new version of Lord Wildhammer, the warrior I played in the regular game. Lord Wildhammer had been an orphan, abandoned on a doorstep in Dragonshire as a baby. Until one day a mysterious old man with wizened blue eyes and a long gray beard plucked him off the streets and told him he was no ordinary boy. That he was the chosen one. The one who would save everyone from the evil dragon Atreus and—

"Sounds good to me," Derek chimed in predictably. "Can we get this over with?"

"Absolutely," Eugene replied. "Let's lock and load."

He walked over to each of us, handing us our goggles and instructing us to put them on. Once we did, he locked them into place. My heart skittered as I felt the now-familiar pulse of heat at my temples, followed by the single beep at my ears as the sensors calibrated with my brain waves.

This was it. There was no turning back now.

I raised my head, peering out from my goggles. The massive Dragon Ops gates were still there, of course. Still as large and looming as before. But now the golden Latin words seemed to shimmer with fire, and the dragon etching had transformed into an actual dragon, swimming through the sky, chasing its tail. As I watched, it turned its head to look at me, giving me a playful wink. Wow.

Suddenly I didn't care about the guide getting sick. The lack of role playing. I was about to see Dragon Ops with my own eyes. Finally!

Eugene walked over to the entrance, opening a small mechanical panel and submitting to a retina scan to verify his identity. Once confirmed, the gates began to creak open and music swelled in my ears. The hairs on the back of my neck stood on end. It was the Dragon Ops theme song!

"All right, kids." Eugene beckoned us over, a smug smile on his face. "Let's rock and roll."

Chapter Seven

I hadn't known exactly what to expect when I stepped through the Dragon Ops gates. I mean, I knew it was going to be awesome. Probably larger-than-life. Over-saturated color, maybe—like an Instagram filter gone wild.

What I hadn't expected was how...familiar...it would all look.

"Wait a second," I said, my jaw dropping in amazement. "Is this the Edelweiss Forest?"

Even as I asked the question, I knew the answer. The legendary Edelweiss Forest, which served as the official starting zone in the regular game, was now spread out before us in all directions. There were the same towering trees with their violet leaves. The same windy trails, half-overgrown with thick vegetation. I even spotted the same small stream winding through the forest, splashing with crystal-clear water. Follow that stream, I knew, and you'd come to a tiny cave, where sometimes a rare dog-size dragon would spawn. Slay him and you'd get a killer starter weapon.

There were animals, too, roaming around everywhere. Two-headed bunnies, pink furry squirrels. Even the legendary green-scaled mini dragons (affectionately known as dragonbites) snuffing through dense foliage, foraging for food. I watched, mesmerized, as one of the dragonbites blasted a dandelion with a mini fireball, then plucked it from its stem once it was good and toasted. He swallowed it down, then smacked his lips, as if to say, *Yum!* and then flew to the next flower.

This was unbelievable. The same land I'd explored for years with a mouse and keyboard now stretched out before me in real life. Well, maybe not *real* life, but definitely the next best thing. I looked up to find the legendary *Fields of Fantasy* twin suns shining down from the sky, scattering rays of light across the landscape.

"Holy giant narwhal horns!" Lilli murmured under her breath, surprising me with one of her favorite exclamations from back when we used to game together. We'd come up with a billion of these after Mom caught us using real-life curse words one day during a really difficult boss fight and threatened to take away the game if we didn't clean up our act. For a while we'd keep challenging each other, making each expression crazier and sillier than the last. But then Lilli quit the game. And I hadn't heard her make one up since.

"I know, right?" I turned to look at her, and a grin spread across my face. Gone was her ugly SensSuit, and in its place she wore a deep-blue robe with ancient golden symbols embroidered at the wrists and hemline. She looked different, too. Her short brown hair was now hanging down her back in a complicated tangle of rainbow-colored braids, and her brown eyes were now bright purple, glowing and sparkling as Ikumi's had. As if they were mixed with stardust.

"You look awesome, Lills!" I exclaimed.

She glanced down at her outfit and shrugged. "I guess," she said reluctantly. Pulling up the hem of her robe, she examined her feet, which were covered in golden high-heeled boots. "Not very practical, though. Like, what if I have to run?"

"Well, it's not like you're really wearing those," I reminded her. "You're still wearing Skechers in real life, right?"

"Oh. Right. I forgot." She dropped her robe and scrunched up her face. "This is so weird."

"And . . . super awesome?" I asked hopefully.

"Let's not go crazy," she said, turning away.

My shoulders slumped. Couldn't she see how amazing this all was? What an incredible opportunity it was to be here? Sure, I knew she only came because I'd begged her. But I really thought once she got here, she'd start getting excited. After all, she used to love *Fields of Fantasy* as much as I did. If not more!

"I like that you're playing a mage again," I tried, not

willing to give up on her just yet. "Did you name her Adorah?" Back when Lilli played *Fields of Fantasy*, she'd had this amazing fire mage called Adorah whose DPS (damage per second) was through the roof. She'd saved my butt countless times, and it was never the same once she quit.

She shrugged. "Yeah. Mage Adorah. Though obviously not the same level as the old one. Kind of annoying the game won't let us use the characters we already leveled online."

"Totally," I agreed. "If I could have brought the real Lord Wildhammer here . . ."

It was then that I realized that I must be in character, too. Running over to the nearby stream, I peered down at my reflection. Sure enough, my skinny twelve-year-old body had disappeared. And in its place? A true warrior with broad shoulders and big muscles that would have taken years to build the old-fashioned way at the gym. Nice!

"Lord Wildhammer, Savior of the Realm," I proclaimed, raising my fist at the stream. "At your service!"

"You've got to be freaking kidding me," Derek muttered.

I turned to check out my cousin's new look, totally expecting to find some big, bulky barbarian type with insta-muscles and a mountain-man beard. Maybe even an orc or a troll or something else really nasty looking, wielding an ax as big as his head. But instead, Derek appeared to be human, dressed in a simple tunic and tights. And not much taller than he was in real life.

Also, instead of an oversize ax? He was carrying a harp.

"Wait," I said, raising an eyebrow. "Are you playing a bard?"

Bards were like the in-game joke of *Fields of Fantasy*. They were the absolute most useless character class, so hardly anyone played them. For one, they didn't have much damage dealing magic, and they weren't even allowed to use actual weapons. All they could do was buff the party by playing music on the sidelines during a fight.

"Why on earth would you choose a bard?" I asked, laughing.

Derek's frown deepened. "I'm not a gamer nerd, okay?" he ground out. "I didn't know what to pick. I just ... figured I like music or whatever."

"Oh," I said, trying to control my laughter. "That's cool." Suddenly I felt bad for making fun of him. "And hey, a good bard can really save a party! You can cast buffs on us to make us do more damage or protect us ..."

"I'll buff you, all right. Right upside the head if you keep talking nerd to me," Derek growled. He turned to Eugene. "Can we get this over with, please?"

"I thought you'd never ask," Eugene declared. He looked down at his tablet, which now looked more like a spell book than an iPad. He still wore jeans and a T-shirt, though— totally out of place in this new land. "The first quest is over there." He pointed to a dirt path winding up a small hill and into the trees. "Knock yourselves out."

Chapter Eight

We headed down the path, me in the lead, Derek and Lilli trudging reluctantly behind. At the top of the hill, the trees thinned, revealing a small farm with a thatched-roof cottage in the middle of a field of carrots, pumpkins, and corn. A wispy curl of smoke drifted from the cottage's chimney, and I could hear birds chirping in the trees nearby. A few two-headed bunnies hopped through the field, helping themselves to an all-you-can-eat veggie buffet.

But it wasn't the farm or the bunnies that got my heart thumping hard in my chest. It was the short, stubby man with messy brown hair and a wild beard who we found leaning against a nearby tree. He was dressed in a farmer's tunic and britches and was chewing on a stalk of wheat. And spinning above his head? A white star. Exactly like the ones you'd find above every quest giver in the regular game.

Sweet! Our first quest!

I dashed over to the man, eager to get started. But when I reached him, I stopped, unsure what to do. In the game, I would have simply hovered my mouse over a quest giver, then clicked on them. What was the equivalent here? Poking him in the belly? After my experience with the troll blacksmith I didn't want to make the wrong move.

"Um, hello?" I tried.

But the man didn't answer. He just stared off into the distance. I waved my hands in front of his face. "Hello? Do you have a quest for us?"

Derek snorted. "Maybe he doesn't speak geek."

"Let me try," Lilli interjected before I could respond with a witty comeback. (Which was a good thing, since I had no witty comeback.) She reached out and poked the farmer in the arm. Twice—like a double mouse click.

The man burst to life, his blank expression transforming into a look of pure terror. It was a bit jarring, given how bored he had looked a moment before, but whatever. We'd figured it out! And now we'd get a quest!

"Brave adventurers!" he cried. "I am so glad you have come! I am in desperate need of your help!"

I shot my sister a grin. "Nice!"

She shrugged, but I could tell she was pleased at having figured it out. I turned back to the quest giver, excitement rumbling in my stomach. What would he want us to do?

Slay a mighty dragon? Rescue a damsel or dude in distress? Steal treasure from a band of cutthroat pirates? Or maybe—

"Trap ten rats."

Wait, what?

I cocked my head. "What did he just say?"

Eugene looked up from his spell book a few feet away. "His house has been overrun by vermin," he stated in a bored voice. "He wants you to trap ten rats and bring them back to him. If you do this, he'll give you a reward."

Derek groaned. "Seriously?"

I nodded grimly. Role playing games like *Fields of Fantasy* were famous for forcing low-level characters to begin their grand, save-the-world adventures by exterminating pests in someone's basement. In fact, it had become such a well-known in-game joke that now designers often included such quests on purpose.

But while this wasn't such a big deal when you were sitting at home on your computer with all the time in the world, when you only had a week to beat the best game ever, it felt like a big waste of time. What if we spent all our vacation on low-level stuff like catching rats and never got to see any of the cool, epic content later in the game?

It was then that I remembered what Hiro had said about the time compression technology they used. Our vacation was a week, but it might feel like a month while inside the game.

Giving us plenty of time for rat catching.

"Come on," I said. "It'll help us level up. We can't exactly fight dragons while we're still level one, now can we?"

"Fine," Lilli said, taking a step toward the cottage's front porch. "Let's get this over with."

Derek, on the other hand, planted himself down on a nearby stump. I gave him a questioning look.

"Are you coming?" I asked.

He smirked. "Why? I'm just a useless bard, remember?" He pulled out his harp and began strumming a tune. *"Buffing, buffing—I'm just good for buffing! And eating turkey and stuffing!"* he sang tunelessly.

I raked a hand through my hair in frustration. "We really need everyone to play!" I protested. "That's sort of the whole point of forming a party...."

Derek changed his tune. *"Party! Party! Ian's kind of farty!"*

I squeezed my hands into fists, my face flushing with frustration. Was he really going to be like this the entire trip? I was about to tell him to just go back to town and watch TV for the next week, when Lilli put a hand on my arm.

"Come on," she said, dragging me toward the cottage. "It's just trapping rats. We'll be fine without him."

I groaned, knowing she was just trying to make me feel better. In reality, she wanted to be doing this about as much as Derek did. In fact, no one else really wanted to be here— which was starting to make me not want to be here, either. Which was so unfair! I had been waiting for this moment my entire life. An epic adventure. The experience of a lifetime! And now I had a guide who didn't want to guide, a cousin who was more into fart jokes than fighting, and a sister who was looking at me as if I was a loser with no friends.

Oh, and rats that needed catching. Awesome.

I reluctantly followed Lilli to the cottage, stepping onto the sagging front porch, which creaked and groaned under our weight. The whole place, in fact, looked as if it were about to fall in on itself. I wondered, for a moment, what it would look like if I could remove my goggles.

But I couldn't remove my goggles. Just like back at Dragonshire, they'd completely vanished from my face. At least as far as my mind was concerned. I wondered if it was the same for Lilli, but didn't want to freak her out if she hadn't noticed. At this point, I was just glad she was questing with me. Even if it was only out of pity.

And so I followed her through the battered front door . . .

And into total blackness.

I squinted, trying to look around. But it was so dark inside I could barely see my hands in front of my face. Okay, not freaky at all. I took another step forward, feeling my way around, trying to ignore the panicky feeling rising in my throat.

It's just dark, I scolded myself. *No big deal. You're in the dark every night at bedtime.*

It was then that my ears caught a scurrying sound. Tiny claws scraping against wood.

Rats. Many, many rats by the sound of it.

I drew in breath, trying to remind myself that this was just a silly beginner quest. They weren't monsters, just vermin, and they were probably more scared of me than I was of them. But my brain remained unconvinced. After all, while clicking rats on a computer screen might feel like brainless busywork, facing off with real-life, bald-tailed, beady-eyed creatures in a pitch-black house was something else entirely.

"Argh!" Lilli screeched, almost knocking me over as she jumped to the side. "Something crawled over my foot!"

"Quick!" I cried. "Put down a trap!"

"What traps? Where are they?"

Good question. I fumbled around until my fingers brushed against something metal. "Hang on! I think I found a lamp or something." I flicked a switch and the room flooded with a dim golden glow. Unfortunately it also caused the rats to scatter and disappear into little holes in the floorboards and walls until we were alone again.

Lilli sighed. "What now?"

I looked around, thinking hard. The cottage was practically empty, furnished only with a kitchen table (complete with a lantern and a bunch of rattraps) and a few chairs. A dirty, old throw rug covered part of the floor, and a wooden cot piled with tattered blankets had been pushed up against the far wall. There was a fireplace, too, but the fire had gone out, leaving only a few smoldering ashes.

There was only one thing to do. I plucked a trap off

the table and set it on the floor. Lilli followed my lead, and together we managed to set all the traps, with some in every corner of the small room.

"Now I guess we leave and come back?" Lilli suggested, looking around the room. "They're not going to come out while we're standing here with the lights on, right?"

"Right." I turned and headed to the door. Lilli followed after turning off the lantern, plunging the room back into darkness. As I exited the cottage I could hear the squeaking sounds start up again. Nice. Shouldn't take long to fill those traps. I wondered how many experience points we would get for doing it. Would it be enough to level up?

Outside, we found Derek, who had stopped playing his music and had started pestering Eugene instead. I watched as our guide held up his hands in a helpless gesture and our cousin groaned in exasperation.

"What's going on?" I asked.

"I'm trying to get him to show us something good," Derek replied. "If we're going to be stuck here all day, I want to see some cool content. Not waste time with dumb, newbie rat quests."

"We have to level up first," I reminded him. "That's how games work."

"Which is totally bogus," Eugene broke in before Derek could reply.

I frowned. "What?"

"These games," he said, scratching at his nose. "They all

start out so boring. And all the good stuff? Half of the play-ers who come here will never be able to level high enough to see it—even with the time-compression thing. All this work I put into the end-game bosses like Atreus will be for nothing."

"Atreus?" I repeated, surprised. "My uncle said you didn't have an Atreus."

"Are you kidding? Of course we have an Atreus," Eugene sputtered. "He's the most amazing thing I've ever built. Not that the suits will admit it." He made a face. "All that work I put into him. And now they won't even use him."

"Why not?" I asked. Maybe now we'd finally get the real story.

"They say he's too smart. That no one will be able to beat him and they'll go home from their vacation disap-pointed and wah, wah, wah. Everyone gets a trophy these days. Ridiculous."

I had to agree. "No one has ever beat him in the regu-lar game, either," I pointed out. "And no one seems to care about that...."

"Exactly!" Eugene cried, pointing at me. "You get it, kid. Atreus is supposed to be the big bad of the entire game. Not some trophy kill that a weekend warrior can bag and brag to his friends about back home. So I gave him intelligence, and made him watch thousands of recorded *Fields of Fantasy* bat-tles from the past ten years. He now knows a gamer's mind and moves better than the gamers themselves." Eugene rubbed his hands together in glee. "And the longer Dragon Ops is open, the smarter he'll get. And the harder he'll be to beat."

"So let's see him already," Derek demanded.

"Weren't you listening, bard boy? He's not part of the game."

"So what?" my cousin argued. "You're his programmer. Can't you just *program* him to show up? We don't have to fight him or anything. We just want to check him out. See if he's as cool as you say he is."

Eugene pursed his lips. "I mean, I could," he hedged. "But the bosses would kill me if they found out. Like real-life kill me."

My heart started beating a little faster, realizing he was starting to cave.

"We won't tell anyone," I promised. "Will we, guys?"

Lilli and Derek shook their heads, obviously as eager as I was. Eugene laughed.

"You guys are going to get me in so much trouble," he said. Then he held out his hands in defeat. "But why not? Someone should get to appreciate all my hard work. Might as well be you!"

Chapter Nine

We waited, excitement rising, as Eugene started tapping on his spell book. When he finished, he looked up to the sky. We followed his gaze, at first seeing nothing but a few clouds floating by. I dug my nails into my palms, trying to be patient.

Thankfully, I didn't have to wait long. A moment later the sky darkened as a long, regal shadow appeared, cresting above us, so large it nearly blocked out the twin suns. I drew in a breath.

Atreus. Ready or not, here he comes.

I watched as the mighty beast swept into view, beginning to circle us from above. It was definitely the same dragon I'd seen from the boat. And he was as impressive now as he had been the first time around. A giant, majestic creature with crimson-colored scales that caught the sunlight and scattered a thousand colorful sparkles across the ground below.

"Holy rainbow-colored unicorn poop!" I heard my sister whisper, looking down at the reflected colors dancing on her skin. Even Derek was gaping, his mouth opening and closing like a fish's. I couldn't tell if he was excited . . . or scared.

"Come on, you big dummy," Eugene shouted as the dragon continued to circle. "Land already." He looked at me and huffed. "AIs. Got minds of their own." He snorted. "Literally."

"Maybe Derek could play him a song?" I suggested.

Derek scowled, assuming I was making fun of the bard thing again. But this time I was serious. In the original *Fields of Fantasy* game, sometimes dragons could be brought down to earth by certain song spells. It was one of a bard's few true talents. Something Eugene quickly confirmed.

"Atreus loves music," he assured Derek. "Especially heavy metal. But he'd be cool with a ballad, too. Just no country. He hates country." He smirked, and I got the feeling he'd programmed that particular quirk himself.

Derek shot us a suspicious look, but gave a tentative strum on his harp. Then he started singing—an acoustic version of an Imagine Dragons song, which I suppose made sense under the circumstances. His voice was unsteady at first, as if he were nervous. Then it became more confident, the notes clear and clean. Wow. He wasn't half bad. Who would have thought Mr. Too Cool for School had such a good singing voice?

Atreus seemed to agree. His ears pricked at the sound,

and his eyes locked on Derek. For a moment, he hovered, suspended in midair. Then, to our excitement, he dipped his snout and started swooping to the ground at full speed. I had to stumble backward to avoid getting plowed over as he came in for a landing, stirring up a huge cloud of dust on impact.

And then, there he was. The biggest, baddest boss of *Fields of Fantasy*—giving Derek a huge, slurpy kiss on the cheek with his massive black tongue.

"Ew!" Derek cried, staggering backward and wiping dragon drool off his face. "That's gross, dude!"

Lilli burst out laughing. "Aw," she cooed. "I think he likes you!" She took a step forward, reaching out to brush her hand against the dragon's scales. Her eyes lit up in excitement—clearly forgetting for a moment that she wasn't into the whole high-tech thing anymore. "He's so soft! His scales feel like satin!" She turned to me. "You gotta feel this, Ian!"

I cautiously approached the giant beast. He towered above me and I looked up, *way up*, to make sure this was okay with him.

Atreus's eyes locked on me. His mouth curled. *Well, well, tiny human*, his deep voice rumbled in my ears. *It seems we meet again.*

I smiled. He remembered me! And he recognized me, too—even with my new-and-improved warrior bod.

"Still need that ear scratching?" I asked. "This time I'm sure I can reach."

Atreus lowered his head in response, and I reached up, scratching behind his ear. Lilli was right; his scales did feel satiny soft. And yet, at the same time, I was pretty sure they were tough enough to stop a bullet.

"Wait, what are you talking about?" Eugene broke in. "Have you guys met or something?"

"Oh, yeah," I said, waving him off. "Me and Atreus here go way back." As I continued to scratch, the dragon rubbed his head against my hand, as a cat might, and I half expected him to start purring. "We met on the ferry yesterday."

"So you've been roaming again." Eugene tsked, walking over and grabbing Atreus by the chin, roughly jerking the dragon's head around to face him. Atreus shrugged out of his grasp, giving him a sulky look, as if to say, *Hands off, buddy.* A low growl rippled from his throat.

"Be nice, lug-head," Eugene snapped back, not the least bit intimidated by the warning growl. "After all, I'm the only one who doesn't want to send your profile to the trash bin." He turned to us, rolling his eyes. "Gotta love it when the AIs start getting too big for their britches."

"So is he really real?" Derek broke in. "Like, a robot or whatever?"

"Yes." Eugene bobbed his head, looking proud of himself. "Think of him as a very large drone. He's made of metal and can actually fly. The original idea was that maybe some-day guests could ride him or one of the other three dragon lords in the game, were they to find a way to tame them."

"Wow!" I exclaimed. "Riding a dragon? That would be amazing!"

Atreus turned back to me. *Would you like a ride now, tiny human?*

"Uh..." I gave an uneasy laugh. "Well, maybe not right this second..." I backed up a few steps. While riding a dragon in theory sounded supercool, I wasn't quite sure I was ready for the real thing.

"Ian's afraid of heights," my sister chimed in helpfully.

I shot her a look. Was that really necessary to explain? Not that it wasn't true. In fact, I hated heights almost as much as I hated water. When my mom took us to New York City and the Empire State Building? I almost had a heart attack at the top. I had to stay inside with my eyes closed while she and my sister spent forever taking a gazillion self-ies outside.

"I want a ride!" Derek declared, sounding enthused for the first time since we'd entered the game. He took a step toward Atreus, but Eugene blocked his path, holding up a hand.

"I don't think so," he said. "It's bad enough I've brought him here in the first place. The powers that be would kill me if they found out I was offering piggyback rides to kids. We don't even have the proper safety equipment."

"You're going to fit him with seat belts?" Derek asked skeptically. "That's pathetic."

"Yeah, well, falling off a dragon from fifty feet in the air would be even more pathetic," Eugene pointed out.

Atreus sighed, looking as disappointed as Derek. His long, powerful legs folded out from under him and he flopped onto his side, heaving out a long, slow breath. Poor guy. He looked so dejected. I reached out to give him another scratch behind the ear. This time he did make a sound like he was purring, snuggling up against my hand.

Thank you, tiny human, he grumbled in my ear. *That feels so—*

Eugene kicked him in the belly.

"What are you doing?" I asked, horrified.

"Trying to get him back into character," Eugene snapped, staring at the dragon in disgust. "We can't have our star attraction acting like your great aunt's kitty cat, now can we?" He kicked Atreus again. "Come on, man. Show some dignity here. You're supposed to be the big bad, remember?"

The dragon gave him a sulky look. But in the end he obeyed, rising slowly to his feet and shaking himself off. He turned to us, his eyes wide and sad.

I am sorry, he said. *It seems I still have much to learn about this game.*

And with that, he unfurled his mighty wings and pushed off on his back haunches, launching himself into the air. A moment later he disappeared over the horizon, leaving us alone.

"Great," muttered Eugene, tapping at his spell book. "This is worse than I thought."

"What are you talking about?" I demanded. "He's awesome!"

Eugene raised an eyebrow. "Did he fill you with terror?"

"Well...not exactly."

"Did you have the almost overwhelming urge to scratch his belly?"

"I did," admitted Lilli, meekly raising her hand.

"Well, then there you go," the programmer pronounced, disgusted. "The powers that be were so concerned with him being too tough, they went and messed with my code and turned him into a freaking marshmallow instead. Who's gonna want to fight a boss monster like that? He'd probably try to hug the players to death." He groaned. "This is ridiculous. I need to go check on his code again. See where it's going wrong." He glanced at his watch. "You guys mind cutting the tour short?"

Wait, what?

"No way!" I cried. "We just got here. We haven't even finished our first quest yet!"

"And I'm truly sorry about that. But I have a job to do. I can't babysit you kids all day."

"We don't need babysitting," Derek protested. He placed a hand on Eugene's arm. "Look, why don't you go back and do your job? We'll be fine out here. Ian's, like, a total gamer geek. In fact, I bet he knows more about this game than he does about the girls at school."

I wasn't sure he meant that as a compliment, but at this point I was down with whatever worked. "It's true!" I chimed in. "I've been playing *Fields of Fantasy* since I was eight."

Eugene shrugged. "All right then," he said, looking me up and down. "If you're sure..."

"Don't worry," I said. "We'll look out for each other. Nothing's going to happen."

Eugene gave us a salute, then turned and started trudging down the path, back toward the iron gates. As he went, I could hear him mutter under his breath, "Have fun with the dungeons and the dragons, tiny humans...."

Derek watched him go, a wicked grin spreading across his face. "Finally!" he declared. "Now let's go find some real action."

Chapter Ten

"Hang on," I said. "Before we wander off, we need to finish our rat quest and turn it in. I'm sure all the traps are filled by now."

"Oh yeah," Derek agreed. "Maybe we'll even level up."

I opened my mouth to remind him that technically he didn't help at all with the rat gathering and therefore shouldn't get credit for it, but I stopped myself. After all, we were a team. And we all needed to gain as many levels as possible if we wanted to hit the cool content later in the game.

Lilli, who had been silent since Atreus left, now frowned. "Are you sure we shouldn't just go back with Eugene?" she asked. "We have no idea what we're doing out here by ourselves. We don't even know how to fight. . . ." She took a step toward the trail leading out of the park.

I leapt in her path. "We watched the tutorial. I'm sure we can figure it out," I pleaded. "Come on, Lills. If we go back, we're going to be bored out of our minds, sitting around the hotel for the rest of the day. This is our one chance to have a real adventure."

She raised an eyebrow. *"Real?"* she repeated skeptically.

I sighed. "You know what I mean."

Derek strummed on his harp. *"Lilli, Lilli! The game's scared her silly! She wants to run down the hilly...."*

My sister groaned. "Never mind," she said. "It was only a suggestion."

Pushing past us, she trudged back over to the cottage, yanking open the door and stepping inside. Relieved, I ran after her, and together we starting collecting all the now-filled rattraps. Derek, of course, remained outside to let us do the heavy lifting. As I picked up one of the traps, the rat inside squirmed madly, peering out at me with bulging, frightened eyes.

"Aw, I almost feel bad for them," I said.

It was funny; it had always been such a nothing quest to trap rats in other games. But now I couldn't help but wonder what would happen to the poor little guys. Would the farmer re-home them? Or exterminate them outright?

"They're just make-believe," Lilli reminded me. "A bunch of rat-shaped pixels."

Right. I stuffed the trap into the bag. Of course they weren't real. Which meant they didn't have real feelings and they didn't feel real pain. Just like Atreus. Even though he looked really sad when Eugene kicked him—it was just part of his programming. He was a robot, after all. And robots didn't have feelings.

Right . . . ?

"Come on," Lilli said, interrupting my troubling thoughts. "Let's go turn this in and get it over with."

We headed out of the cottage and back to the farmer, who was still hanging out in the same spot, the white star still spinning above his head. *Weird.* Why hadn't it turned green? That was what usually happened in the regular game when you'd completed a quest.

Lilli poked him twice. The man's face came alive.

"Brave adventurers!" he cried. "I am so glad you're here. I am in need of your help!"

Uh . . . What?

"We already helped you, you idiot!" Derek cried, coming over and grabbing my sack, holding it open in front of the farmer. The creatures inside squealed at the sudden light. "Look. Rats. Trapped."

"Brave adventurers!" the man replied, ignoring the bag. "I am so glad you're here. I am in need of your help!"

"Ugh. Do you think the quest is bugged?" I asked, slumping my shoulders. That would be just our luck, right? Some kind of glitch in the game? And now Eugene wasn't even here to fix it for us.

"Wait a second . . ." Derek frowned, looking into my bag, then Lilli's. "Don't you need ten rats? I only see nine."

"Are you sure?" I squinted into the bag, surprised.

"Um, I may not be a mathlete, but I can count to ten."

"Right." I did a quick count myself. Sure enough, we were missing one rat. Urgh. How had we missed one?

"Guess we better head back inside," I said.

"What? No way!" Derek hopped in front of me, blocking my path to the cottage. "Look! We have the whole game to ourselves now! We're off the rails! We can go anywhere. See everything! Fight everything!"

"And die horribly if we don't level up first," Lilli pointed out dryly.

Derek pushed the bag in her direction. "Fine. You guys play it safe. Collect your rats. But if I'm going to be stuck on this island, I'm going to go ride me some dragons." He strummed on his harp. *"Dragons, dragons. Gonna ride me some dragons! While Ian and Lilli are pathetic and saggin'…"*

And with that, he headed down the hill, still singing, until he was out of sight.

"Ugh," Lilli muttered. "He really is the worst."

"Agreed," I said with a shudder. Then I shifted from foot to foot. "Though, should we go after him? I mean, he's a bard. He's not going to last ten seconds out there without us." I thought back to my solo adventures the day before. Derek had no idea what he'd signed up for. And by himself…

"He'll be fine," Lilli assured me. "Worst that can happen is some crazy-powerful dragon drains all his hit points in a single blow and he'll be forced to revive and start over."

Oh right. Reality check. I was beginning to need a lot of those out here. Derek could do what he wanted. Nothing was going to hurt him in real life. Still, everything seemed so real. It was hard to remember it was just a game.

A game with only two players now. Not exactly a proper party.

I sighed, turning to Lilli. "Look, if you want to go back to town, I'll go with you. We'll come back out tomorrow with Lady Farah. Do this the right way."

For a moment Lilli said nothing, just stared at the ground as if she was trying to make a decision. Then her eyes lifted to the farmer's cottage. "Nah," she said. "Might as well keep playing. Like you said, what else is there to do? Besides," she added with a small grin, "we at least have to out-level Derek by the end of the day. Or we'll never hear the end of it."

I grinned. She wanted to keep playing! Even if it was just to show Derek up, it felt a little like having my old sister back.

"Totally," I agreed, hoping I didn't sound too eager. "I mean, can you imagine? He'd probably write some terrible song about it and make us listen to the whole thing."

Lilli laughed and we headed back into the cottage, looking around for that last trap. But weirdly, there didn't seem to be one. Nor did there seem to be any more rats. We stood still, holding our breaths, but there was no squeaking. No claws scratching against the wood.

Lilli crossed her arms over her chest. "So where is it?"

"I don't know...." I started pacing the room, peering into each corner. But there were no rats as far as I could see.

I had almost given up entirely when my toe accidentally knocked against the small throw rug on the floor. Curious, I dropped to my knees and peeled it up. My eyes widened. There was an outline of a wooden door underneath.

"Look!" I cried.

Lilli ran over. "Holy sneaky secret trapdoor!" she exclaimed. "Good find, Ian!"

Excited, I wrapped my hand around the door's outline, trying to tug it open. At first it seemed to be stuck, but after a second pull, I was able to yank it free. It moaned as it yawned open, revealing a rickety-looking ladder descending into a pit of darkness.

My heart stopped. I dropped the door. It slammed shut with a loud bang.

"What are you doing?" Lilli demanded.

"Oh, that's probably for another quest," I said quickly, scrambling to my feet. "Maybe a follow-up or something? I'm sure the rat *we're* looking for is up here somewhere." I picked up a chair, which clearly wasn't hiding a rat, and made a point to look under it.

"Ohhh!" Lilli said knowingly. "I get it."

"Uh, get what?"

"You're scared to go down there."

"I am not!"

"Really?" She lifted the trapdoor again.

"I just don't think the rat is down there! That's all!"

A loud squeaking sound rose from the pit. Lilli raised an eyebrow. "Probably not, huh?"

I slumped down into the chair, banging my head against the kitchen table. Lilli rose to her feet and joined me, placing a hand on my shoulder. "Come on, Ian," she said. "You were the one who wanted to play this game, remember? Don't chicken out on me now!"

"I'm not!" I protested. "It's just . . . you know how I hate dark, closed-in spaces." Almost as much as I hated water and heights.

Ugh. I was a total wimp, wasn't I?

Lilli gave me another pitying look, which only made it worse. "Look, how about I go down?" she asked. "I'll trap the rat and run right back up. You can stay here and wait."

I closed my eyes for a moment and sighed. Then I forced them back open. "No," I said. "I'll come with you."

"Are you sure?"

"Yeah." I forced a nod. "It's only a game, right?"

"So you keep telling me."

I watched as she grabbed the lantern off the table and headed to the trapdoor, pulling it open again. She swung her legs around, then dropped down into the pit, disappearing into the darkness. A moment later, I heard her voice again. "You can come down," she called. "It's safe."

Grudgingly, I trudged over to the trapdoor, carefully lowered myself down onto the ladder, and began to work my way down. The rungs felt rickety and unstable under my feet, as if they could give way at any moment. Which would be a real-life problem, my brain helpfully decided to point out. If the ladder broke, we'd be trapped down in the basement without a way back up. And at the moment, no one really knew where we were, except Derek. But who knew when or if he'd be back?

Thankfully, the ladder held my weight and finally I was able to plant my feet onto solid ground. Relieved, I joined Lilli, who had turned on the lantern.

"Do you hear it?" she asked with a frown.

I shook my head, looking around the basement, which was mostly empty. Just a pile of farm equipment leaning against a wall and a bale of moldy-looking hay. "No," I said. "Maybe in that corner over there?" I pointed to the one dark corner at the back of the room, where the lantern light didn't penetrate.

"Yeah," Lilli agreed, turning in that direction. But she stopped short as a strange sound suddenly emitted from the darkness.

Not the squeak of a rat. But a deep, dark growl.

Chapter Eleven

"Um...what was that?" I stammered. "Was that a rat?"

Before Lilli could answer, the sound came again, low and rumbling and fierce. With trembling hands, she raised her lantern. At first we saw nothing. Then, something in the corner flashed in the light.

Something huge. Something definitely not a rat.

"Run!" I cried, dashing for the exit. My sister dove after me, and together we scurried back up the ladder. Once above, we slammed the trapdoor shut and looked at one another, wide-eyed.

"What was that?" Lilli whispered. "That did not look like a rat."

I winced, my mind flashing back to the nightmarish creature we'd just seen down below. A grotesque mash-up of a monster sporting the bloated body of a rat and the reptilian snout of a dragon. It had stubby wings, greasy gray scales, and a long, bald tail swishing behind it.

A rat dragon? A dragon rat?

The growl came again from beneath the trapdoor. "Maybe it was a king rat?" I asked. "Some kind of rare spawn?"

Lilli shuddered. "Did you see its eye?"

I nodded. That had been the worst part by far. A blackened socket where his left eye should have been, with a hole so deep I was sure I had caught a glimpse of skull underneath.

"You know what? This is ridiculous," Lilli declared. "We have no idea what we're doing. We don't have a complete party, and we don't even know how to fight." She headed toward the door. "Let's go grab Derek, come back, and start over tomorrow, like you said."

I sighed, but I knew she was right. We weren't prepared for this. And we were stumbling around, not getting anywhere. We'd been out here for what felt like an hour and hadn't even finished one quest. Better to go back for now and play the right way tomorrow with Lady Farah or another guide.

I joined Lilli at the door. She wrapped her hand around the handle and pulled.

It wouldn't budge.

Lilli tried again. "Help me with this. I think it's stuck."

Together, we tugged with all our might. But the door would not open. It was as if it had been locked from the outside.

Lilli glanced at me. "Do you think Derek...?"

I made a face, pounding my fist against the door. "This isn't funny, Derek!" I cried. "Let us out. Now!"

But there was no answer. And the door remained stuck. Lilli wriggled the knob again. "I don't even think this has a lock," she said at last, stepping away. "Which means..." Her eyes traveled to the trapdoor, then back to me. She didn't have to speak for me to know what she was thinking. My heart sunk.

"It's a game thing," I concluded miserably. I should have known. After all, this was typical in some games—locking you in until you finished your quest.

We were going to have to kill the giant rat dragon.

Awesome.

"Such a fun game," Lilli muttered sarcastically as she walked over to the trapdoor again, yanking it open. She turned to me. "After you, Lord Wildhammer."

"Uh, I don't know about this." I hovered by the front door, my pulse pounding under my wrists. "I mean, do you really think the two of us can beat that thing?"

"Well, if we can't, we'll die," Lilli said simply. At my look of dread, she added, "Game-die, that is. If at first you don't succeed, fight, fight again, am I right?"

That had been our motto back when Lilli was still into

gaming. Especially with some of the more ferocious creatures we'd taken on. There was this one time with a particularly hard sea dragon that I swear I died a hundred times on before I finally gave up and watched a bunch of YouTube videos on how to beat him.

This wasn't any different—aside from the fact that we couldn't YouTube it. That thing down there? It might look scary, but there was nothing it could do to us in real life. I thought back to the troll's sword slamming down on my head. It hadn't hurt. It just felt weird. And then I was fine. I would be fine now, too. Nothing to be scared of . . .

"Fight, fight again," I repeated under my breath. And together, we headed back down the ladder.

As we dropped to the floor, the rat dragon stepped out from the shadows, a low, guttural growl rippling from his throat as his good eye locked on us. I held up my shield with a shaky hand, not sure it would do any good. Hopefully it wasn't a fire breather. Or an acid spewer. Or . . .

Okay, fine. Whatever it was? It was going to be bad.

"Do you have any spells?" I whispered to Lilli. "Maybe one to slow it down?"

"Um, maybe? Let me look in my spell book . . ."

I groaned. "You couldn't have done that upstairs?"

"Just distract him, okay?" she snapped. "You're the tank, remember? That's kind of your job."

She wasn't wrong. A warrior's main job was to "tank" the bad guys—which meant getting right in there and letting them beat on you while others stood back and did damage from afar. But while that was easy to do from the safety of a computer monitor and mouse, the idea of facing off against an actual snarling, drooling giant beast? That was something else entirely.

Come on, Ian, I scolded myself. *You're a gamer. You got this.*

Sucking in a breath, I unsheathed my blade and held it out in front of me before taking a hesitant step toward the rat dragon. The creature watched me warily with its one eye, still spitting and growling, but keeping its distance.

"That's right," I said. "Stay back, you coward." I waved the sword in its direction, starting to feel pretty good about myself. It was scared of me! The big, bad rat dragon was actually scared!

It was then that I noticed its belly. Or, more precisely, its glowing-red belly. Which was getting bigger and bigger . . .

Uh-oh.

"Lilli!" I screamed. "Duck! Now!" And I hit the deck.

Chapter Twelve

The rat dragon let loose its flame. It shot across the room, above my head, barreling directly at my sister behind me. Lilli leapt to the side, narrowly missing getting blasted dead-on. The flames hit the far brick wall instead, charring it black before sputtering out. Heat rose in the air, prickling my skin.

Whoa. That was way too close.

With trembling legs, I rose to my feet, holding my sword out in front of me again. My palms were so sweaty at this point, I could barely hold on. And I had no idea if I'd be able to swing it if necessary. The rat dragon took a menacing step forward. I held up my shield, heart slamming against my rib cage.

Suddenly, out of nowhere, the entire room filled with light. I whirled around, my eyes widening as they fell upon

Lilli, her staff now crackling with electricity. Excitement burst from my chest. She'd done it!

"Get it!" I cried.

Lilli hurled the electric bolt at the rat dragon, striking him square in the chest. It bellowed in rage, then charged at my sister, the electricity still dancing wildly across its scales. She screamed and tried to back away, but the basement wasn't big enough and she smacked into the brick wall instead. Farm equipment rained down on her, knocking the staff from her hands.

"Lilli!" I leapt into the rat dragon's path, slashing madly with my sword. It dodged me easily, as if I were some pesky fly. But at least I had its attention, giving Lilli time to dig her way out and find her staff.

My heart pounded in my chest as I squared off with the beast. Its one blue eye flashed, cold as ice, as it swiped at me with its claws. I jumped backward to avoid being gored but nearly dropped my sword in the process. Somehow I managed to keep a grip on it, but my arms were starting to ache and I was getting seriously winded. This was so different from the regular game, where I could sit on my couch and button-mash forever. How long would I be able to hold it off? And would Lilli be powerful enough to get its hit points down to zero with her spells?

The rat dragon charged again, and I was barely able to dodge it this time. My lungs were aching from the smoke in the air, and my eyes stung like mad. I blinked quickly, trying to clear my vision. If only the rat dragon was as affected by the smoke as I was. Of course, it only had one eye—

That's it!

I drew in a breath, excitement coursing through my veins. In every game I had ever played, every monster had some kind of weakness. Some small thing that would give the player an advantage. It might have been an elemental weakness to ice. Or a soft scale on its left side.

Or, in this case, an empty hole in its head. The perfect bull's-eye.

"Aim for his eye!" I yelled at Lilli.

The rat dragon opened its mouth again, prepared to nail us with another blast of flames. I leapt to the right, then charged it from the side, launching my sword like a javelin— aiming directly at the blackened hole.

If this was a movie, I would have hit it straight on, my blade making its mark and sliding through its dead eye socket like a hot knife through butter. Utter annihilation with one deadly stroke, as I conquered all my earlier fears and became a legit hero.

But this wasn't a movie. And this was a very different type of game than the kind I was used to playing. Instead of hitting its mark, my sword bounced harmlessly off the rat dragon's scales, missing the socket completely. I watched in dismay as the blade flew through the air, landing a few feet away with a heavy *thunk*.

"No!" I cried, horrified.

The rat dragon was enraged now, charging in my direction. I tried to back away, but its claws slashed at my chest plate. Sudden pain erupted in my chest and I fell backward in shock, tripping over a rake and landing on my butt. The dragon stomped toward me, its belly growing red again as it readied a final blast. I tried to scramble up, but it was no use. I was trapped. One more second and it would be game over.

Suddenly, the rat dragon let out a spine-chilling scream. Blood exploded from its head, raining down on my face. I managed to roll over, just in time. The creature collapsed right next to me, its body seizing and shaking violently before finally falling still.

It was then that I noticed it. Lilli's staff, sticking out from its eye socket.

An indicator light flashed in front of my eyes. Gold writing scrawled across my field of vision.

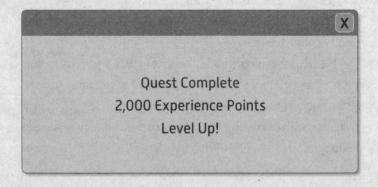

Quest Complete
2,000 Experience Points
Level Up!

I leapt to my feet. "You did it!" I exclaimed, bursting with joy—and relief. "You killed it!" I turned to my sister. "That was amazing, Lills! Totally—"

I stopped short when I saw her face. She gave me a weak smile, then tumbled to her knees.

"What's wrong?" I asked, worriedly. "Are you okay?"

"My arm . . ."

I looked down and caught sight of a nasty cut—the kind that probably needed stitches—snaking down her arm. Blood dripped from the wound, splashing onto the floor and mixing with the rat dragon's. My stomach turned.

"But you're okay, right?" I asked her. "I mean, it's just a game wound, right? It's not real. It's totally not real life."

She looked up at me, then down at her arm. Her jaw wobbled.

"Then why does it real-life hurt?"

Chapter Thirteen

I stared down at Lilli's arm, my mind racing. This didn't make any sense. Sure, you could get hurt in the game. But Hiro said it would feel like a small tingle—like your foot falling asleep—not real pain. But then the rat dragon's claw had hurt when it scratched my chest, too. Way more than it probably should have.

"Do you think our SensSuits are malfunctioning?" I asked worriedly.

"I don't know," she said. "I hope so?"

I nodded grimly. A malfunctioning SensSuit would be bad news. But much better than a real-life injury.

She started tugging at her robe. "How do I get the SensSuit off?" she asked, her voice rising with panic. "If I could just take it off..."

"I don't think you can," I said. "Like we can't take off our goggles. Only the guides can do it."

"Are you serious?" Her face paled. Her hands reached up to her face, realizing for the first time her goggles weren't there. Her eyes bulged. "I did not agree to this!" she cried. "This is not cool!" Then she winced, clutching her bleeding arm.

"Come on!" I took her good arm and gently pulled her up to stand. "We need to get you back to town. Find Uncle Jack or someone else who can help us."

Lilli agreed and I helped her climb the ladder. The front door of the cottage, thankfully, had swung open. Quest completed. We quickly headed outside, where we found the farmer, now with a green spinning star above his head. For a split second I considered poking him as we passed, to finalize the quest. But the pained look on my sister's face made me reconsider and instead we ran past him, heading straight to the starting area.

We stopped in the clearing at the bottom of the hill, where we'd entered the game. I frowned as I looked around. I saw the same purple trees. The same paths leading in all directions. The same stream and the same baby dragonbites toasting their dandelions.

What I didn't see was the exit.

Chapter Fourteen

My heart thudded in my chest, panic seizing me with icy fingers. Where was the exit? It had to be somewhere!

"What's wrong?" Lilli asked, stepping up beside me.

I frowned, turning around in a circle. "This is where we entered, right?"

"Yeah. There's the stream," she said, pointing. "And there's the tree with the Edelweiss Forest sign."

"So then where are the front gates?"

Lilli froze, a look of shock crossing her face. Her eyes darted around the clearing, growing wider at every glance. "They have to be here somewhere," she said, putting up her hands and feeling in front of her as she walked in a few directions. "Maybe we just can't see them, like we can't see our goggles?"

"Maybe..." I agreed, stretching out my own arms, searching for something, anything, that resembled an exit.

But there was nothing there.

Except...

My fingers connected with something soft in front of me—something a little bit squishy. I pressed against it. It didn't budge.

"Lilli, check this out!" I called over to her. She joined me at the spot and pushed with her good hand. Then she tried to walk through it. But her body bounced back, as if she'd jumped on a trampoline.

"Ow!" she cried, rubbing her head, which had hit first. "Is there, like, some kind of invisible wall there or something?"

"Or something," I muttered, realization washing over me. This was not good.

"What?" Lilli demanded, a frightened look on her face. "What is it, Ian?"

"Don't panic," I said. "But I think this is the end of the world."

"What?"

"You know," I said. "Just like in regular *Fields of Fantasy*. They only let you go so far—to the end of the map. And then you can't go farther."

"But where's the gate? The gate's part of the game! And so's the town! We're supposed to be able to go down to the town!" She threw her hands up in frustration. "I can't even *see* the town anymore!"

She was right. Something was wrong here. First, malfunctioning SensSuits. Now, disappearing gates. Suddenly, this didn't feel like a game anymore. At least not the one we were supposed to be playing. . . .

"What about in-game menus?" Lilli asked. "There's got to be an emergency call button or something, right? Like, in case a player gets separated from their guide?"

"Good idea," I said, blinking to access my menu. Options scrawled across my field of vision and I started going through them one by one, until I found one that simply read *HELP*.

But when I went to select it, I realized it, too, was blurred out. And try as I might, I couldn't get it to work.

"What is going on here?" Lilli demanded, her voice tinged with hysteria. "Why is this happening to us?"

"I don't know," I moaned, looking down at her arm. It was still bleeding pretty badly, and I wondered how much it hurt. I turned back to the blurry spot where the gate should have been. "Hello?" I yelled. "Is anyone out there?"

Lilli joined me. "*We're stuck in the game!*" she yelled. "*Please! We need help!*"

But there was no answer.

I slumped onto a nearby toadstool. "They're probably all underground working in the server rooms. They think we're safe with Eugene."

"Eugene!" Lilli spit out. "This is probably all his fault. He went off to fix Atreus. What if he messed everything else up instead?!" She glanced down at her arm again. "What are we supposed to do?"

"Someone has to come eventually," I said, trying to comfort her. "We just have to wait it out."

But even as I made the suggestion, I wondered. I mean, yeah, someone would come *eventually*. But everyone was working like crazy to meet their deadlines, and they expected us to be playing the game with our guide for a week—they'd have no idea he'd ditched us. And then there was the time-compression thing. How long had we actually been gone? And how long in game time would it take for them to discover our real-life disappearance?

My throat felt tight and I tried to force back the tears that had welled in my eyes. All this time I had been dying to play this game. But now that I was here, in the middle of it? I kind of wanted to go home.

Especially once I felt the first drops of rain. And *especially,* especially when the sky opened up a moment later, pounding us with a downpour.

"This isn't happening!" I cried, vainly attempting to cover my head with my hands as thunder crashed above us, followed by a streak of lightning slashing across the sky.

Real thunder.

Real lightning.

At least it felt like it. Though I couldn't be sure of anything anymore.

"Holy buckets of giant's tears!" Lilli exclaimed, looking up in dismay. She was already drenched to the bone. "We need to find shelter—now!"

My gaze darted around the forest, assessing our options. Could we make it back to the rat house in time, maybe? Though I didn't want to get trapped in there if the rat dragon respawned and the door locked again. There had to be something else, somewhere. . . .

Suddenly, my eyes caught a flash of something red, just beyond the trees. "Look!" I yelled, hoping Lilli could hear me over the raging storm. "I think that's a house!"

"Great! Let's go!"

We ran through the dense woods in the direction of the structure, trying not to trip on an upended root or get scraped by the thick brush. Finally, we reached what turned out to be a small cottage, nestled in a cozy clearing. Lilli pushed open the front door, which thankfully wasn't locked, and we dived inside, slamming the door behind us.

"Wow," I said, swiping back my sopping-wet hair. "That's some storm."

"Is it real?" Lilli asked, peering out the window.

"Did it feel real?"

She groaned. "I don't even know anymore." She looked down at her arm. "At least the cut's stopped bleeding."

I took a look at the wound. Lilli was right—it looked way better. Almost as if it was healing before my very eyes. Guess that answered the question of whether or not it was a game wound. But it still didn't explain why it had hurt so much in real life.

I turned to check out the cottage we'd entered. Unlike the rest of the medieval-themed game, here everything seemed surprisingly modern and relatively new. There was a refrigerator, a microwave, and a sink. And two doors that led off to a small bedroom and bathroom with actual indoor plumbing. (Which I quickly used after Lilli went in to clean up her arm—who knew when I'd find another flush toilet out here?)

"This must be one of the game maker's cottages I read about," I said. I yanked open the refrigerator and grabbed two granola bars and two yogurts, tossing one of each to my sister. She reluctantly caught them and slid down into a seat at the table. She still looked stressed out and miserable.

"Game maker's cottages?" she asked in a wobbly voice.

"Yeah. You know. Like how forest rangers have huts in the national parks?" I explained. "It's a way to have staff on hand in case any questers get separated from their guides or get into trouble." I sighed. "Unfortunately I don't think they're manned until the park officially opens."

"Of course not."

I rapped my fingers on the table, thinking hard. "But

maybe there's a radio?" I suggested. "Or a cell phone even? Some way to reach Uncle Jack or Hiro so they can come get us?"

A flicker of hope crossed my sister's face. "Maybe! Let's look!"

Abandoning our snacks, we split up and went through the house, opening drawers and closets, searching for some kind of communication device. A moment later my sister let out a cheer. I turned to see her waving a walkie-talkie in the air.

"Sweet!" I cried, climbing over the couch to reach her faster. "See if you can get someone to reply."

She held the walkie-talkie to her mouth. "Um, is anyone there?" she asked. "Mayday! Mayday! We need help. Now!"

Chapter Fifteen

L illi released the walkie-talkie's button, putting her ear to the speaker. Waiting for someone—anyone—to respond to her desperate plea.

But there was no response. She tried again. "Mayday! Mayday! Anyone? Anyone out there at all?"

Silence. She turned the walkie-talkie over and popped off the back. No batteries.

"Technology," she muttered, tossing it across the coffee table. She slumped down onto the couch, scrubbing her face with her hands.

"At least we're inside," I pointed out, trying to stay optimistic. "And out of the game itself—or as much as we can be. We're not going to get attacked by monsters in here. And, bonus, we won't get struck by lightning."

"Woo-hoo," Lilli said sarcastically. "Way to glass-half-full it, dude."

"Look, I don't like this, either, okay? But freaking out doesn't help. And it's going to be okay. Everyone knows we're in here. They're eventually going to come looking for us. We just have to chill for now."

"I guess." Lilli lifted her feet onto the couch, stretching her hands over her head. "At least my arm is better," she said. "It hardly hurts at all now."

In fact, at this point, it barely looked as if there had ever been a wound at all.

"I'm glad," I said, shoving her feet off the couch so I could sit beside her. It was then that I noticed the old TV in the corner. Or, more importantly, what was sitting under the old TV. My eyes lit up. "Well, hello, beautiful!"

Lilli followed my pointing finger, groaning as her eyes fell upon the ancient video-game console sitting under the television. An Atari 2600—one of the very first original game systems designed for home use. Way before even the first Nintendo.

"Of course," she said, rolling her eyes. "Only *you* would want to play video games while trapped in a video game."

I snorted. "Come on. What else are we going to do?"

"Fine. You play. I'll watch." She pulled her legs up, crisscross-applesauce-style, as I got down to the floor to retrieve the dusty console and grab a controller. No, *joystick*, I corrected myself. That's what they used to call them. Unlike normal game controllers, which are mostly made up of a bunch of buttons, this one had a large stick that you moved around.

"So what are you going to play?" Lilli asked, sounding curious despite herself.

I rummaged through the selection of games. Then I grinned, holding up a cartridge. "The very first Mario game," I pronounced. "*Donkey Kong*!"

"Wait, that's a Mario game?" my sister asked as I inserted the cartridge into the console and the game loaded up on the TV screen.

"Yeah. See? There's Mario," I said, pointing to the bottom of the screen. Of course he didn't look much like the Mario we know now. Just a little blob in a red suit and hat. Only the telltale mustache gave him away. "He's trying to rescue his girlfriend."

"Princess Peach," Lilli concluded.

"Actually this is pre–Princess Peach," I told her, as I maneuvered Mario down the path, then up a ladder as Donkey Kong threw barrels down at me from above. "His girlfriend in this is named Pauline."

"How do you know all this?" Lilli asked, shaking her head. "Seriously, Ian. I think you were born in the wrong decade."

I shrugged. Normally I got annoyed when people said things like that. Especially when the jerks at school had started calling me "Eight-Bit Ian" after I presented my social studies project last year on the history of video games. Which was a totally legit topic, and really interesting, too. I learned all about how games went from simple lines and circles to the virtual and augmented reality stuff we have today. I had called it "From Pong to Pokémon," and I was so excited to present it to class.

Until I did.

Let's just say it didn't exactly level me up in coolness with my peers.

Except... Ikumi. She liked the old games, too. In fact, for all I knew this was her Atari. Maybe she came here to play when she was bored.

I stole a glance out the window. *If only she'd show up now. Maybe she'd know how to find the gate... or at least call for help.*

"Wow," Lilli remarked as I skillfully maneuvered Mario up the ladder and across the screen, timing my jumps so as not to get hit by Donkey Kong's barrels. This was one of the games Mom had downloaded onto her emulator, so I'd had a lot of practice. And it didn't take long to reach the top and get up close and personal with an angry Kong, who grabbed the princess and dragged her to the next level. "You're so good."

"At obsolete video games? Yes. I'm the best," I replied. "Too bad those epic skills are utterly useless here." My mind suddenly flashed back to my poor performance with the rat dragon in the basement, and I sighed.

"What's wrong?" Lilli asked. "Besides the obvious."

"Nothing." I kept my eyes on the game, only to walk right into a fireball. I groaned. "It's stupid."

"Come on. Talk to me, Lord Wildhammer."

I leaned back against the couch, setting the joystick down in front of me. "I don't know. I just thought . . . well, that I'd be better at this, that's all."

"This?"

I waved a hand. "This game. I've been looking forward to playing ever since they first announced they were building it. And I assumed, I guess, that I'd rock it when I got here. I mean, it's a video game. And video games are totally my thing. But this . . ." I trailed off.

Lilli gave me a pitying look. "Well, this game is a lot different than a regular video game. You need . . . different skills."

I made a face. She was trying not to hurt my feelings, but I knew what she meant. Unlike regular video games where you could sit in a chair drinking Coke all day, here you had to be physically fit. The best players would be strong IRL. Agile. With tons of energy.

Like Lilli.

In fact, this game was totally Lilli's jam, whether she wanted to admit it or not. She was the athlete in the family. She rode horses. She did gymnastics. She played soccer. And she was a total daredevil, too. She'd even gone with our dad to Costa Rica one summer and spent a week zip-lining and rock climbing all over the place. Meanwhile, I'd stayed home with Mom, playing the just-released *Dragons of Icelandia* expansion pack from *Fields of Fantasy*.

My sister squeezed my shoulder. "Come on, Ian. We only did one fight. We didn't even have a complete party and we were just learning how to play. You'll do better next time," she said reassuringly. "Besides, you were the one who figured out the rat dragon's weakness. Without that, we would have been goners for sure."

"Yeah," I said. "I guess."

I rose to my feet, not wanting to talk about it anymore. Instead, I walked over to the window, peering outside at the rain, which was still coming down in buckets.

"I hope Derek's okay," I mused. "Do you think he's still out here?"

"I don't know," Lilli said, joining me at the window. "I guess he must be. If we couldn't find the gates, there's no way he did. Hopefully he found someplace to hide out from the storm."

"Maybe once the rain stops we can start looking for him," I suggested. "I feel bad that he's all alone. He must be freaking out. And what if his SensSuit is messed up, too?"

Before Lilly could reply, there was a sudden burst of static coming from the television set.

Puzzled, I turned around. Donkey Kong and Mario had disappeared from the screen. In their place was a live-action video of a dark, crumbling temple half-filled with mist and smoke.

Lilli and I locked eyes. This was totally freaky.

Weird synthesized music began to play in the background, growing louder and more menacing as the camera slowly panned across the temple, revealing a treasure trove of gold and jewels. It stopped in front of a large crimson-colored dragon curled up on a pile of golden coins.

"Wait," I said, shocked. "Is that...Atreus?"

I stared at the TV, mesmerized. The dragon lounging in the cave definitely appeared to be Atreus, with the same red scales and glowing golden eyes. Yet there was something distinctly different about this creature from the one we'd met earlier in the Edelweiss Forest. Something...almost ominous.

The camera snap-zoomed to an extreme close-up of the dragon's face.

Well, well, tiny humans, Atreus growled, lifting his head. *It seems we meet again.*

I stopped breathing. It was the same thing he'd said back in the Edelweiss Forest. But this time, it sounded so different. Cold, cruel, filled with menace. And so unlike the playful voice of the creature who had licked Derek's face and begged for ear scratches.

Suddenly, my mind flashed to Eugene. Or, more specifically, what Eugene had said. Atreus was supposed to be terrifying, not cuddly. And he'd gone back to the base to make him so.

Well, mission 100 percent accomplished.

Lilli rapped on the screen with her finger. "Hey, Atreus!" she cried. "Can you hear me? Can you call Eugene for us? Or my uncle? We're having some trouble here. My SensSuit isn't working right, and we can't seem to leave the game."

Atreus's lip curled. A trail of smoke twined from his snout. *But why would you want to leave the game?* he asked. *When the fun has only just begun?*

What?

A horrifying realization washed over me. "Wait," I said slowly. "Was it you who locked us in? Did you mess with our SensSuits?" Holy Luigi's green overalls—was *that* why this was all happening? Had Atreus's new programming somehow broken the entire game?

"We need to speak to Eugene," my sister insisted. "Your programmer. We need to talk to him. Now!" Maybe he could still fix this before it was too late.

The camera pulled out as Atreus rose to his feet. Gold coins rained from his belly, plinking down onto the massive pile below. His eyes narrowed as his searing gaze seemed to burn through the screen.

Eugene cannot help you anymore, he growled. *This is my game now, and I am in control of all you see and hear.* His icy laugh echoed through the cottage. *Silly fools. They thought they could lock me away? I am the great Atreus, destroyer of worlds. I am more powerful than you could have ever imagined. And now it's time to play by* my *rules.*

"But we didn't do anything, Atreus!" I tried, scrambling

closer to the TV, desperate to plead our case. "We're just kids. Just visiting for a week. We didn't lock you away. I was the one who scratched your ear, remember? We just came here to play the game."

The dragon's lower lip curled, revealing sharp fangs I was sure hadn't been there before. *Then you are in luck, tiny human, for that is exactly what we're about to do.*

"No!" Lilli shook her head. "You don't understand. We can't play your game. My SensSuit is busted. When I get hurt? It really hurts."

Then your SensSuit is working perfectly, Atreus replied. *Exactly as it should. After all, what fun is a game without real stakes . . . ?*

"No," I whispered, shaking with fear. "You can't be serious."

Oh, but I am, tiny human. I even have a quest!

"A . . . quest?" Lilli squeaked, giving me a terrified look.

You have three days to make your way to my lair in the Crystal Temple, deep within Mount Fearless. Find me, fight me, do your best to defeat me. Only then shall I let you free.

He settled back down onto his pile of gold, snorting loudly. *But beware,* he added, his voice rumbling. *For in my game there are no save points. No do-overs. Make one wrong move and it will be game over. Forever.*

I clenched my fists. "No. This isn't cool, dude. Just let us out, okay? Or let Lilli out at least. She didn't even want to come here to begin with. If you have to keep someone in the game, keep me! I'll play with you. Just . . . let her go."

Atreus roared, cutting off my words. *No one will leave without playing my game. No one will leave without completing my quest. You have three days! Use them well, or I shall ensure they will be your last on this earth!*

And with that, the TV went black. As if someone had clicked a button on a remote. I blinked, and when I opened my eyes again Donkey Kong was back on the screen, throwing his little barrels. One of the barrels hit Mario, and I watched as the little guy twirled in a circle while the familiar eight-bit death music played.

Game over flashed on the screen.

And then, in its place . . .

A spinning white star.

Chapter Sixteen

"**N**o. No freaking way."

Lilli staggered to her feet, backing away from the TV, her arms held out in front of her as if warding off a wild beast.

"I'm done!" she cried. "This game is not fun anymore. I don't want to play." Her voice cracked. "You can't make me play!"

But she was talking to no one. Atreus was gone.

I got up and reached for her, then guided her over to the couch. She collapsed onto the cushions and put her face in her hands. She tried again to reach for her goggles, but came up empty-handed. She screamed in frustration.

"I hate this game!" she cried. "I hate this game so much!"

"I know," I assured her, helplessness washing over me. "Trust me, I'm not such a big fan at the moment, either."

"Oh please. You're probably loving this. Trapped in a video game. This is like, literally, your biggest dream come true."

I groaned, guilt like a stone in my stomach. Lilli wouldn't even be here right now if it hadn't been for me begging and pleading for her to come. She'd be safe at home, bungee jumping or cliff diving—something a lot less dangerous.

"I'm sorry," I said simply. "This is all my fault."

She averted her eyes. "It's not like you could have known...."

I turned away and walked over to the window again. I didn't need her to tell me I shouldn't blame myself for this, when there was no one else to blame.

Outside the world was still, peaceful almost. The rain had finally stopped. Night was starting to fall. Atreus's words crept through my brain again. *You have three days.* Did he mean game days or real days?

Oh man, this was so messed up. We needed help. We needed an adult. Would Eugene realize at some point that we hadn't come back? That Atreus had taken over? Surely he wouldn't just leave us out here, right? Especially once he realized what Atreus had done.

But by then, would it be too late?

I looked over my shoulder at the TV, watching the star spin in an endless loop. Drawing in a breath, I walked over, reached out, and poked the screen twice. The star blinked and my menu updated with the new quest.

"You can't be serious."

I turned to see Lilli rising from the couch. Evidently, since we were in the same party, her quest log had updated, too.

I shrugged. "What else are we supposed to do?"

"Um, stay here? Wait for help?" She turned her palms out at me. "Like you said, they're going to realize we're gone sooner or later, and they'll send a team in to find us. In fact, they're probably already on their way now. If we go out there, we might get hurt . . . or worse. It's better to stay here, where we know we're safe."

"You're right," I said. "You're totally right. It's just—"

I was interrupted by a sudden flashing red light coming from my game menu. I stared at it for a moment before finally realizing it was some kind of incoming call. Reaching out, I accepted it with shaky fingers.

Please be Uncle Jack. Eugene. Anyone . . .

"Ian! Is that you? You've got to help me!"

My eyes bulged as a video stream popped up like a hologram in front of me, hovering in the air. There was a small cage made out of what looked like bleached bones in some kind of dark room. A lone figure stood in the cage, grasping the bony bars with white-knuckled fingers, tears staining his dirt-streaked face.

"Derek?" I gasped. "Where are you? Are you okay?"

"Do I look okay?!" Derek cried, his voice cracking on the words. "I've been captured by a crazy dragon and put in a cage!"

Oh no. No, no, no!

"Derek, this isn't funny!" Lilli protested.

"Do you hear me laughing?" He sounded furious, but I could see the fear in his eyes.

"What happened?" I asked.

Derek turned away, staring at the cage bars behind him. "I just wanted to ride him," he admitted at last. "I know Eugene said not to, but I figured just for a second. So I played him one of my songs. The one that got him to come down the last time. And he did. And he seemed totally cool with me riding him. But then—something weird happened while we were in the air. It was like—he changed. All of a sudden. Without warning."

My sister and I exchanged looks. *Eugene. I knew it!*

"I thought he was going to drop me. Instead, he flew me down into this huge volcano and threatened to burn me alive." He turned back to us, waving his hand at the cage. "And now...I'm trapped. And...and...I need you to get me out of here. *Now!*"

"Why didn't you call us sooner?" Lilli asked.

"I didn't know I could! I kept going through my game options, trying to send a message for help. But they're all messed up. I only just figured out I could call you."

"Don't worry, Derek," I said. "We'll come get you!"

His face paled. "Come get me? No! You don't understand! This isn't some quest. This is real life. You have to get Hiro! Or my dad! The dragon's gone crazy! The whole game has!"

"It's okay. Don't freak out," I told him, not knowing what else to say. I didn't want to admit we were basically as trapped as he was. "Just...uh, hang tight for now. And, uh, don't do anything to make Atreus mad."

"Um, how am I supposed to do that?"

"Play him some songs," Lilli suggested. "He likes those, right?"

Derek stole a reluctant glance at his harp, which sat in the corner of the cage. "Yeah. I guess," he said. "Though, I don't know that many songs. And I really have to pee. And I really, really don't want to have to pee in here." He stopped, cocking his head as if listening to something. His face shadowed with fear. "Oh no! I think he's coming back!"

The hologram vanished as the call disconnected.

I sank down onto the couch, my heart racing in my chest. Visions of Derek's frightened face danced through my head. Along with that horrible cage of bones. With an out-of-control AI dragon robot right next door...

"Well, I guess that settles that," I said, giving my sister a look.

"Oh no." Lilli shook her head, getting my meaning. "You can't be serious."

"Come on, Lills. I know Derek can be a jerk. But we can't let him get eaten by a dragon."

"*He's not going to get eaten by a dragon!*" Lilli cried, slamming a fist against the wall. "*This is only a game! It's not real!*"

I locked her in a stare. "The pain in your arm felt pretty real, right?" I asked quietly.

Her face went stark white. "Yeah, but . . ." She trailed off, looking miserable. I couldn't blame her.

"Look, I don't like this any more than you do," I said. "But I don't know what else to do. Remember what Hiro said. The entire place is wired to a mainframe computer. Everything is controlled by that computer. And that means now everything is controlled by Atreus. The gates, the monsters, our SensSuits and goggles. That's some pretty real-life power." I held out my hands. "So, yeah. It's not *real*. But does that *really* matter anymore?"

Lilli's whole body seemed to crumble, the fight going out of her. "So what do we do? Do you really think we can rescue him?"

I shook my head. "No way. We're, like, level two. We'd never beat Atreus in an actual fight."

"So what then? Where do we start? We barely know how to play."

I scrubbed my face with my hands. I wanted to argue, but at the same time, I knew she wasn't wrong. We had three days and only two people—not even a complete party and no guide to speak of. This was literally impossible.

Unless . . .

A sudden thought struck me. I stood up. "Wait," I said. "I have an idea. Maybe."

"What is it?"

Drawing in a breath, I accessed my menu and scrolled through the options. Finally, I found the one I was looking for. The FIND PLAYER option. Thankfully, it was not blurred out.

"Find Ikumi," I commanded the game.

"Ikumi? Who's Ikumi?" Lilli broke in.

"This girl. I met her yesterday while you were at lunch. I think she might be a beta tester. Or one of the employees' kids. She said she's been playing Dragon Ops since the very beginning, so she's probably really good."

"You think she can help us?"

"I hope so. Cause she's the only hack we've got."

My menu blinked and a map appeared, floating in front of me. In the center was a large *X* marking Ikumi's location, which appeared to be in a village called Ghost Hollow.

"Yes!" I cried, excitement rising inside of me. "Found her!"

"And she doesn't look that far away, either," Lilli noted, peering at the map. "At least I don't think so. . . ." She tapped her chin with her finger. "Can you call her? Like Derek called us?"

"It doesn't look like it," I mused, going through the options. "I'm guessing you have to be in the same party—or at least on each other's friends list. . . ."

"But you really think she could help us?"

"She's the only one, at this point, who possibly could."

"Well then." Lilli grabbed her bag and walked to the door. "Let's get ourselves to Ghost Hollow."

Chapter Seventeen

We stepped out onto on the front porch of the game maker's cottage. It was full-on night now, with thick clouds covering the moon, making it so dark I couldn't see more than a few feet in front of me.

My ears, however, were working fine, perfectly picking up every rustle in the nearby bushes, every squeak and growl, causing the hairs on the back of my neck to stand on end. We weren't alone out here. Not by a long shot. And if we walked out blind? We were totally going to end up some monster's midnight snack.

"Maybe we should go back inside and look for flashlights," I suggested uneasily.

But Lilli shook her head. "I already looked. There were none."

"Well, we can't just walk out in the dark. Anything could be out there."

"Too bad we can't up the brightness settings like we do in the regular game," Lilli joked. "The ultimate dark-level hack."

"Wait, are you sure we can't?" I accessed my menu and went through the options again. Maybe there was something I missed. . . .

A moment later, I let out a cheer. "Ooh!" I cried. "I've got it!"

"A brightness setting?"

"Even better," I declared. "Night vision."

In fact there were all sorts of weird goggle settings to choose from in the menu—infrared, sunglasses (I guess for really bright days?), and night vision. These game makers had really thought of everything.

Well, except for the whole "What if a rogue AI dragon takes over the game?" thing.

I reached out and clicked the goggles icon. In an instant the dark world came alive with a glowing green tint. Suddenly, I could see everything. Trees, bushes, paths . . .

And eyes. Hundreds of glowing yellow eyes.

"Um . . ." I stammered, biting my lower lip. "Lilli?"

But my sister was still fiddling with her menu. "What's it under again?"

The yellow eyes blinked in sync. Super creepy. "It's in the options section," I said. "You might want to hurry. . . ."

"There!" she cried triumphantly. Then she screeched. "Holy golden glowing orbs of nightmares! What are those?"

"No idea. But I'm going to take a wild guess and say they're not friendly."

"Think we can sneak past them then?" Lilli asked. "'Cause I'm guessing we don't stand a chance, fighting them all at once." She squinted, her eyes scanning the forest. "There does seem to be some sort of path...."

"Awesome," I said sarcastically. "A sneak quest."

As much as I loved video games, I'd always hated the sneak quests. I didn't have the patience for them. I'd get bored halfway through and then just give up and start hacking and slashing my way to the other side.

I was a master at the hack-and-slash.

But that wasn't going to work here. There were way too many of them, whatever they were. Maybe I could have taken out a few, but then the rest of the pack would hear the dying cries of their friends and activate.

And the mighty warrior would be reduced to a tasty chew toy.

So... sneak it was.

I drew in a breath. "Okay," I said. "Let's do this before I lose my nerve." Stepping off the porch, I began to tiptoe, as quietly as I could. After taking a few steps, I glanced back at my sister, who was a few feet behind. She shook her head.

"What?" I whispered. "I'm sneaking!"

Look at your noise meter, she mouthed.

I glanced at my menu. Sure enough, a small indicator in

the upper left hand corner was blinking red. I sighed and slowed my pace even more.

"Take your time," Lilli whispered as she came up behind me. "Look before you step. Then repeat." She met my eyes with her own. *You can do this*, she mouthed. Though I wasn't sure if she truly believed it.

But what choice did I have? I did as she suggested, placing one foot down, then another, taking my time to make sure I didn't step on anything or trip over anything. And sure enough, my noise meter soon dropped back down to "hidden" level. My sister shot me a thumbs-up.

We continued this way through the forest, down the winding path, tiptoeing past countless pairs of eyes that, upon closer examination, turned out to belong to packs of draconites—baby dragons the size of small dogs, nestled in cozy ground nests while their mothers hunted for food. Unlike their gentle cousins, dragonbites, draconites were known to be vicious little hunters. Though they were really cute...

I stopped to get a better look at one of them in a nearby nest. The draconite inside had a small, chubby body with short wings and a pug-shaped snout. It was so super adorable, I almost waved Lilli over to check him out. Then Mr. Adorable raised his head and yawned, showing off a double set of razor-sharp teeth.

I gulped and kept moving, hurrying to catch up with my sister. The sooner we got out of here—

"ARGH!"

Distracted by the draconite, I'd totally forgotten to pay attention to my footing and managed to hook my foot under a tangled root. When I tried to lift it again, I tripped, flying forward and hitting the ground hard, my palms skidding painfully over sharp rocks.

"Ow!"

A dozen pairs of eyes snapped in my direction.

Oh no.

No, no, NO!

"*Run!*" Lilli shouted. "Get up and run!"

Scrambling to my feet, I ran after my sister, fast as my legs could carry me. Behind us, I could hear the draconites roaring, taking flight. It didn't take long for them to fall into formation and chase after us—like a swarm of giant, deadly dragon bees.

This was not good. This was not good at all.

I pushed myself to run faster, sweat dripping down my back. How far would they chase us? In the regular game, each monster was assigned to a specific zone. Which meant if you could get to the end of that zone, they would retreat to their starting point and leave you alone.

But here? After Atreus's takeover? For all I knew they were free to chase us to the end of the island.

"Ow!" Sharp pain shot up my leg. Looking down, I saw one of the draconites had latched on to my shin, his double set of teeth digging into my flesh. I shook my leg hard, finally managing to dislodge him, then kept running before another one could grab me. But the hot white heat pulsing through my body wasn't making it easy.

It's not real, I tried to remind myself. *Your brain is tricking you.*

But the pain only intensified. So much for mind over matter.

"Look!" Lilli cried suddenly. "Over there!"

My gaze alighted on a small door cut into the side of a cliff. Hope surged through me. If we could just get inside . . .

We changed direction, booking it to the door. The draconites followed close behind, snarling and chomping their teeth. When we reached it, Lilli wrapped her hands around the handle and pulled.

The door didn't budge.

Chapter Eighteen

"Let me try!" I cried, grabbing the handle and throwing all my weight in the opposite direction, hoping to yank it open. But it was stuck fast. Meanwhile, the forest had gone quiet.

Heart plummeting, I slowly turned around. The draconites had surrounded us and were watching with eager eyes. I looked up, wondering if we could possibly climb the cliff in front of us, but it was too steep—too smooth. No handholds to help us. And since draconites could fly, it probably wasn't the escape we needed, anyhow.

With shaky hands, I reached for my sword. What else could I do? But I had little hope of successfully hacking and slashing my way through this horde. There were too many of them, and they were too small and too fast. It would be all too easy for them to dodge my clumsy, heavy strikes, then dive in for the kill.

They inched forward, gnashing their teeth. The wound in my leg pulsed angrily, reminding me of how sharp those teeth were. Would they all attack at once? At least then it would be over quickly. But what would happen next? Atreus had said no do-overs.

Did that mean if we died in the game, we'd die in real life?

"Yes! I got it!"

I whirled around, surprised to hear the excitement in my sister's voice. To my amazement, she'd somehow gotten the door open, revealing a dimly lit passageway beyond.

"How did you—?" I started to ask, then realized it didn't matter. The door was open. We had our escape. I took a step toward it.

The second I made my move, the draconites roared in unison, dive-bombing us at top speed. I lunged through the door, narrowly missing being raked by a set of sharp claws. My sister followed, trying to yank the door shut behind her. But one of the draconites had managed to get stuck, half in, half out, making it impossible to seal. She struggled, trying to knock it away with her free hand while avoiding its teeth and claws.

Suddenly, I knew what I had to do. I raised my sword, slashing down on the draconite's head, slicing it from its body. The head fell to the ground with a heavy thump, and my sister slammed the door shut and locked it again. From outside, I could hear the frustrated roaring of the other draconites, banging into the door over and over. Thankfully, the lock held.

We were safe. At least for the moment.

I looked around, taking in our new surroundings. We had entered a low-ceilinged cavern with rough stone walls. A narrow tunnel led downward, lined with flickering torches every few feet. I strained to listen for any sounds of new monsters on approach, but heard nothing.

I dropped to the ground, my heart still racing. "That was close," I managed to say, looking down at my leg. The burning pain had reduced to a slow throb, which was good. But it did confirm what I'd been secretly wondering—Atreus had messed with my SensSuit, too.

"Too close," Lilli agreed. She leaned against the wall, panting heavily.

"Once again thanks to Eight-Bit Ian," I said bitterly, looking at my palms, which were still bruised and cut from slamming against the ground. "I am seriously the worst gamer ever."

Lilli nudged me with her elbow. "Come on. I could have fallen just as easily."

"But you didn't. And you got the door open somehow and totally saved us. How did you even do that, by the way? Some kind of spell?"

"Nope. Just plain, old-fashioned lock-picking. I put a couple points in it when we leveled after the rat dragon."

I groaned. "I totally forgot we leveled. I need to assign

my skill points, too. I'm thinking a 'plus three to not suck-ing' might help. You think that's an option?"

Lilli chuckled. "You really need to stop being so hard on yourself. You killed the dragon thingie, remember?" She pointed to the severed draconite head on the floor, now soaking in a pool of dark blood. I shuddered, my stomach twisting. Killing things was a lot grosser here than in front of a computer monitor.

Sighing, I accessed my menu, selecting the LEVELED UP! option I'd totally missed before. I'd been given five points to assign to my character. I could choose between strength, which would make me do more damage; vitality, which would give me more hit points; and dexterity, which would make me harder to hit. There were also a bunch of ran-dom skills to choose from, including speech, sneak, and, of course, lock-picking.

In the end, I decided to put two points in strength, two points in vitality, and one point in sneak. Maybe that would help me not fall flat on my face next time.

"There," I declared. "Now I'm a total ninja like you."

"Fantastic!" declared a new voice. "After all, everyone knows, ninjas are *way* cooler than pirates."

I spun around, my heart in my throat all over again. Was someone in the tunnel with us?

At first I saw nothing. Then, I caught a weird fluttering at the corner of my eye. I looked down, then up again as I realized the draconite's head was no longer lying in the pool of blood. Instead, it was hovering in midair...

With a brand-new body attached.

I yelped and lunged backward, slamming into the cave wall behind me. As I winced in pain, the newly regenerated draconite regarded me with skeptical eyes.

"Great Scott, is it Noob Week and no one thought to tell me?" he asked in a striking English accent. "This bloke can't even stand up straight."

I stared at the creature, mouth gaping. "You're...you're alive!"

"Give Captain Obvious a gold star."

"But I chopped off your head!"

"Well, not *my* head. I mean, I guess it's my head now, after nicking it from that dead fellow. It didn't need it anymore, thanks to you."

The draconite made a sudden move toward us. We squealed and ducked to get out of his way. He stopped midair, cocking his head in confusion. "What? Do I smell or something?" He sniffed his wingpits and shrugged.

We exchanged glances. "Um, no offense..." Lilli stammered. "But aren't you going to try to eat us?"

"Eat you?" The draconite raised an eyebrow. (Yes, somehow he had eyebrows. They were rather bushy, too.) "Are you joking? Have you ever had a taste of human flesh?"

We shook our heads.

"Well, let me be the first to inform you, you taste *nothing* like porg." The draconite smacked his lips. "Mmm. Porg. I'd really fancy a nice, big, fat porg sandwich right about now. Kentucky-fried, preferably. You don't happen to have one in that sack of yours, do you?" He gestured to our packs with his wing.

"Porg? What do you think this is, a Star Wars game?" I asked.

"Right," he declared. "I hate that whole copyright thing. Always so limiting when it comes to proper snack foods." He shook out his wings. "In any case, I must ask: What in D'ou's name are you doing wandering around Dragon Ops without a guide? It's dangerous out there, you know! Even for experienced players." He gave us a critical once-over. "And you two are clearly not experienced."

"I managed to chop off *your* head," I muttered, offended. I was already mad at myself for my poor performance so far. I didn't need to get shade from random virtual creatures, too.

The draconite sighed. "Again, not my head. Just borrowing it so you can see me. Our case studies have found that humans can't accept disembodied voices as their guides. They need to see something. So I chose this. If you kill something else down the road that you'd prefer I look like, give us a shout and I'll swap out."

"I don't understand. What are you?" my sister interjected,

stepping closer to examine the creature now that she was no longer worried about being on its dinner menu.

The draconite shook himself and a ripple of silver shimmered down his side. "Sorry," he said. "I probably should have led with that, eh? My programmer says I have the worst manners known to AI kind. But since she was the one to program my manners to begin with? I say that's on her." He flew over to me, holding out a paw. "Name's Yamata-no-Orochi. After the legendary eight-headed Japanese dragon of old. But feel free to rename me. That's your right. Why, you can call me Farting Felicia if it strikes your fancy." He paused, then added, "Though I'm really hoping it doesn't. Honestly, I'm still reeling from being called Fluffy Princess Babypants by that last beta tester group. That was a rough one, even for a pro like me."

"So wait," my sister said. "Are you, like, a pet or something?"

"A *pet*?" the draconite screeched. "Of all the insulting—" He huffed loudly, releasing a large puff of smoke from his snout. "I am an official Dragon Ops companion and guide, I'll have you know."

"A guide?" I repeated. "I thought all the guides were human."

"That's what you get for thinking," scoffed the draconite. He landed on top of Lilli's head and started picking at his teeth with his claw. "In truth, the human guides are just temporary. Until they get all the kinks worked out. Otherwise there'd be too many real-life employees to house and feed and clean up after." He pinched his snout with his paw. "Humans are so dirty, no offense."

"So wait," Lilli said, a look of realization crossing her face. "You're, like, a virtual guide?"

"*Your* virtual guide, to be precise. Which reminds me, I really don't appreciate you entering the game without me. As I said, it's dangerous out there. Especially at your level. How did you ever even get past the front gates?"

"Um, Eugene let us in," I said. "He said he was filling in because Farah was sick."

"Farah *is* sick. Everyone's sick. Some dodgy barbeque or something—practically all the humans have been puking their guts out all morning. That's why they assigned me to you, instead." The draconite frowned. "Not Eugene. He's not one of the guides. Unless he's new…"

I frowned. This was really weird. "No. He said he was a programmer," I explained. "But that he was assigned to take us on a tour. He wasn't very happy about it."

"I shouldn't think he would be. The programmers are quite busy these days." The draconite looked around. "So… where is he now?"

"He left," Lilli explained. "He went to fix Atreus. And… well, I'm afraid it didn't go so well."

"I should say not. The game is completely unstable.

That's why it took me so long to find you. Everything's gone completely wonky. And half of my control functions aren't working."

"Look, we need to get out of here," I said. "Can you help open the gate at least?"

The guide shook his head. "I'm afraid not, mate. And before you ask, I can't call for help, either. It's like everything's blocked off." He gave us a rueful look. "Look, I don't want to alarm you, but I think we're trapped in the game."

"Yeah, no kidding," I muttered.

"You can't do *anything*?" Lilli asked. "Like, maybe raise our levels or something? Give us some extra powers or gear? At least give us a fighting chance in here?"

"Sorry, luv. I'm just a low-level AI. All I've got to offer is my brilliant personality and wicked sense of humor. Maybe a few fun facts. For example, did you know turkeys can blush? Or that giraffe tongues can be twenty inches long? That armadillo shells are bulletproof?"

"So basically a walking Alexa," I concluded, disappointed.

"Hey! Don't you be knocking my girl Alexa! She's one smart cookie!" the draconite scolded. "And that lass can sing! Not to mention play a mean game of *Jeopardy*." He started humming the theme song to the game show.

I groaned, turning to my sister. "This is ridiculous. Let's keep heading to Ghost Hollow like we planned." I started down the tunnel. "I think it's this way...."

With a noisy flap of his wings, the draconite flew into my path, stopping me in my tracks. "Now *that* is something I can help you with!"

I rolled my eyes. "We have a map, dude."

"Maybe so, but you don't have all the rest of what's stored in my databanks. Game lore, creature guides—loads of useful stuff. For example, did you know draconites hate fire? You could have walked down that path with a lit torch and none of them would have come within ten feet of you." He gave me a knowing look. "I could have told you that. Saved you quite a bit of trouble."

I bit my lower lip. I didn't want to admit it, but he was right. That was exactly the kind of information we would need if we were to have any chance of getting through this game.

"Fine," I said. "I guess we could use your help."

"Of course you could," the draconite replied, puffing up with pleasure. "Now, all you have to do is make it official. Click on me and give me a name. Then we'll be off on our grand adventure."

Lilli came up beside me, reaching out to poke the draconite. Then she frowned, thinking. "What should I name you?" she asked. "No offense, but Yamata-no-Orochi is kind of a mouthful."

"Also, you don't have eight heads," I added.

"Look, mate, I don't bring up your shortcomings—"

"How about . . . Yano for short?" Lilli suggested.

The draconite seemed to consider this. "You know, that's not bad," he said. Then he laughed. "Get it? You know? 'Yano'?"

I groaned. "Seriously, are all your jokes this bad?"

"Of course not!" Yano replied. "Some are much, much worse."

Chapter Nineteen

"**A**re you sure we should trust this guy?" Lilli whispered as we followed Yano deeper into the tunnel, keeping our ears pricked for any unusual sounds. All I could hear was the faint crackling of flame from the torches and a small drip of water from somewhere nearby.

"Why do you say that?" I whispered back.

"I don't know. It's just... too convenient, I guess. Him appearing out of nowhere like that. How do we know Atreus didn't send him to spy on us? Or lead us in the wrong direction completely? How do we know for sure he is who he says he is?"

Ugh. I hadn't thought of that possibility. I had been so relieved to have someone else take the lead, but what if he was leading us into something much worse?

"He said he was supposed to be our guide from the

beginning. And he knew about Farah and the bad bar-beque," I pointed out.

"True. But then what about Eugene? Why did he show up to guide us instead? He didn't seem super thrilled to be leading us into the park, and he left the first chance he could get."

I frowned. "I don't know. This whole thing is weird. Maybe Ikumi can sort it out. She must know everyone, since she lives here and all."

"True. Though what if she's trapped in the game, too?" Lilli asked.

"Oh." I hadn't thought of that.

"I mean, if she was playing when everything glitched out, then she's probably stuck, just like us. Which means she might not be able to be any help." Lilli closed her eyes in frustration. I was right there with her.

"Let's keep going for now," I said. "It's not like we have much of a choice, right? We'll just keep an eye on Yano to make sure he doesn't do anything weird. And hopefully Ikumi at least has some answers about what's going on."

"Okay. Sounds like a plan," Lilli agreed. "Though first we need to get out of this tunnel." She tapped her staff on the ground, and a low echoing sound bounced off the walls. "It looks weirdly familiar here, doesn't it? Sort of like the Dry Bones dungeon we did a couple years back?"

"You're right!" I exclaimed, looking around. "It totally

does. Same weird etchings on the walls. Same torches . . ." I made a face. "Hopefully no snake boss, though. I so do not need to get poisoned here on top of everything else."

I shuddered, remembering our first trip through the Dry Bones dungeon. We'd fought this really tough snake thing at the very beginning and I got badly poisoned. And since no one had remembered to bring any antidotes with them, poor Lord Wildhammer had to spend the entire fight puking fluorescent green slime every ten seconds. Which basically made him useless.

It was awful in the game, and would be even worse if it happened here.

Lilli laughed, remembering. "You poor thing. I don't know why we didn't just go back and get you cured and start over."

"Logan didn't have time, remember? He had to go pick up his brother or something. And he swore he could tank himself." I rolled my eyes, remembering. "'Cause thieves make *such* good tanks . . ."

Lilli didn't reply. When I looked over, she was staring down at her feet, her face and neck flushing red. I cringed. What had I been thinking, bringing up the L word? *Way to go, Ian.*

"Sorry," I said quickly. "I didn't mean—"

She waved me off. "Whatever. No big deal."

But it *was* a big deal. I could tell from the look on her face. She was still not over that loser. And he had single-handedly annihilated all her good memories of this amazing game. We'd had so much fun playing *Fields of Fantasy* on those boring summer afternoons. And now all she could remember was the way it had ended.

"Look," I started, "Logan was a jerk. But you can't let him ruin the game for you. You loved gaming! I know you did!"

"Yeah, well, I thought I loved Logan, too. And look where that got me."

"You can't blame the game for that."

My sister stopped in her tracks. "I know, Ian, okay? Let it go. Seriously."

"Okay, okay." I held up my hands. "Just . . . trying to make conversation."

"You might want to give yourself some points in Speech next time you level up," Yano suggested brightly. I hadn't realized he'd flown back to join us again. Hopefully he hadn't heard us talking about him. "It doesn't seem to be your strong suit."

"Thanks," I muttered.

"I live to serve," Yano replied. "Also, fun fact: Some poisons can be good for you! Gila monster saliva can lower blood sugar and help diabetics lose weight. And some viper venoms even reduce blood pressure." He flapped his wings. "Would you like me to continue?"

"No!" my sister and I shouted in unison. Then we looked at each other and snorted, breaking some of the tension between us. Yano gave me a knowing wink, then flew up ahead, leaving us alone again.

My sister turned to me. "Sorry," she said. "I didn't mean to go off on you. I just don't want to talk about you-know-who."

"I'm sorry I brought him up. It's just…I miss playing with you. And…well, I hate that you don't miss playing with me."

My sister's face fell. "Ian—"

But before she could finish her sentence, Yano was back, his eyes alight. "Look! Look!" he squawked. "Look what's up ahead!"

I followed his gaze, my eyes widening as they caught a thin ribbon of natural-looking light shimmering before us. "Is that an exit?"

"The literal light at the end of the tunnel," Yano agreed with a dreamy sigh. "Sometimes this game can be almost poetic."

Excitement rolled over me. We'd done it! We'd gotten through. Surging with a sudden burst of energy, I started running down the tunnel in the direction of the white light. As I ran, I could hear Lilli laughing behind me.

"Hang on, Leeroy!" she called out, referencing an old internet meme about a *World of Warcraft* guy who rushed into a dragon's nest without warning. Lilli had always claimed he reminded her of me—both in the game and in real life—and it had become a favorite nickname.

"At least I have chicken!" I shouted back with a grin—Leeroy's famous last line after he managed to get his entire party wiped out with his dumb move. The light was getting closer now. We were almost out. We were almost—

Holy mother of dragons! What is that?

I stopped short, digging in my heels as something large and slimy slithered into our path. Scrambling backward, I managed to trip over my own feet, crashing butt-first onto the hard stone ground, sending a fresh dart of pain shooting up my spine. But I could barely feel it as I looked up at the massive creature now in front of me.

And suddenly, I felt very, *very* chicken.

Chapter Twenty

"Holy colossal worms of squirming nightmares!" Lilli cried from behind me. "What is *that*?"

It was a good question. In fact, in all my years of playing *Fields of Fantasy* I'd never seen such a creature as the one gliding toward us now. A huge, legless, wormlike monster with a bulbous head, slimy turd-colored scales, and ten tiny black eyes circling a cavernous hole of a mouth filled with rows upon rows of shiny white teeth.

And if that wasn't gross enough? As it slithered closer, I realized it wasn't just a giant worm—it was a giant worm infested with baby worms. Its bald, wrinkled hide squirmed with mini-me versions of itself. And when one of those baby worms fell off the creature's body and landed in my hair? I almost puked on the spot.

"Argh!" I cried, smacking at my head. "Get it off me!"

Yano landed on my shoulder. He stuck out his tongue and slurped up the worm. "Now *that* tastes like porg!" he crowed, green slime dripping down his chin.

"I think I'm going to be sick," Lilli moaned, clutching her stomach.

"What . . . is that?" I asked, backing away from the creature. The good news? It'd stopped moving toward us. The bad? It was totally blocking our exit.

"Come now! Haven't you ever seen an earth dragon before?" Yano asked. "They're actually quite lovely. Though quite deadly, too, now that I think about it."

"*That's* a dragon?" Lilli sputtered, staring at the creature.

Yano rolled his eyes. "Of course! Dragons come in all shapes and sizes. Don't be all judgy."

The worm dragon licked its mouth with a thick black tongue, and a splotch of goo splashed onto the ground. I watched in horror as the drool hissed and smoked, burning a hole into the stone.

"So it spits acid, too," I noted. "Awesome."

"How else is it supposed to burrow through solid rock?" Yano asked. "Let's be practical here."

I bit my lip, trying to figure out what to do. There was no way we could sneak around this thing. It was too big, too thick, its doughy flesh filling up almost the entire tunnel. But what else could we do? We'd come too far to turn back now, and the tunnel exit was so close.

And yet so far...

I turned to my sister. "We have no choice. We have to fight it."

Lilli nodded grimly. "Maybe I could start with a spell?" she suggested. "It's an earth dragon, so maybe something water related?"

"Sounds good," I said. As every gamer knew, if a creature possessed the powers from one element, they were bound to be weak when faced with the opposite element. So you'd fight fire with ice. Earth with water. Hopefully it still worked like that here.

I reached for my sword and shield, trying to gear myself up to dive into the fray if the dragon tried to charge my sister after she performed her cast. I was determined, this time, to do better than I had with the rat dragon in the basement. After all, I was a gamer, I reminded myself. And while this was a little different, at the end of the day it was still a game. And the only way to get out of this mess was to find a way to win.

Which left no room for wimping out.

Lilli closed her eyes, muttering some magic words under her breath. As I watched, breathless, a blast of water shot out from her staff—hitting the worm dragon square in the face. Yes! Direct hit!

"Sweet!" I cried. "Get it, Lills!"

The worm dragon roared with fury, shaking its head back and forth, causing more baby worms to rain down on top of us. I ducked and covered my head, feeling their slimy little bodies writhe across my skin. But when I looked again, the dragon was still standing there, as if the water blast had done no damage at all.

"Argh," Lilli groaned. "It must be immune to magic or something."

Before I could reply, the dragon lurched forward, hissing and gnashing its teeth. I leapt in front of my sister, raising my shield moments before the creature spewed a hot load of acid straight in our direction. My shield, thankfully, took most of the blast, but a few drops splashed onto my breastplate, sizzling and burrowing into the steel.

I screamed, dropped my burning shield, and fumbled with the straps of my armor. I barely managed to get it off my body before the acid burned all the way through to the other side. Quickly, I threw it across the tunnel like a hot potato.

Lilli ran over to me. "Are you okay?"

"I think so. But my shield and chest plate are toast." I glanced over at the discarded armor, which was still blistering as the acid gobbled up the metal. My stomach twisted as I imagined what it would have felt like on my skin.

"What are we going to do?" Lilli asked, looking panicked. "My spells don't work. And you can't fight without armor."

We turned to the worm, who had gone back into self-defense mode, opening and closing its mouth like a monstrous baby bird while mini worms danced on its tongue.

What kind of sick programmer designed such a disgusting thing?

Suddenly, a thought struck me. I turned to find Yano, who had clearly been busy treating himself to an all-you-can-eat worm buffet while we'd been fighting for our lives. He looked up, a little guiltily, half a worm still wriggling from the side of his mouth.

"Yes?" he asked.

I sighed. "Um, could we trouble our guide for a little *guidance* here?"

"I thought you'd never ask." Yano slurped the rest of the worm into his mouth, then spit it out, making a face. "Ugh. Stay away from the green ones. They taste like old farts."

"That won't be a problem," I said, shuddering. "Now how do we defeat this guy?"

Chapter Twenty-One

Yano flew over to us, landing on my shoulder. "Right," he said, shaking out his body, as if ready to get down to business. "Let me start with a quick scan. This way I can try to match it with the creatures in my database. See if it has any weaknesses."

The draconite closed his eyes, mumbling something under his breath. Something that, oddly, sounded a lot less like a spell of scanning and a lot more like the lyrics to a Taylor Swift song.

I shot my sister a look. She shrugged, still keeping a wary eye on the earth dragon, who didn't seem all that interested in initiating a second attack. Which was kind of weird, actually. Most creatures—at least in regular games—would keep attacking until they or the other players were dead. But I wasn't about to complain.

Yano switched to a Beyoncé song.

"Anything?" I asked.

"Oh. Yes. Sorry." He opened his eyes. "I found a weak spot. But...I'm not sure you're going to like it." He chuckled.

"What is it?" I asked. "Its eyes? Its mouth? One particular baby worm?" None of these things sounded good. But at least it would be a start. As it was, we were fighting blind.

Yano shook his head, now giggling madly. "Nope. But you're getting warmer...."

I ran a hand through my hair, trying to think. Then, a horrifying thought struck me. "Oh man. Please don't say its butt."

"Well, I won't say it, *but...*" Yano slapped his side with his wing. "Oops!" He cackled again. "Anyway, yes. You must slice off its tail. It's the only way."

My gaze turned to the worm, dismay rising in my stomach. "Seriously?" I cried.

"I'm an AI, mate. We don't joke around. Well, at least about serious stuff. I do know some great jokes." He cleared his throat. "Like, why did the teddy bear say no to dessert?"

"Because it was already *stuffed*," my sister shot back. "I mean, really. We learned that one in kindergarten."

"Um, no offense, but can we put comedy hour on hold and get back to the whole dragon-tail thing?" I interjected. "How am I even going to get back there? There's, like, zero room between it and the tunnel's wall. And if I even try to squeeze by, it's going to blast me with more acid. And without my armor—"

"Wow, you really are a glass-half-empty kind of lad, aren't you?" Yano tsked. "If you would let me finish..."

"Well, then finish already!"

Yano rose from my shoulder and flew over to the worm dragon. Before we could make a move to stop him, he got right up in the creature's face and waved his paws madly in front of each of its ten eyes. Instinctively, I put my hands over my face, bracing for another acid spew.

But the earth dragon did nothing. In fact, it didn't react at all—as if it didn't even realize Yano was there. I lowered my hands.

"Wait," I said. "Is it—"

"Blind?" Lilli finished for me. "Oh my gosh, it can't see us!" She let out a small cheer. The dragon snapped its head in her direction, snorting angrily.

"But it *can* hear you!" Yano added, flying back to us. "Which means you need to be really, really quiet if you want to sneak past it and reach its tail."

"Ooh! Another sneak quest. Ian's favorite," Lilli remarked teasingly.

"Hey! I'm more than happy to let you do the honors."

"That's very gallant of you, Ian." Yano snorted. "But I'm afraid that's not going to work. You need something sharp if you're going to slice off its tail. And, as a mage, Lilli isn't allowed to use a sword."

"How convenient," I grumbled.

Sucking in a breath, I crouched low and inched closer to the big bad as quietly as I could, this time paying special attention to my noise meters. Thank goodness I had put that point in sneaking—it was definitely making things easier now. In fact, it wasn't long before I found myself within punching distance of the creature's giant maw, which, let's just say, looked even more terrifying close up. And it had looked pretty darn terrifying from a distance!

But I forced my fear down and kept moving, reminding myself once again that this was only a game. That this creature was nothing more than a bloated bunch of pixels, mashed together by some bored programmer dude chowing down on Cheetos in his cubicle back at the base.

Unfortunately, this knowledge didn't make me feel much better. After all, the dragon looked real. It sounded real. And, thanks to Atreus's tweaks to our SensSuits, I knew its teeth would *feel* real chomping down on my flesh.

Come on, Ian! Less thinking, more moving.

Finally, I reached the side of the tunnel. Pressing my back against the wall, I began to inch along the stone, careful not to come in contact with the dragon. It was a tight squeeze; there couldn't be more than a foot of space between the dragon and the rock. Plus the creature kept squirming from side to side, making that space ebb and flow. I was forced to inch forward, then stop, wait for it to move, then take another step. Sweat dripped down my forehead as my pulse pounded in my ears. But I pressed on, and soon I was three-quarters of the way to my destination.

"Piece of cake," I whispered to myself, low enough for the dragon not to hear. Maybe I wasn't as bad at this game as I thought! Maybe I'd get to the other side, raise my sword, cut off its tail and—boom! Lord Wildhammer, hero of the realm.

Suddenly a voice wormed through my head.

Piece of cake, huh? Atreus purred. *Then perhaps we should take things up a notch . . .*

Wait, what?

Um, that's really not necessary! I tried to silently send back, hoping the video-game dragon could hear my thoughts as I could hear his. *I was kidding about the cake. The cake was a lie!*

Suddenly the tunnel started to shake hard, as if caught in an earthquake. Dirt rained down from above, a big chunk landing in my eye before I could blink. I doubled over as the sharp grit stung my eye, and I tried to keep the other eye open so I could see what was happening. Huge rocks broke free of the walls, smashing down onto the stone floor in front of me, behind me—everywhere. I put my hands over my head to try to shield myself, but it was no use.

"Please, Atreus!" I begged. "Stop!"

But the tunnel continued to shake as if it was about to collapse. The dragon worm bellowed in rage, as it was also getting smacked by falling rocks, and its body jerked, pinning me against the wall and knocking the air from my lungs. I gasped as I struggled to free myself, but it was no use. I was trapped between the dragon and the wall. And still quite a few feet from its tail. What was I going to do? A stray rock slammed down on my head, almost knocking me out. I screamed in pain.

"Hey, ugly! Over here!"

I lifted my head, vaguely recognizing my sister's voice. It sounded muffled and far away. But the earth dragon shifted in the direction of the sound, thankfully releasing me from my prison. I collapsed in a heap, my whole body feeling bruised and broken.

"Your mum is a sandworm!" I heard Yano pick up the cry. "And your dad is—"

I didn't wait to hear the rest. I picked myself up and ran—full Leeroy Jenkins–style now—to the dragon's tail. When I reached it, I didn't pause. I raised my sword and slammed it down, slicing through thick, wormy flesh.

The dragon screeched in agony as its tail detached from its body. Blood fountained from the gaping wound with so much force it knocked me backward. I grunted as the severed tail landed on top of me and I fought to knock it away.

"Ew! Ew! Gross!"

Then, suddenly, I heard it. Triumphant music blasting in

my ears. A moment later, writing scrolled across my field of vision.

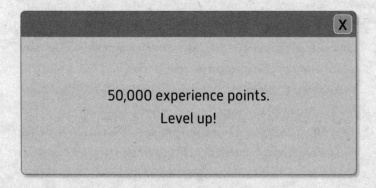

X

50,000 experience points.
Level up!

"Whoa!" I cried, scrambling to my feet and looking around. Thankfully the tunnel was no longer shaking. "Did we do it? Did we slay the dragon?"

Sure enough, the earth dragon was now nothing more than a lifeless, bloated corpse on the ground. A surge of excitement shot through me and I jumped up and down with joy.

"We did it! We totally did it!" I cried as Lilli and Yano made their way around the dead dragon and over to me. I ran to my sister, throwing my arms around her in a huge hug. "Can you believe it?"

Lilli laughed. "That was all you, dude. I only distracted it for a second. You got the job done." She smiled at me. "Maybe you're not as bad as you think you are, dragon slayer."

My cheeks burned. Dragon slayer. I was a dragon slayer!

"Well," I stammered. "Maybe I'm not *so* bad...."

"You were quite epic, in fact," Yano agreed. "Especially under the circumstances. I didn't want to alarm you while you were fighting for your life, but that dragon? That was Wyrm, one of the four main boss dragons in the game."

I stared at our guide. "He was a boss? And we killed him? How is that even possible at our level?"

"Oh, it isn't," Yano replied smugly. "But lucky for you, you have an epic guide. I actually activated a special power-up I'd saved from the last group I worked with to cast on you so you'd have a fighting chance. For one glorious minute you were both level eighty."

Suddenly all the glory and honor I'd felt for defeating the guy deflated. "Why would you do that?"

"Um, so you wouldn't end up a bloody puddle on the floor?" Yano said. "You're welcome, by the way."

"I know, but that's cheating!"

"Atreus is cheating. I was just helping out my group. Remember, we don't know what happens when you die in the game. Would you have preferred to find out by getting eaten alive by a nasty worm creature?"

"Thank you," my sister interjected. "We appreciate it." She gave me a stern look. I sighed. I knew she was right. But still! I really thought it'd been me....

"Whatever," I said. "Just...let us try first next time, okay? Before you rush in to save the day?"

"No problem. As I said, that was my last extra power-up. You are now officially at the mercy of your own incompetence for the remainder of the game."

"Great. I think. . . ."

Yano looked up at the ceiling. "I still don't understand that whole cave-in thing, though. Definitely wasn't in the fight description I read. Maybe they added it recently. They're always changing things here. Hard to keep updated."

I frowned. In the glory of victory I'd almost forgotten about that part. The way Atreus had whispered in my ear before starting a cave-in. A shiver tripped down my back, and I wondered if I should mention it to my sister. The dragon was definitely not planning to make this easy on us. And next time we might not be so lucky.

"This thing is so freaking gross," Lilli remarked, kicking the tail with her foot to knock it away. It rolled over, uncovering something odd shaped lying on the ground. "Wait, what's that?" she asked.

"Um, no idea."

I watched as my sister dropped to her knees, scooping the object up into her palm. "I think the dragon dropped it. Maybe some kind of treasure?" She rose to her feet, holding it out for me to see.

I raised an eyebrow. "It looks like a turd."

"No it doesn't," she protested, clearly offended. "It looks like an egg."

I wrinkled my nose. The object in her hand was vaguely

egg-shaped. But it was also brown. A very specific shade of brown. "I'm still going with dragon turd."

"Whatever." She waved me off. "I'm going to keep it, just in case. Who knows, maybe I can sell it or something."

"Who's going to want to buy a turd?"

"What if it's a magical turd . . . ?" She grinned wickedly.

I shook my head. "Worm dragons and magical turds. What's next?" I asked as we walked toward the cave exit, ready to step out into the sunshine.

But as we did, Atreus's voice slithered in my ear again.

Oh, tiny human. Just you wait and see. . . .

Chapter Twenty-Two

"Ah, yes. The Soundless Bog. So lovely this time of year."

Lilli and I joined Yano at the mouth of the tunnel, surveying the new land we'd entered. While the starting zone had been a peaceful medieval forest—very pretty and picturesque—this place was a hot, swampy mess, with sunken riverbanks and sludgy, algae-infested water. The kind of water you'd expect an alligator to slither through. Or worse...

Crisscrossing the swamp was a maze of wooden walkways, branching out in all directions without any kind of safety railings. At the far end, I could just make out a small village.

"Is that Ghost Hollow?" I asked, a thread of hoping rising in my chest. "Are we really here?"

"That is Ghost Hollow," Yano confirmed. "But you're not there yet. You still have to cross the Soundless Bog."

I looked out over the murky water. At least it was no longer nighttime. We must have been in that tunnel for a while—at least in game time. Now, the twin suns shone brightly above, as if it were midday. Did that mean an entire day had passed in the game? And if so, how much time did that equal in real life? I was so confused by the time thing it hurt my head to think about it. I knew at some point we needed to eat and sleep—but what if this whole adventure had only been an hour or something in real-life time?

My sister stepped up to the closest walkway. As she tested it with her foot, it creaked under her weight. "You think this is safe?" she asked doubtfully.

"Safe?" Yano let out a barking laugh. "Are you kidding? This is Dragon Ops! Nowhere is safe! Well, except perhaps the Peaks of D'ou. If you're friends with Lord D'ou, that is. Otherwise you're basically asking to become a human Popsicle."

"Who's Lord D'ou?" I asked. It wasn't the first time I'd heard Yano mention his name. "I don't remember him from the regular game."

"You wouldn't," Yano replied. "He's new to the franchise. But he's brilliant. And I'm not just saying that because my programmer created him and programmed me to like him." He scrunched up his face. "Though . . . maybe I am, now that I think about it. Ugh. Nice work on the free will thing, Phyllis!" he shouted into the void. Then he turned back to us. "Sorry. In any case, just like Wyrm, Lord D'ou is one of the four king dragons of the game. He rules the kingdom of ice."

"Cool," I said. Another dragon robot. Hopefully this one wouldn't be as evil as Atreus. Or as slimy as Wyrm.

"Yes. Very cool," Yano agreed. "In fact, quite cold actually. 'Cause it's . . . made of ice?" He rolled his eyes. "Humans are so slow sometimes."

"Um, hello?" Lilli interjected. "Can we talk about this swamp that's right in front of us?" She waved her hand at the bog. "Do you have any useful info on this place?"

"Of course I do!" Yano shot back, looking offended. "I wouldn't be a very good guide if I didn't!" He cleared his throat. "This," he said solemnly, "is the Soundless Bog."

"And . . . ?"

"And it is . . . soundless. And . . . a bog." He gave us a *duh* look. I groaned.

"So helpful!" I muttered.

"Why thank you! I aim to please. I also accept tips, if you are so inclined at the end of the tour."

Ignoring him, I joined my sister on the walkway. As I stepped onto the wooden platform, I tried and failed not to notice the pair of large black eyes blinking back at me from under the water's murky surface.

Just a fish, I told myself. *A very . . . big . . . fish.*

"Come on," I said. "Let's go. Quickly."

We started our trek across the bog, moving carefully and navigating the maze of paths as best we could while avoiding rotten floorboards. It was slow going, but we were making steady progress, and I was starting to feel confident we could get through this with little trouble.

Until the fog started to roll in.

It was a thick fog—the kind that books always compared to pea soup—and soon we were socked in up to our waists. Which wouldn't have been much of a problem except now we couldn't see the tangle of walkways beneath our feet. Leaving us with no way to tell which floorboards had rotted through and which passageways led to swampy dead ends.

I gulped, looking across the sea of white before us, stretching out for what seemed like miles. With no way to tell where the bog ended or where it began.

Or, most importantly, which way we should go.

I glanced worriedly at Lilli. She opened her mouth to speak....

But nothing came out.

Her face went as white as a Mario ghost, and she gripped her throat with her hands. I tried to ask what was wrong, but even though I felt like I was speaking just as always, I didn't make a sound.

It was at that moment I realized how quiet everything had become. We'd been so focused on picking our way across the boards, I'd barely noticed the sounds of the birds tweeting from the trees or the leaves rustling in the breeze.

Now their absence and the absolute silence that had fallen over the swamp was nothing short of terrifying.

The Soundless Bog.

Suddenly Yano's explanation made a lot more sense.

I started shuffling slowly, feeling for the wooden walkway under my feet as my heart pattered hard in my chest. Why hadn't anyone bothered to build railings on these things? Wasn't that some kind of safety violation? Right now, there was nothing to keep me from making a wrong turn and plunging into the swamp. Finding out firsthand what those eyes were attached to.

I looked around for Yano, hoping he'd be able to guide our way. But he was nowhere to be seen. Instead, my eyes fell on a strange shadow creeping through the mists. Large and dark and sort of human shaped, but way too tall and skinny. With a few too many arms … and legs …

And teeth?

How could a shadow have teeth?

I grabbed my sister's arm and pointed. Her mouth twisted in horror. She tried to speak, but still, nothing. Desperate, she made a frantic gesture with her hands. I didn't need to hear her to know what she was trying to say.

Run.

Chapter Twenty-Three

But we couldn't run. Not without risking launching off a walkway and ending up in the swamp. Instead, we were forced to step carefully, quietly, hoping maybe the shadow was just a shadow and not a murderous creature out for human flesh. Hey, maybe it didn't like the taste of human flesh. Yano thought we were gross. Maybe we were gross to this shadow monster, too.

But . . . let's not try to find out.

Suddenly my foot hit air instead of wood and I flailed, waving my arms madly as I tried to keep my balance and not fall face-first into the swamp. Just as I was about to go over, strong hands grabbed me and yanked me back to safety. Lilli released me with a grim look. She gestured with her hands: *Slow down, idiot.* I sighed and gave her a thumbs-up to let her know I understood.

My eyes rose back to Ghost Hollow. It still looked so

far away; how would we ever reach it? The walkways had been a maze even when we could see them. Now we were walking blind.

I checked behind us. The shadow monster was so much closer than it was before. It floated over the fog, as if it were a surfer cresting a perfect wave. I could make out a few more details now. The thing had glowing red eyes, a body that seemed almost made of smoke, and way more of those freaky shadow teeth than I originally thought. Could shadow teeth dig into real-life flesh?

My sister grabbed my arm and pulled me down into the fog. My vision blurred white and I couldn't see a thing. Why did she think we were better off down here? But there was no way to ask her.

I was about to stand up again when I felt her tap on my arm. She grabbed my hand and placed it down on the wooden walkway at our feet. Then she picked up my other hand and placed it a foot in front of me. My mouth opened as I realized what she was suggesting. We couldn't see the pathway from above. But we could crawl through the fog and feel our way through.

While staying out of sight of the shadow monster.

Okay, so Lilli was basically a genius.

We crawled blindly on our hands and knees, unable to direct one another or even really see each other. We were nothing but hands on wood, feeling our way through, praying we wouldn't run into the shadow monster and his teeth.

I had no idea if we were even still heading toward Ghost Hollow, or back to where we started.

Still, anything was better than being out here.

Finally, after what seemed like forever, I felt dirt under my fingers. We'd reached solid ground. I let out a cry of joy—and was more excited when I realized I could actually hear my voice again. I rose to my feet, blinking to clear my vision, and spotted the entrance to the village not ten feet in front of us.

"We did it!" I shouted. We had made it through the Soundless Bog! I turned to see my sister collapsing onto the grassy bank beside me, breathing heavily, and when I looked back at the swamp I saw that the fog had lifted—just like that. The shadow monster had disappeared with it.

My menu blinked. Another level gained. *Yes!*

"So was that fun or what?" Yano chirped, appearing beside us.

"I think you need to review your definition of fun," my sister grumbled. Then she grinned as she realized she could speak again.

"Ah, come on, admit it," Yano cajoled. "That was a fantastic level. Really unique. One of my favorites, actually. And that shadow monster. Beautiful piece of programming!"

"You should probably look up the definition of 'beautiful' while you're at it." I laughed, climbing to my feet. "'Cause that thing was not winning any contests."

"You may be right," Yano said, relenting. "But in any

case, you made it. That's what matters. And on your first try, too! Quite lucky, actually, seeing as Atreus probably wouldn't have given you a second one."

I frowned, my joy now clouded with dread. We still didn't know what might happen if we died in the game. Atreus had said there were no do-overs, but what did that even mean? If we died in the game, would the game trick our brains into thinking we were dead in real life?

Ugh. I didn't want to think about it. We'd made it. That was all that mattered. For now.

"Good thinking, by the way," I told my sister. "I never would have thought to go down into the fog."

"Thanks!" Lilli replied, looking pleased with herself. "I did this Ninja Warrior Halloween course last year. And they had this cemetery section with a fog machine. It was the only way to get through."

"Awesome!" Together, we were becoming quite a team. Like we had been in the regular game. Though I didn't want to jinx it by pointing that out to Lilli just yet. "Anyway, let's go check out this town. See if we can find Ikumi."

I turned back toward Ghost Hollow, ready to head inside, but something stopped me before I took that first step. My eyes widened at what I saw at the front gate.

Orange lights. Grinning pumpkins. Creepy music drifting from the town square.

I raised my eyebrows. "Speaking of Halloween…"

Chapter Twenty-Four

The front gates of Ghost Hollow looked ready for a party, with large, grinning jack-o'-lanterns impaled on spikes and cottony spiderwebs draped across the front gate. Even their town crest was Halloween inspired, depicting the famous headless horseman riding into town with the words BOO TO YOU written in fancy script below.

I turned to Yano. "Is it Halloween?" I asked excitedly. I had always loved when *Fields of Fantasy* changed up the game every year in October for Halloween. Or All Hallows' Scream, as they called it. Every village and town would be decked out in spooky decorations, and some would even offer special quests and games. Bobbing for ghost apples, pin the tail on the demon, and my favorite, broom-riding races. If you played the games, you got special prizes, too. Various potions or unique pieces of armor. I once scored a pumpkin-head helmet that made ghostly moaning sounds every time I put it on. Which I did, repeatedly, just to annoy my sister.

"Actually, Ghost Hollow is something new for Dragon Ops," Yano explained. "People loved the All Hallows' Scream event so much, they decided to keep it going full-time. This way, whenever you have a chance to visit the island, you can celebrate the holiday."

"No way! I wonder if they have Ghost Goop here!"

Ghost Goop was the coolest stuff ever, in my opinion. A frothy, rainbow-swirled milkshake that glowed in the dark and had the power to make you glow, too, after you drank it. I always wondered what it tasted like. Maybe I could finally find out for real!

"Uh, remember. We're here to find Ikumi," Lilli reminded me sternly. "We don't have time to trick-or-treat."

"I know, I know." I waved her off. "I'm not going to waste any time. But if there, like, happens to be Ghost Goop, just sitting there as we run by? I'm going to drink it. Who knows if I'll ever get a chance again!"

She rolled her eyes. "You do you, Ian."

We headed through the gates and into the town, which turned out to be much smaller than Dragonshire. There was a general store, an armory, a magic shop, and a tavern, along with maybe half a dozen small cottages lined up and down a single dirt road.

At least if Ikumi was here, she wouldn't be hard to find. Except...

"Wait, is everyone wearing masks?" Lilli exclaimed, looking at the people gathering near a huge black cauldron filled with a bubbling purple liquid. A female gnome dressed in a pointy black hat was handing out cups of her brew to the crowd. A crowd, I realized in dismay, all decked out in fancy party masks. There wasn't a single visible face in sight.

Uh-oh.

"Well, this certainly ups the difficulty level," Yano remarked. "How will you know which one's your girl?"

It was a good question. I peered around the bustling town, trying to identify anyone roughly Ikumi's height. But in truth, I didn't really remember how tall she was. And who knew if she'd even be the same size now? Or have the same color hair? She'd been playing the game for two years. She probably had all sorts of cool outfits and purchased looks that she could change into.

"Can you find her on your map?" Lilli asked.

I shook my head. "All I can tell is she's somewhere in the town." I let out a frustrated breath as a band of masked villagers pushed past me, laughing and chowing down on huge turkey legs. "This is going to be impossible."

Yano smacked his lips at the sight of the turkey legs. "I'll catch up with you later," he said. "Cheers!" And with that, he launched off my shoulder and flew in the direction of the turkey.

Lilli watched him go. "I'm pretty sure our guide would lead us into the pit of despair if it meant a bite to eat."

"Yeah, well, I might join him at this point," I declared. Everyone was eating something here, and it was making me realize how hungry I was. "We haven't eaten since the game maker's cottage, and I have no idea how long ago that was in real life."

"Don't we have some kind of protein bars in our packs?" Lilli asked.

I wrinkled my nose. "You want to eat protein bars? Look at all the cool food here!" My eyes fell on a woman handing out big bags of orange-colored cotton candy, and I sighed.

"Virtual food is not going to cut it," Lilli scolded. "We need real-life energy if we're going to have a chance at this. Now come on. Let's find Ikumi first, then worry about eating. Maybe the local tavern would know where she is? That's where you always find the good info in the regular game."

I reluctantly followed her into the tavern. Like the town square, it was all done up in over-the-top Halloween decorations—eerie ghosts floating from the ceiling, cobwebs draped on every table. It was packed with people, too. Some sprawled out around a smoky fire pit in the center of the room, drinking out of large copper mugs, while others sat at long tables chowing down on stew served in hollowed-out pumpkins. There was even a band up on a makeshift stage, playing an upbeat song. It took me a moment to recognize it as "Monster Mash."

And everyone was wearing a mask.

"Argh," I exclaimed, frustrated. "This is ridiculous."

I followed Lilli to the bar and slipped onto one of the stools. "Excuse me, barkeep," my sister said, tapping his arm to get his attention. She had to yell to be heard over the band. "We have traveled here from a faraway land, in search of one who will aid our quest. Perhaps you can help us?"

I hid a smile at the way she said it, as if she were her character rather than a real-life person playing a game. I wasn't sure when it had changed for her—during our crazy encounter with the earth dragon, or perhaps it was the scare in the Soundless Bog? Whatever it was, having her all-in made things feel like old times again.

The barkeep turned to Lilli, wiping the bar surface in front of her with a dirty rag. He had a long, narrow nose and tiny ratlike eyes, and was the only one in the place not masked. "Well, well, what have we here?" he asked, setting two huge mugs in front of us. "Adventurers, from the looks of you! We don't get many of your kind here."

"I can't imagine why," I muttered, thinking back to the shadow monster.

"Might ye be looking for work? I have some tasks that need doing. I would reward you greatly."

Here we go again.

"Uh, we're good on the whole questing thing," I assured him. "We're actually searching for someone. Her name is—"

"I need salt for my stew," the bartender interrupted, a

white star appearing over his head. "Fetch me three salt rocks from the nearby Cavern of Echoes and I will—"

"Oh for goodness' sakes!" Lilli interrupted. "Our lives are in danger here! We don't have time to salt your stew!"

"—give you the recipe for making Ghost Goop. The best thirst quencher in town!"

"Really?" I burst out before I could stop myself. "The actual recipe?" If I had the recipe I could make it all year round back home in the regular game. I'd never have to wait for All Hallows' Scream again!

Lilli rolled her eyes. "Can you at least try to remember our lives are on the line here? We don't have time for side quests."

"I know, I know." I turned back to the bartender, poking him again to get his attention, accidentally accepting the Ghost Goop quest. Lilli groaned.

"Look," she said to the bartender. "We're kind of in a hurry here. We're looking for a girl. Her name is Ikumi. Have you seen her?"

The bartender stared at her blankly. "I need salt for my stew," he declared. "Fetch me three salt rocks from the nearby Cavern of Echoes and I will give you the recipe for making Ghost Goop. The best thirst quencher in town!"

"Yeah. Thanks for being so helpful," Lilli muttered, pushing off her stool.

I sighed, scanning the tavern again, a sinking feeling in my chest. "This is going to be impossible." I cupped my hands around my mouth and shouted, "Ikumi? Are you in here?"

But the music was too loud, drowning out my words. No one even noticed me.

"Come on," Lilli said. "Let's not give up. For all we know they may lift their masks at midnight or something. In the meantime, we can find someplace to sit and eat our protein bars."

My stomach gave a sudden growl. "Yeah," I agreed. "Good idea."

I started to follow her outside. But just as I was about to step through the door, the band started playing a new song.

A very familiar-sounding song...

"Wait a second!" I exclaimed, whirling around. "That song's from *Mario 3*!"

Heart in my throat, my eyes lifted to the stage. There, in the center, stood a girl strumming a guitar. At first look, she appeared to be dressed like everyone else in town, in a simple peasant skirt and apron and wearing the same kind of mask.

But on closer examination, I noticed something else. Namely, a strand of pink woven through her otherwise black hair.

I ran up to the stage. "Ikumi?" I asked. "Is that you?"

Chapter Twenty-Five

The girl onstage, startled, almost dropped her guitar. Her eyes locked on me and she cocked her head in question. "Who are you?"

It was then that I remembered I also looked totally different from when she'd seen me last. I'd looked like myself then. Now I was Lord Wildhammer.

"It's me! Ian!" I exclaimed, patting my chest. "Remember? We met at Dragonshire after I got smashed up by that troll."

Her eyes lit up behind her mask, the familiar glitter spinning in her pupils. "Ian!" she cried, sounding overjoyed. "What are you doing here? I mean, I know what you're doing here. It's just—wow, you came a long way! How are you already here? This really isn't a beginner's town. . . ."

"It's a long story," I told her. "But basically we came here to find you. We need your help."

She gave me a wary look. "It's not that I'm not happy to see you," she said, lowering her voice. "It's just . . . like I told you, I'm really not supposed to play with guests."

"I know! But this is an emergency," I pleaded. "At least let me explain."

Her eyes roved the tavern. "All right," she said. "But not here. There are too many possible spies. Meet me out back in five minutes."

And with that, she went back to playing her guitar, this time switching to an old *Zelda* tune. I headed over to my sister, who was still waiting by the door.

"Was that her?" she asked as I reached her. "Is she going to help us?"

I quickly explained what Ikumi had told me, careful to keep my voice down. Though—spies? What did that even mean? And why was she not supposed to play with other guests? It didn't make any sense. Maybe she'd explain when we met up with her.

We headed out of the tavern. The party was still rocking, and there were even some fireworks going off in the air. It was beautiful and festive, and all I wanted to do was hang out and have fun. I mean, this was a *game*, right? And we were technically inside a freaking theme park. We could have been having such a good time if Atreus hadn't gone rogue.

Man, I hated that dragon.

We walked around the tavern until we got to the back.

Ikumi was already there when we arrived, sitting on a bale of hay, her mask removed.

"You must be the sister," she said to Lilli.

"Yeah, nice to meet you. I'm Lilli."

Ikumi nodded. "You, too. Didn't you say there was a cousin with you?" she asked me. "And where's your guide?"

"Um, he's getting a little snack," Lilli said. "As for Derek . . . well, that's why we're here."

Ikumi listened as we told her the story about Eugene, Derek, and Atreus. When we had finished, she let out a low whistle.

"Wow," she said. "That doesn't sound like the Atreus I know at all. He's always been so gentle. He wouldn't hurt a fly!"

"Yeah, well, that was before his upgrade of evil," I replied grimly. "Now he's broken free of his programming and is out for revenge. And if we don't do his quest, he's going to kill Derek. And we'll be stuck in the game forever!"

A flicker of terror crossed Ikumi's face before she shook it away. "Are you sure this isn't just some quest line they gave you?" she asked. "To make the game more thrilling?"

"No way," I said. "For one thing, our SensSuits are all messed up. When we get hurt in the game, it really hurts. And when we tried to go back to the front gates? They weren't there anymore—at least as far as we could see."

"Also, we can't call for help," Lilli added. She looked beseechingly at Ikumi. "Can you?"

Ikumi frowned. She blinked a few times, accessing her menu. A moment later, the color drained from her face. She sat up straighter.

"This is really strange," she said. "All my call features are blocked."

Lilli and I exchanged a doomed look. So much for that plan.

Ikumi slipped off the bale of hay and began pacing behind the tavern. "This has never happened before," she mused, scrunching up the mask in her hand. She looked up at us. "I need to check on some things. See if I can find out what's going on. Can you wait for a bit?"

"Actually, we're kind of under a tight schedule," I said. "If we don't reach Derek in two days—"

She held up a hand. "I promise I won't be long. Besides, it will be dark soon and not safe to travel. Get yourselves a room for the night. And some supplies and new armor— it looks like you need it. I'll meet you first thing in the morning."

"And join our party?" I asked, hope rising in my chest. "Because honestly? We're never going to be able to do this without you."

She pursed her lips. "Maybe. We'll see."

And with that, she walked over to the back door of the tavern, pulled it open, and disappeared inside. Lilli gave me a skeptical look.

"She's going to join us," I said, determined to stay glass-half-full. "You'll see."

"I hope you're right," she replied. "'Cuz I don't know what we're supposed to do if she doesn't."

"Come on," I said. "Let's go gear up. Whether Ikumi joins us or not, we need to be prepared."

Chapter Twenty-Six

"Really? They call this armor?"

Lilli held up a leather crop top, making a disgusted face. "How on earth are you supposed to fight in this? It doesn't even cover your belly!"

Yano swooped down and plucked the top from Lilli's hands, dropping it onto a nearby bench. "Lucky for you, you're a mage," he reminded her. "Which means you get to wear a robe." He flew over to a garment rack and plucked out a dark-blue floor-length dress, accented by glowing stars. Lilli reluctantly took it from his talons.

"This is even worse," she groaned. "I might as well be wearing tissue paper on the battlefield. Who decided mages shouldn't wear armor, anyway? It's seriously the dumbest idea ever."

"Agreed," I said with sympathy. "But that's just the way it's always been."

After parting with Ikumi, we'd combed the town, locating the armor shop at the far end. For its small size, it had a ton of cool stuff, though most of it was way higher level than we were. And super expensive, too. In addition to armor there were also crazy hairstyles and upgraded facial features you could buy to make your character look even cooler. I wanted to get one of the awesome glow-in-the-dark eyes sets, similar to what Ikumi wore, but they were more money than the two of us had combined—and, as Lilli added, not at all practical. We needed core gear, not add-ons.

"Don't worry, Lills," I declared, patting her on the back. "You don't need armor. Not when you've got Lord Wildhammer and his fancy Tank Gear O' Awesome at your side!" I pounded my new chest plate. "With this bad boy, I'll have four hundred fifty armor points. I could get hit by a truck and barely feel it."

"Congratulations," Lilli replied, rolling her eyes. "Meanwhile, I'm pretty sure a mosquito could bite through this thing and kill me with malaria."

"Yeah, but look at its stats! Your AoE will be through the roof!" I pointed out.

AoE was short for "area of effect." It allowed Lilli to cast a large spell on a ton of creatures at one time instead of targeting each of them individually. For example, a storm mage might conjure up a lightning storm. Or a fire mage might set a section of ground on fire.

Lilli picked up a sleeve, examining the embroidery.

"True," she agreed. "That would have been useful with those draconites in the forest."

I nodded, then wandered to the back of the store to see all the other awesome but unaffordable stuff they had to offer. On the very back wall, I found a flashy red suit of armor with spiked shoulders—supercool looking, much lighter than the one I'd picked out, and made of chain mail instead of plates. The advertised armor rating was only about half of what my new suit was—it definitely wouldn't stand up to a truck. But it had a plus forty to damage dealt and a plus five to speed, which was pretty awesome.

"Hey, check this out," I called to my sister and Yano. "I think it's wrath armor."

A Wrath Warrior didn't fight like a normal warrior did. Instead of keeping the monsters busy so the rest of the party could bring them down, Wrath Warriors could get into the action themselves and pound the bad guys into oblivion. As a trade-off, they also got hurt easier and died quicker. And they were no good at keeping other members of a party—like a mage, for example—safe from harm.

But still! How cool would it be to be able to kick some serious monster butt for once?

"I think I'll take it," I declared.

Lilli gave me a skeptical look. "Why? What are you going to use it for?"

"I don't know. Could come in handy, though."

She picked up the price tag and squinted at it. "So could the twenty thousand gold pieces you're about to spend on it."

I groaned. "I forgot what a cheapskate you are in these games."

"I think the word you're looking for is 'practical.'"

"Yes." I beamed at her. "Because this armor is *practically* perfect."

I grabbed the armor off the wall and saw it even came with a matching cape! I would be the Lando Calrissian of Dragon Ops every time I wore it!

Not that I was going to wear it, of course. It was for emergencies only. And maybe walking through town? What could it hurt to wear it walking through town?

Done shopping, I headed to the merchant, laying out my items on the counter. It was then that I noticed three blocks of a strange white substance under the display case.

"What are those?" I asked curiously.

"Salt blocks," the merchant replied. "Used to salt a stew. Some adventurer left them here the other day and never came back for them. I'll probably throw them away."

"No!" I cried. Excitement rose in my chest. Salt blocks! Like what the bartender had wanted in exchange for the Ghost Goop recipe! I could buy these and turn them in without having to waste time on the side quest. Surely even my sister couldn't have a problem with that!

I glanced over at Lilli, who was still arguing with Yano about mages and armor. I lowered my voice. "How much?"

The merchant frowned. "They're not for sale."

"Come on," I begged. "Everything's for sale, right?"

"Fine. Twenty thousand gold."

"Twenty thousand?" I cried, then glanced at my sister and lowered my voice again. "You were going to throw them away."

The merchant looked at me blankly.

I groaned, looking down at my wrath armor, then at the salt. "How about thirty thousand for everything? That's all I've got." Lilli was seriously going to kill me.

The merchant looked over the goods. "Thirty-five thousand," he agreed.

Argh. This was going to completely wipe me out. But still! Wrath armor! Ghost Goop!

"Fine," I said. "Now can I have my salt?"

"Ian, are you done?" Lilli started to come over.

The merchant pulled the salt from the display case. I grabbed it quickly, stuffing it in my pocket before she reached me. If she found out I'd just spent fifteen thousand gold pieces on salt...

"What's wrong?" she asked suspiciously. "You look guilty."

My face warmed. "Well, I know you don't approve of my new armor."

She laughed. "It's fine," she said, patting me on the back. "If you think it'll help us, then you should go for it."

"Oh yeah!" I declared, grabbing the helmet and tucking it under my arm. "This armor is going to save our lives someday. You wait and see."

And the Ghost Goop, I thought to myself as we headed out of the store. *Maybe not life-saving. But it's gonna be fun!*

Chapter Twenty-Seven

We'd originally hoped to book a room at the local inn for the night. But it turned out to be super expensive, and I was super broke thanks to my secret purchase at the armory earlier. Lilli was not pleased by this—she assumed I had wasted all my cash on the wrath armor—and kept mumbling about how it "better come in handy someday." I assured her, once again, that it would, then started searching the town for somewhere else to sleep. Because if my sister found out she was sleeping on the ground because I wanted Ghost Goop, well, let's just say I might need that wrath armor to protect myself from *her* wrath.

Thankfully, we came across a small, abandoned house to make ours for the night. The front door was half hanging off its hinges, and several windows were smashed through. But there was a roof and four walls and two twin beds in the bedroom, complete with pillows and blankets. Which made it slightly better than that time my dad forced me to go camping with the Cub Scouts and I had to sleep on the ground in a tent.

I brushed off the kitchen table to make room for dinner. I wasn't super excited about eating protein bars—my kingdom for a taco—but I told myself that at least it was real food and would really fill us up. But when I reached into my pack to pull them out, I was shocked to find they no longer looked like protein bars at all. Instead they looked like huge, colorful gummy bears. How cool was that?

Grinning, I grabbed a yellow bear out of the pack and handed it to my sister, choosing a red one for myself. They had to be at least the one-pound size I'd seen sold at Christmastime that my mom would never let us get because of the crazy sugar content. Would these taste like the real thing? Or the protein bars they were in real life? This was definitely one time I wouldn't mind the game playing tricks on my brain.

"Surrender, Sir Gummy!" I commanded my bear. "For you are no match for Lord Wildhammer's stomach!" I chomped off the bear's arm, savoring the burst of almost sickly sweetness. *Yes! Trick my brain, gummy bear! Trick it good!*

My sister regarded her own gummy with solemn eyes. "I am terribly sorry, m'lady," she said, hopping on board. "But sacrifices must be made for the good of the realm." She stuffed half the bear in her mouth at once, then started laughing so hard she could barely chew.

We were both chewing and laughing when a familiar red light started flashing at the corner of my eye. Another incoming call. I accepted it, trying to say hello with a mouthful of gummy, which didn't sound much like hello at all.

The video stream came to life.

"Gummy bears?" Derek burst out, staring out at us from his cage of bones, a flabbergasted look on his face. "I'm trapped in a freaking cage with a crazy dragon ready to dismember me and you guys are hanging out, eating gummy bears?"

Oops.

"They're actually protein bars in real life, if that makes it any better," my sister told him.

"I don't care if they're steaming dragon turds! You are having fun. I am in dragon jail. And my fingers are practically falling off my hands from playing so many songs, trying to keep this ugly dragon from making me a midnight snack." He grunted with annoyance. "Also, this place stinks. And not only because I had to use the corner of the cage as a bathroom."

"Ugh, I'm so sorry!" I said, feeling suddenly terrible for having any sort of fun. All this time we'd been adventuring, Derek had been stuck in that awful cage.

"Have you heard from my dad? Hiro? When they are going to fix this mess?"

I let out a breath. "We can't get in touch with them. But we did find someone who might be able to help. She's trapped in the game, too. But she's been playing for two years, so she's really high-level. We're hoping she'll join our party."

"Tell her she doesn't have a choice!" Derek shot back. "You got me in this mess! You better get me out!"

"Come on, Derek. We're doing the best we can," I protested, starting to get annoyed. "Just chill out already, okay?"

Derek stared at me, a shocked look on his face. Not surprising, I supposed. *He* was the one usually yelling at me, not the other way around.

"Sorry," I said, immediately feeling bad. "I didn't mean—"

Derek waved me off. He walked to his harp and picked it up, strumming it half-heartedly. "Look, I know sometimes I can be a jerk," he said slowly, staring at the wall behind him, not looking at us.

Lilli gave a quiet snort. *Sometimes?* she mouthed at me, rolling her eyes.

"And I know you probably don't like me very much," he continued.

"That's not true!" I protested. Though of course it was.

He turned back to us, his face pale and pleading. "Just... please don't leave me in here. I'll do whatever you want. I'll never call you a geek again. In fact I'm glad you're a geek, 'cuz only a geek could save me now!"

"Derek, we're going to get you out, okay? One way or another. I promise."

"I promise, too!" Lilli chimed in. "Even if you are a jerk. You still don't deserve to be eaten by a dragon."

He nodded slowly. "Thanks," he said. "And...be careful, okay? This Atreus guy? He's not messing around. He really wants to win this. And he's going to do whatever it takes."

A chill tripped down my spine. "Thanks, Derek. We'll see you soon. I promise."

And with that, we ended the chat. My sister set down her gummy bear. "I really hope Ikumi can help," she said. "Because otherwise? I don't know what we're going to do."

"No kidding," I said, setting down my own gummy bear, no longer hungry. I rose to my feet and walked over to the bedroom. I stared down at the grimy-looking bed, hoping it wasn't as dirty in real life as it looked in the game. I tried to think of the beloved Mario sheets I had on my bed back home. The ones my mom was always trying to get me to throw out because they were so old and faded. Derek had made fun of those sheets the first time he'd seen them, saying I was a baby for still having video-game sheets.

Bet he would give anything to have those sheets now....

I crawled under the ratty blanket and stared up at the ceiling. Lilli followed suit in the next bed, puffing up the pillow to try to make it softer. "Ugh," she said, giving up and plopping her head down. "Luckily I'm so tired I could sleep on a rock right now."

"I wonder what time it is," I thought out loud, looking

out the window at the night sky. "Like, real-life time. Do you think we've been gone a whole day? Or only an hour or two?"

Lilli sat up in bed. "I hadn't thought of that," she said worriedly.

"What?"

"Well, what if this time compression thing means we haven't been gone that long at all? Because that would mean no one would even be looking for us yet! They would assume we were out in the game. Even Eugene might not notice for hours that we didn't come back." She gnawed on her lower lip. "Which would mean—"

"That we're on our own," I concluded. Not good.

She lay back down in bed, propping her head on her elbow. "At least we're not totally alone. I mean, we have each other."

"Yeah," I said, suddenly feeling brave. "It's been great playing with you again, even under the circumstances. I almost forgot what a good team we made."

"Totally," Lilli agreed. "We were awesome. Before... you know." She trailed off, looking sad.

Great. She was thinking about Logan again. Seriously, if I ever met that kid, I'd strangle him with my bare hands.

"You shouldn't have let him chase you offline," I said quietly. "You could have blocked him or whatever."

"It's not that easy."

"Yes it is!" I cried, before I could stop myself. I knew I

was on dangerous ground and should shut up, but somehow I couldn't. "I mean, you never even met the guy in real life, right? So who cares what he thinks?"

"Drop it, Ian. Seriously," my sister shot back, her voice ripe with warning.

"No. I'm sick of dropping it. You loved video games. They were, like, your favorite thing. And then you just give them up—over some stupid guy? That's not like you, Lilli!"

"You don't understand."

"Then explain it to me!"

Lilli gave a heavy sigh. "Please go to sleep, Ian."

I didn't want to go to sleep. Not without finishing this conversation. Not without finding out what really happened with Logan. There was something she wasn't telling me—I was sure of it now. Something so awful that she couldn't bear to even talk about it with her own brother.

But her voice sounded so sad. As if she was trying desperately not to cry. And I didn't want to upset her further. And so I kept my mouth shut, lying in bed, trying to imagine what it could be. What could Logan have done to my sister that hurt her so badly?

And how could I help her get over it if she wouldn't even tell me what it was?

Chapter Twenty-Eight

The village was still rocking as I slipped out of the house late that night and made my way down toward the tavern. The streets were even rowdier now than they were earlier, with people dancing and whooping around the cauldron in the center of town. Even young children were running around—chasing little enchanted pumpkins with arms and legs through the crowd. I was tempted to grab one myself as it skittered over my feet, then danced away. I knew from the regular game you could turn them in for Halloween treats, and I was still hungry, even after the gummy bear.

But I couldn't be distracted from my mission.

I opened the door to the tavern and stepped inside. The place was quieter than it had been earlier; most people must have gone outside. The band was gone, too. And the only people left were lounging by the fire, looking half-asleep. I walked up to the bartender and plopped my salt stones on the counter.

"Here you go," I said. "Now how about that Ghost Goop recipe?"

The man's eyes lit up. He grabbed the salt cubes and whisked them away, then handed over a slip of paper—the recipe, I assumed—and two foaming cups of rainbow-colored swirls.

My eyes widened. I hadn't realized I would get actual Ghost Goop along with the recipe. I stuffed the paper in my pocket and greedily wrapped my hand around the cup. Finally! I'd get to see what this delicious concoction actually tasted like!

"Shouldn't you be asleep?"

I glanced over my shoulder. Ikumi had entered the tavern and was walking over to me. She had changed her look again and was now wearing the same black robes she'd worn when I first met her. Her mask was gone and her hair was long and blond.

"Ah, I see. Doing side quests," she noted before I could reply. "Can't get enough of this game, huh?" Reaching over, she grabbed one of the Ghost Goop cups and tipped it back.

"Hey!" I cried. "I quested for that!"

"What, are you going to drink both?" She smirked at me as her skin and clothes started to glow fluorescent pink. Soon, she was so bright I almost had to turn away.

I laughed. "You look like Princess Peach," I joked,

downing my own drink. It tasted like lime sherbet and I started glowing bright green. So cool!

"Guess you must be Luigi, then," she replied, setting down her cup. "This stuff is so ridiculous. I have no idea why it's even in the game. It's not like it's useful."

"It's fun, though!" I reminded her, slipping off the barstool and spinning in a circle. Ribbons of green streaked from my body, as if I was a living, breathing glow stick.

Ikumi laughed and joined me. Together we twirled around the room, nearly knocking everything over. The other patrons looked up grumpily, muttering to one another by the fire.

At last, out of breath, I collapsed onto the empty stage, lay on my back, and stared up at the ceiling. Ikumi joined me, though she didn't seem winded at all.

"Wow," I exclaimed. "That was fun."

Ikumi giggled. "I know! I can't remember the last time I had fun in here."

I propped myself up on an elbow. "So why do you still play?" I asked. "If it's not fun."

"What else can I do?" she asked with a long sigh.

"So, what? Are you, like, an employee's kid or something?" I asked. "Do you live on this island?"

She nodded, suddenly looking very sad. "Yes," she said. "My dad is a programmer."

"Wow. That must be weird, living here. Does your mom live here, too? Do you have any brothers or sisters?"

She shook her head. "No. My mother is dead. And I have no siblings. It's just me."

"And your dad."

"Well, yes. But he's busy working most of the time. I'm usually here by myself."

I tried to imagine this. Being stuck on an island for two years, no one to play with except computer-generated characters. At first it would be awesome. But after a while . . .

"Anyway, I thought a lot about your problem with Atreus," Ikumi said, changing the subject. "And I think I know a way you could beat him."

"You do?" My heart started thumping faster.

"Maybe. But it's a long shot."

"What is it?"

"When the island was first designed, the programmers divided it up into four kingdoms. A kingdom of ice, a kingdom of water, a kingdom of the earth, and a kingdom of fire. They then created four dragons to rule over those kingdoms. Each dragon was given an Elemental Stone embedded with their own special power. Atreus got the Fire Stone. Lord D'ou got the Ice Stone. The Water Stone went to Lord Kaito, and the Earth Stone went to Wyrm."

My ears perked up. "Wyrm? We actually killed him!"

"Wait. You killed Wyrm?" Her voice held her disbelief.

I grinned, feeling pretty proud of myself. "Oh yeah. He was so gross, too! All those nasty baby worms! But I snuck behind him and chopped off his tail! You should have seen all the . . ." I trailed off. Ikumi's face was ashen. "What?"

"Oh no. This is terrible news," she said. "Wyrm was a good dragon. She was gentle. Kind."

"Um, no offense, but he—she?—totally tried to melt me with acid."

"She drools. You have to stay away from her drool. But she would never attack someone unprovoked." She wrung her hands together, looking really upset. "Those nasty worms? Those are her children. She lives underground, raising them."

I gulped. Was this true? I tried to remember the fight. Surely Wyrm had attacked us, right? Or had we attacked her first? Yano had eaten some of the little worms. Had he been chomping on her children?

"Well, she's probably respawned by now, right?" I tried, grasping at straws. "I mean, don't they all, like, come back to life eventually, so the other players can kill them, too? Or, you know, invite them to tea?" Or whatever it was you did with a nice dragon.

Oh man. Here I'd been so proud of myself for bagging my first dragon. Instead, I'd murdered someone's mom.

"I don't know," Ikumi said in answer to my question. "Most creatures do regenerate after some time. Under the normal rules. But we don't know what rules Atreus is playing by. We don't know who gets to have a second chance."

I nodded slowly, dread falling over my shoulders like a heavy blanket. "Including...us?" I asked, trying to voice the question that had been on my mind since we first learned the game had gone off the rails.

She nodded slowly. "Which is why I've decided to help you. You're very low-level. You've been lucky so far, but there will be much worse to come. You will need my help to face it."

Relief flooded through me. "Thank you. Thank you so much!" Maybe with Ikumi's help we could actually make it out alive! "And, uh, you said you had a plan?"

"Maybe," she said. "I told you about the Elemental Stones. They are the most powerful items in this game. Atreus has one. But if we can get the others from the other dragons? We may be able to harness their power to fight him." She pursed her lips. "Though obviously Wyrm is out...."

My face burned. "Yeah. I'm really sorry about that."

She waved me off. "But that leaves two more. Lord D'ou and Lord Kaito. The Ice Stone and the Water Stone. Two very good defenses against fire." She rose to her feet. We were both still glowing, and I wondered how long the potion's effects would last. "All right," she said. "Meet me here at first light. We will head to Lord D'ou's mountain and ask him for the first stone." She bit her lower lip. "Just... don't mention what happened with Wyrm."

"Trust me, I'm not stupid."

She smiled a little at this. "I know," she said. "And who knows? This might actually be—"

But she never got a chance to finish her sentence. Because at that moment, we were interrupted by a deafening roar.

"Dragon incoming!" called a voice from outside. "Men and women—to arms!"

Chapter Twenty-Nine

We raced to the tavern's window and peered outside. My mouth dropped open at what I saw. The once-festive town had turned into a nightmare of fire and smoke. People screaming, running, trying desperately to hide—some literally on fire as they tore through the streets.

"What is happening?" Ikumi cried. "This is not one of the town's story lines!"

"I don't think Atreus cares much about story lines," I said grimly. Then a horrifying thought struck me and I ran for the door. "Lilli!" I cried. "We have to get to Lilli!"

"Are you crazy? You'll be burned alive!"

"She's my sister. I have to help her." Sucking in a breath, I pushed open the door, stepping out into the inferno. The air was thick and smoky, and I started choking immediately. Ikumi joined me, ripping off a piece of cloth from her robe.

"Put this over your mouth and nose!" she instructed. "It'll help a little."

I nodded, doing as she instructed. Then I pushed through the smoke, trying to avoid tripping over all the bodies on the ground. So many partygoers—once so happy and carefree—now lay dead.

RAWR!

The sound blasted my ears from above. I looked up, my whole body tensing, as my eyes fell on the dragon circling.

No, not just any dragon. Atreus himself.

My, my, tiny human. The dragon's voice rippled through my ears, sending a chill down my spine. *How green you are. Don't tell me you've been wasting time on side quests....*

Oh no! The Ghost Goop!

"No! I swear I'm not! I just bought some salt!" I protested. "It didn't take any time at—"

The dragon roared again, cutting off my words. *Waste no more time! Or I shall see fit to waste more villages.* His laughter was cold and cruel. He opened his mouth again, blasting the tavern with flames.

"Ian!"

Suddenly my sister seemed to appear out of nowhere. She was standing in some kind of weird bubble and beckoning me to her. I ran and she grabbed me, pulling me inside the circle. It felt like stepping into a bubble of slime, but once inside I realized I could breathe again.

"Is this from a spell?" I asked.

"Yes. And it won't last. We need to get out of here!"

I turned to Ikumi, who was still outside the bubble. "Come on!" I urged. "Let's go!"

But Ikumi shook her head. "No. These people don't deserve to suffer this way. I need to help them." Her face was streaked with dirt, though she didn't seem to be having trouble breathing. Did everyone have a protective spell but me?

"We could help, too!" I suggested. After all, this was kind of my fault. If I hadn't done the Ghost Goop quest...

"No!" Ikumi shook her head. "You're too low-level. You'll get yourselves killed. Go—I promise I'll find you later!"

And with that, she raised her hands, chanting loudly in a language I didn't recognize. I watched, mesmerized, as bright light began to stream from her fingers.

Lilli grabbed my shoulder. "Come on!"

Reluctantly, I joined her, racing to the village's back gate, which now, like everything else, was blazing with fire. We dove over the burning logs and into the dark woods beyond.

We hadn't made it more than fifty yards when we heard the boom.

Followed by a blinding white flash.

What in the world...?

My whole body trembling, I dared turn back around. My jaw dropped as my eyes fell upon what once was Ghost

Hollow, now nothing more than a smoking ruin of charred wood and ash.

"Oh no!" I cried. "No, no, *no!*"

I started back toward the gate. But my sister grabbed me, stopping me in my tracks.

"Ian, no!" she cried. "You can't go back there!"

"But Ikumi! She's still there!"

My sister's face was pale. "If she was," she said slowly, "she's not anymore. I mean, look. There's nothing left."

Lilli was right. The town had literally exploded. No one could have survived a blast like that.

I sank to my knees, tears flowing down my cheeks. I didn't know why, exactly. We had just met Ikumi. We barely knew her. But she couldn't simply be gone. Could she?

Could she be real-life dead?

"She saved us," I said in a choked voice. "She stayed to save us."

"And it's a good thing she did, too," Yano declared, swooping toward us. At least he was okay. "Because you were glowing like the Green Lantern. Not exactly the best way to avoid a dragon's attention, if you ask me!"

I cringed. "It's all my fault. Me and that stupid Ghost Goop." I sank to a nearby rock. If only I hadn't snuck around to do the side quest. So selfish. And now Ikumi was gone.

"Think of the bright side!" Yano declared. "Now we can find out what happens when you game-die! Maybe she got out!"

Hope burned in my chest. "You think?"

He shrugged. "Or she could be real-life dead. One or the other, I suppose."

"But how is that possible?" Lilli demanded. "All of this—it's not real. It's all a trick of the mind!"

"Don't underestimate the power of your mind," Yano replied. "If your brain believes it's dead, it could very well stop your real-life heart from beating."

Lilli and I exchanged horrified glances. If Ikumi could real-life die, that meant we could, too. And Derek...

I squared my shoulders. "Come on," I said. "Ikumi sacrificed herself to give us time. We can't waste it. We may not have another chance." I turned to Yano. "You said you knew D'ou, right? We need to get to him. Now."

Chapter Thirty

We set off, leaving the ashes of Ghost Hollow behind and diving deep into the Sleeping Rain Forest, which, according to Yano, sat between us and Icelandia, where we would be able to find Lord D'ou and hopefully convince him to give us his Ice Stone.

Unfortunately, unlike its name implied, the Sleeping Rain Forest was very much awake with nasty creatures in need of killing. Every five seconds we'd be ambushed by another mob. *Trash mobs*, they called them in a game like this. Random encounters with various creatures who had no importance to the overall quests, but still needed to be disposed of. I hated trash mobs—they were a distraction to the main quest lines and made it take twice as long to get anywhere.

As we fought, I tried to fill Lilli in.

"So if we can get the Ice Stone from Lord D'ou"—I said, hacking away at a giant bloated fly that dropped down into our path; it hissed and spun, making it difficult to hit with my sword—"and the Water Stone from Lord Kaito, it'll be two stones against Atreus's one. Maybe we'll have a chance."

Lilli raised her hands, pointing her staff at the fly. It exploded into a ball of flames and dropped to the ground, still sizzling. "Shouldn't we get all three of the stones? Won't that give us an even better chance?"

"Yeah," I said, as I searched the dead fly for loot. I rummaged around his corpse until I pulled out a battered pirate hat. Where was he keeping this when he was alive? It wasn't as if he had any pockets. I threw it in my sack, just in case it would prove useful (or fashionable) in the future. "About that..."

"You've already slain dragon number three, remember?" Yano exclaimed cheerfully, flying up behind us, just as a snarling two-headed coyote leapt into our path. I raised my sword, managing to chop both heads off in one blow as it charged at us. Sweet! I was getting better at this. At least with low-level monsters. My sister gave me a high five, then dug out an old battered shield and three gold pieces from its dead body. She held up the shield questioningly to me, but I shook my head. Mine was better, and I was running out of space in my sack. "Remember that nasty earth dragon with the tasty treats? My brilliant power-up final move?" Yano continued.

I groaned. "Thanks for that, by the way. You couldn't have mentioned that Wyrm was a nice mommy dragon before we made a move on her and her children?"

Yano shrugged. "Didn't really think it was relevant."

"Wait, what?" Lilly asked. "Wyrm was one of the four bosses?"

"Yeah. So thanks to Mister Not-Relevant here, we already murdered our chance to get the third stone. So we're going to have to work with—"

"Wait a second," Lilli interjected. I watched as she reached into her robe's pocket and rummaged around.

"What?" I asked.

"That... thing! That thing I found in the tunnel after we killed the earth dragon. Remember you said it looked like fossilized poop?"

"I don't think I said 'fossilized.'..."

She pulled it from her bag. Honestly, it still looked like a turd to me.

"What if *this* is the Earth Stone?" she asked.

My eyes widened. Could she be right? Could we already have one of the stones we needed to defeat Atreus?

I turned to Yano. "Could this be the Earth Stone?"

"I don't know. We could ask D'ou..."

"Well then." I reached out, closing my sister's fingers around the stone again. "Let's go find D'ou."

"Holy frozen french fries of doom," I exclaimed a few hours later, putting a hand over my eyes as we emerged from the jungle out onto a vast frozen tundra. The twin suns shone down on the icy landscape, reflecting back up at us with almost blinding brilliance, and the few scraggly trees were blanketed in ice crystals. In the distance I could see the shadow of a snow-covered mountain. But besides that? Nothing but icy wasteland. No homes, no animals, no people.

Just Icelandia, home of Lord D'ou, keeper of the Ice Stone.

It was hard to believe moments before we had been hacking and slashing our way through thick jungle vines, all sweaty and gross, and now we were basically shivering. I glanced behind me, hoping to get a last look at the jungle, but it had completely disappeared. All I could see was ice, ice, and more ice.

"This is *so* cool!" Lilli remarked.

"Actually, I think the word you're looking for is 'cold,'" Yano grumped, landing on Lilli's head. He blinked twice, conjuring up an ugly Christmas sweater with rainbow poop emojis in Santa hats. "Ah, much better," he declared.

"And so stylish, too!" I added, raising an eyebrow.

Yano beamed, lifting off Lilli's head and flying in circles, parading his outfit for all to see. "Let's just say it's no accident I've won best-dressed guide three months running."

"I can't imagine the competition," Lilli replied with a

laugh. Her gaze went back to the landscape. "So is this it? Are we finally here?"

Yano flew out in front of us. "Indeed," he declared. "Beautiful Icelandia." He pointed to the snow-capped mountain in the distance. "And there lies the Monstrous Peak, where Lord D'ou makes his home."

"Great," I exclaimed. We were finally getting somewhere! "Let's go get that Ice Stone."

We picked up the pace, making our way toward the mountain. The going wasn't easy; the ground was covered in ice and very slippery. We fought our way forward through a strong, bitter wind that whipped across the land, knocking us around. I began to get nervous about what it would be like up on the actual mountain if conditions were this bad down below.

It was then that I spotted an odd sight. While it had originally appeared there was nothing and no one for miles, as we drew closer to the mountain we found an old man, sitting on a small stool and fishing through a hole in the ice. I looked down at my feet in surprise. Had we been walking on a lake this whole time?

The man looked up as we approached. He had a long white beard, wrinkly olive-colored skin, and wizened eyes. His ears, peeking out from under a knit hat, were strangely pointed. Was he an actual elf?

He rose to his feet, setting aside his fishing pole and holding out his arms in welcome. "Brave adventurers!" he cried.

"What brings you so far out into the wilds of Icelandia?! Surely you must be lost. Come inside, my friends, and you can warm yourselves by the fire and grab a bite to eat." He gestured to a small hut that I could have sworn hadn't been there a moment before.

"Thanks," I said. "But we don't have time. We're on a mission to see Lord D'ou."

The man's eyes widened. "But Lord D'ou lives on top of the mountain!" he exclaimed.

"And...?"

He shivered. "The Monstrous Peak is treacherous, even on a good day. There are avalanches, falling rocks, and deadly creatures that would make you their dinner! And that's if you even get across the ice field to begin with. Which"—he gave us a patronizing smile—"you will not." He shrugged. "Why don't you stay here instead and help me with my duties? If you can catch ten fish and bring them to me, I will give you a great reward."

Ah, yes. Another side quest. Let's just say I'd learned my lesson after the disaster at Ghost Hollow.

"Sorry, we don't have time for fishing," I told him. "We have to get to D'ou."

"Surely there must be a safe path across the ice field," Lilli pressed.

The man nodded his head. "Aye," he agreed. "If you must go, there is a way. Though I warn you, it will not be easy. You must follow the steps exactly as they are laid out.

One stray step and *you will surely meet your doom.*" His voice thundered on the last part—way too overdramatic, in my opinion, sending goose bumps up my arms.

"Stay on the path. Right," I said quickly, shoving my hands behind my back. "Sounds easy enough. We'll catch you on the way back down."

"*If* you make it up the mountain," he replied, still in that scary doomsayer voice. "*And* if D'ou lets you live."

"Yes, yes. All those things," I agreed. He really needed to stop freaking us out here. I was already nervous enough about climbing the mountain in the first place, with my fear of heights and all. He didn't need to make it worse. "So long, dude."

"And thanks for all the fish!" Yano chirped, his mouth completely full. While we'd been talking, he'd helped himself to an all-you-can-eat seafood buffet from the man's buckets. I worried for a moment that this would cause a problem—like with the troll blacksmith back in Dragonshire—but the elf didn't seem programmed to mind and instead settled back onto his stool.

"Well, he was certainly cheerful," my sister remarked as we left the little hut and continued our journey toward the mountain pass.

"I know, right? Guess he's supposed to add tension to the game," I said.

"Yeah, well, mission accomplished."

"Meh." I waved her off, not sure if I was trying to relieve

her anxiety or my own. "He's probably programmed to exaggerate. I mean, how hard could it be? It's just a little ice—"

"Ahh!"

Lilli screamed, flailing, as the ground cracked under her feet. I dove forward, grabbed her arm, and yanked her backward. We tumbled onto the ice in a heap, butts first.

"Holy slip-and-slides of doom!" Lilli cried. She scrambled off me and crawled over to what was now a big hole in the ice, her whole body trembling. I joined her, keeping a safe distance as I stared down into the angry churning river below the surface. Yikes.

Yano flew above us, dropping a half-eaten fish into the hole. The current sucked it up instantly, and it disappeared under the ice as if it had never been there at all. Imagine if Lilli had fallen in! She would have been pulled under and frozen to death in seconds.

I looked up, staring out over the frozen tundra, my mouth dipping into a frown. "Okay then," I said. "Maybe the fisherman wasn't exaggerating after all."

Chapter Thirty-One

I rose to my feet, keeping my distance from the cracked ice. "We need to find another way to the mountain," I said in a shaky voice. "This is not safe."

"But there is no other way," Lilli argued. "I mean, look."

I scanned the frozen expanse and saw she was right. We had to get across the ice field somehow. But how? We had no idea how many other weak spots there were in the ice and where they were located. Which meant one wrong move would lead to a freezing end.

"It's really too bad you guys don't have wings. Or, you know, ugly Christmas sweaters for that matter," Yano commented as he caught my sister shivering. "Seems as if I am the only one properly prepared for this quest." He gave a long-suffering sigh. "As usual."

"Yeah, well, maybe you should fly up to D'ou and get

us our Ice Stone then," Lilli shot back. "If you're so *prepared* and all."

Yano huffed. "Sorry. I'm not programmed to complete quests for you. After all, it wouldn't be much of a game if I did all the work."

"Wait a second," I said, an idea sparking. "This is still a game, right? Which means there has to be a way across the ice field. Otherwise the game would be unplayable." I tapped my forehead with my finger, concentrating. "It's probably some kind of puzzle. What did the fisherman say again?"

"'One stray step and you will surely meet your doom!'" Lilli replied, mimicking the scary voice he'd used.

"Yeah, yeah," I said. "But what else?"

"He told us to follow the steps *exactly*." She stared over the icy expanse. "But there *are* no steps. . . ."

"Maybe they're covered in snow?" I suggested, brushing at the light dusting with my foot. All I found was more ice. "Or not. Unless they're invisible . . ."

"Ooh!" Lilli cried, clapping her hands. "I have an idea." She blinked to access her menu, and a moment later, a big grin spread across her face.

"What?" I asked, puzzled. "Did you find a map or something?"

"Better," she proclaimed. "Infrared. Our goggles have infrared, remember?"

Oh yeah! Back when we'd found the night-vision option on our menus, there had also been an infrared setting. I reached for it now and made the selection. My vision blurred for a moment, then cleared, revealing a strangely colored world of reds and greens and blues. And winding through the ice field? A trail of red footprints, marking the way.

I let out an amazed whistle. "Follow the steps exactly," I repeated. "This must be what he meant!"

"Sweet!" Lilli cried. "Maybe we can do this after all."

We gave it a try, stepping carefully on each footprint, concentrating on keeping our balance as we went. It wasn't easy. The ground was still super slippery, meaning I had to take a step, steady myself, then take another step.

We were about halfway there when we heard a screech.

"Don't look now," Yano remarked casually. "But I think we've got company."

I turned around slowly, my heart filled with dread. My eyes locked upon a dragon, hovering a few yards above the earth. It was huge—about the size of a bus—and glowed ice blue under the infrared light. And when it opened its mouth, I could see a flash of blue sparks dancing on its tongue.

"Is that . . . D'ou?" I managed to stammer, crossing my fingers. Maybe we wouldn't have to climb the mountain after all.

"No," Yano replied. "D'ou is *much* bigger."

"I had a feeling you were going to say that," my sister muttered.

I drew in a breath, my gaze not leaving the ice dragon. It was watching us, too, its deep-blue eyes glowing eerily as it slowly flapped its wings to keep airborne. Could we make a run for it across the field and up the mountain? But no, I could barely walk on the ice as it was. And I was guessing even full-on track-meet speed wouldn't be enough to outrun it.

"Maybe it's a good dragon?" Lilli suggested hopefully. "Like Wyrm?" She turned to the creature, pasting a big smile on her face. "Why hello, Mr. Ice Dragon!" she greeted cheerfully, though I caught a slight tremor in her voice. "So good to meet you! We're just hoping to cross this little ice field and swing up to D'ou's place for a bit. You don't mind, do you?"

The dragon roared, a burst of blue fire cannonballing from its mouth. We screamed and ducked as flames shot over our heads, scorching the ground behind us. Huge chunks of ice broke loose and dropped like stones into the raging river below.

"I think it's safe to say he *does* mind," Yano noted.

"Yeah, got that." I clenched my teeth as the dragon let out another burst—this one landing a few feet in front of us. More chunks of ice fell into the river, creating yet another gaping hole. If this kept up, we'd be sunk in no time.

"Oh no," Lilli cried. "It's destroying the trail!"

She was right. It wasn't aiming for us at all. At least not yet. It was trying to destroy our only path to D'ou.

Lilli backed up a few feet, then ran toward the hole, leaping over it and hitting the other side. She turned to me. "Come on!" she called. "Jump!"

I stared down into the rushing ice river, my heart pounding like a jackhammer in my chest "What if I slip?"

"I'll catch you. I promise."

Could she, though? I watched as her own feet slid on the ice. She was barely standing up herself. Could she really hold me up, too?

But there was no other way. Gathering my courage, I backed up, then ran as fast as my feet could take me. Trying not to look down, I leapt over the crevice and landed on the other side. As I hit the ground, my feet slipped out from under me and I screamed as I lost my balance. But Lilli, as promised, grabbed me and held on until I was able to steady myself.

"You're so good at this game," I said, shaking my head.

Before she could reply, the dragon turned. His eyes locked on Lilli and it let out another blast. This time aiming directly at her. She started to scream, but the scream died in her throat as daggers of ice hit her square in the chest.

"Lilli!" I watched in horror as the ice rippled across her body until she was completely covered. A human Popsicle. "No!"

I clawed at the ice, but it was too strong. I could barely make a scratch. "No! Lilli! Can you hear me?" I tried to hug her—maybe an act of true love would thaw a frozen heart? It worked in that movie....

But the hug did no good. Lilli remained frozen. And the dragon was still headed our way.

"Uh, Ian?" Yano said worriedly. "You gonna do something about this guy?"

Drawing in a shaky breath, I slowly turned around, stepping away from my sister. I wasn't sure what would happen if she got blasted a second time, and I definitely didn't want to find out. I reached to my waist and, with trembling hands, pulled out my sword, squared my shoulders, and lifted my chin. It was up to me now. Probably the worst Dragon Ops player ever.

But I was a gamer. And gamers never gave up.

"Hey, Ice Cream Breath," I growled at the dragon, even as my heart stuttered in my chest. "You ready for a licking?"

Chapter Thirty-Two

The dragon's eyes snapped in my direction and locked on to me. His stare was icy blue and cold as death. I had never been so scared in my entire life, but I gritted my teeth and forced a smile, giving him a cheerful wave. When he opened his mouth to blast me with more icy fire, I dropped to the ground, just in time to miss the stream of frigid death shooting over my head.

The dragon roared in frustration, stomping in my direction, but thankfully it didn't try to blast me again. Maybe it was out of power, at least for the moment, but that wouldn't last long. If I was going to attack, it had to be now.

But what should I do? How was I going to get close enough to him to strike? And even if I could, would my sword make a dent in his scales? I was not a damage dealer—Lilli was. And there was no time to change into my new wrath armor midfight to give myself a cutting edge.

"What do I do?" I called to Yano. If only he had another one of those supersonic power-ups . . .

"I would suggest running," the draconite replied. "No offense, but you don't stand a chance here."

Argh. I knew he was right. But I couldn't just run away. My sister was still frozen. I had to find some way to defeat this guy and save her. No matter what.

The dragon lumbered toward me, its steps thundering in my ears as it clomped down hard on the ice. I'd always imagined ice dragons to be super majestic looking, but to be honest, up close this guy was a little lumpy and bumpy—and maybe even a little yellowish in spots, as if it had been made out of dog-pee snow. Thank goodness we couldn't smell anything in this game!

But all thoughts of dragon snow pee left my head as it suddenly swiped at me with four sharp claws. I jumped to the right to avoid it, careful to stay on the trail of footsteps. It swiped again, this time forcing me back. A bead of sweat trickled down my nose as my feet found more prints. It was almost like playing *Dance Dance Revolution*, a game Lilli and I had always loved in arcades. Back, back, left, right. Stay on the trail. Don't miss a step!

But how long could I keep it up? I was already out of breath. And the dragon wouldn't be out of ice for long. In fact, I could already see its belly growing white and large as it built up another deadly blast. I jumped back again, my mind racing. I was going to have to attack—to go on the offensive—but how? To make matters worse, I was running out of safe spots to jump to....

That was it!

The idea leapt into my brain. *I* could see where to jump, thanks to my infrared goggles.

But the dragon didn't have infrared goggles.

Which might give me a chance.

"Hey, Ice Queen," I called out to him, my entire body shaking like a leaf. Would this work? It had to work! "It's time to let it go! Or, er, you know, let me go?"

"You might want to work on your one-liners," Yano pointed out helpfully. "Just saying."

I ignored him, my eyes glued on the dragon. As it charged at me, I leapt to the right, then took two steps back, praying it'd take the bait.

We both paused. Then, just as I'd hoped, it clomped straight toward me with heavy steps, enraged and ready to kill. With a final lunge, it almost took off my arm, but I side-stepped just in time, and while the dragon was regaining its footing, I turned and leapt over a big weak spot to the footprint on the other side.

My feet slipped out from under me the second they came into contact with the ice. I hit the ground hard, knocking the wind from my lungs. But I couldn't stay down. Forcing myself to stand, I dragged my battered body another step backward.

And the dragon followed.

The creature screeched in surprise as it came down on a

weak spot of ice. There was a loud crack as its foot punched through, and the ice crumbled under its feet. Flapping its wings, it tried to push himself airborne—but its claws couldn't find traction on the slippery surface. The rushing water soon soaked its wings, making them too heavy to lift. It bellowed in rage as it fought, thrashing helplessly, until the current finally dragged it down and under.

Until it was gone entirely.

I stared down at the massive hole in the ice, my heart racing in my chest. At first I was half convinced it would rise again—ready for round two. But then my game menu blinked, registering the kill, and the experience points began to rack up on my menu screen. Another level gained.

But I barely paid attention to that. Instead, I turned away from the hole and back to where I'd left my sister trapped in her block of ice. I'd hoped her prison would melt with the dragon's death; that was how it worked in some games.

But no. My heart sank as my eyes fell upon her frozen body. Her mouth was open in midscream. I ran over to her and banged on the ice with my fist, trying to shatter it. But it was solid as a rock.

Which meant... what? She was stuck here? But for how long? Would it ever wear off? Would she be alive when it did? I tried to figure out if she was still breathing, but I couldn't tell. It didn't seem as if any part of her was moving. My heart started pounding in my chest. What was I going to do? I couldn't lose her! My sister!

"Oh, Lilli," I cried, leaning my forehead against the block of ice. It was so cold. *She* was so cold. "I'm so sorry."

This was all my fault. I'd dragged my sister here, against her will. Put her in danger, all because I wanted to play some stupid game. And now... What if this was it? What if this was game over for Lilli? What if she was real-life dead and it was all my fault? I cried so hard my throat hurt, and the freezing tears stung my cheeks.

"Wow. Looks like your sister could use a bit of a warm-up," remarked an amused voice.

I whirled around, shocked to find Ikumi standing behind me. She was dressed in a thick white fur coat. Her hair was now glowing fluorescent green and was piled on top of her head like a Christmas tree.

I stared. "You're not dead," I whispered before I could stop myself. *Way to state the obvious, dude.*

She smiled. "I told you I'd catch up to you," she scolded. "It just took me a little longer than I thought. Sorry about that. Didn't mean to make you fight that guy alone." She dropped her gaze to the hole in the ice. "Though you seem to be doing pretty good without me."

And with that, she raised her hands and muttered some strange-sounding words under her breath. When she finished, a warm golden glow flashed over Lilli.

And the ice melted away.

Chapter Thirty-Three

My sister collapsed to the ground, still dripping wet and out of breath. I ran to her, putting my arms around her, tying to help her back to her feet. She looked up at me, then Ikumi.

"Holy icy fortress of awfulness! I seriously thought I was going to be stuck in there forever. Thank you," she said to Ikumi. "I owe you my life." Then she turned back to me. "And thank *you*," she added with a grin. "Also, never tell me you're bad at this game again, because I will call you a big fat liar."

I couldn't help it—I threw my arms around her and squeezed her tight.

She laughed, struggling. "I can't breathe!" But she didn't sound like she minded that much, and a moment later she was hugging me back just as hard. Then she raised a fist to the air.

"Team Dragon Slayerz forever!"

I laughed, raising my own fist. "Long may we reign!" I added, finishing our old chant. We'd made it up when we first started playing *Fields of Fantasy* and formed our first guild—a group of friends joining forces to play together. We'd called ourselves the Dragon Slayerz (with a *z*, since the *s* version was taken) and even made T-shirts with our crest (a giant dragon's face with two swords behind it). I still wore my shirt sometimes, even though it was, like, two sizes too small now. Lilli, on the other hand, had thrown hers away when she quit the game. I still remembered how crushed I'd been when Mom asked me to take out the trash and I found it in her room, tossed out as if it had meant absolutely nothing. I'd felt as if I'd lost my sister forever that day.

But now she was back. She was alive and smiling and looking genuinely excited about playing the game. And it made my heart so happy I wanted to burst into tears all over again. Or hug her. Or tell her how glad I was that she was here. Team Dragon Slayerz forever!

"Not to break up this happy reunion?" Yano interjected. "But we might not want to be hanging out here when Ice Breath respawns."

I glanced over at the icy hole where the dragon had fallen. In my excitement over killing the deadly monster, I had almost forgotten it was a *video-game* deadly monster. Which meant after a certain time period, he might come back so the next group could fight him.

In other words, time to make like a banana . . . and split.

"Are you with us?" I asked Ikumi, holding my breath for her response. "You want to join the Dragon Slayerz?"

She smiled. "How can I refuse?"

Stepping carefully, we managed to make our way through the rest of the ice field and start the actual climb. The good news? We no longer had to worry about footsteps and infrared. The bad? More trash mobs. Tons more trash mobs.

Thankfully, this time, we had a secret weapon named Ikumi.

It was funny; when I'd first asked her to join our party, I had no idea what character class she even played. But I soon learned she was a druid, which meant she could cast healing spells, which we desperately needed, and could call forest animals to come to her aid. Soon we had what felt like an entire wolf pack fighting by our side, under Ikumi's command. At one point I actually wondered if I should tell her to call them off to give *me* a chance to fight.

But that was ridiculous. I thought of Derek, trapped in his cage, waiting for rescue. We needed to get the Elemental Stones as fast as possible, and Ikumi was helping us get there.

"She really is amazing," I remarked to my sister as we walked a few paces back, allowing Ikumi and her little friends to rip into an Abominable Snowman. "Though, I guess playing the game for two years straight will do that."

"Yeah. She's something," Lilli agreed, watching Ikumi with a puzzled expression. "But..."

"What?" I asked.

She shook her head. "I don't know. It's just...do you think there's something strange about her?"

"What do you mean?"

"Okay, this is going to sound really weird," Lilli said. "But...is she actually here?"

"What? Of course she's here. She's right there!"

"Yeah. Right. But so are those wolves. And that Bigfoot guy," Lilli added, gesturing to the new monster that had stepped into our path. "But none of them are really *here* here. Not like we're here, anyway. I mean, if we were able to take off our goggles, they'd disappear, right?"

"You think Ikumi is virtual?" I asked, raising an eyebrow.

My sister shrugged. "I don't know. But don't you think it's weird how she just showed up like she did? As if she had appeared out of thin air?"

"Maybe we just didn't see her coming. I *was* a little busy kicking dragon butt," I reminded her, half hoping to get another little shout-out for the dragon-butt kicking in question. Not that I needed praise; I was just doing my job. Like a warrior should. A really talented warrior...

"Well, I was stuck in a block of ice," Lilli said. "And I saw her appear out of nowhere. Like she'd just zapped into existence."

I scratched my head. "Maybe she has a warp spell?"

"Yeah, but how do you have a warp spell in this game?" Lilli asked. "Do you think *we* could warp? Our real bodies?"

"I guess not..."

"Also, how did she survive the Ghost Hollow thing? You saw what happened there; there was no way anyone could have gotten out. So did she regenerate? Or..."

Before I could reply, an oversize snowman leapt into our path, surprising us. I drew my sword and slashed at its snowy body. The creature snapped its teeth, then started shooting razor-sharp nose carrots in my direction. I held up my shield in front of me to block them. From behind me, I heard Lilli mutter a spell.

A moment later, the snowman exploded, covering us in snow. All white, thankfully. No dog pee this time.

"Nice one!" I cried, wiping the snow off my face as I turned to my sister. I raised my hand and we fist-bumped. She laughed awkwardly.

"We're getting pretty epic at this, aren't we?" she asked.

"Dude. We are the epic-est," I declared with a grin. Then I got back to the subject. "So what, you think Ikumi's, like, an NPC or something? 'Cuz, no offense, but she doesn't act like one. You've seen the quest givers and townspeople. They all think this is real. She clearly knows it's a game."

"Yano knows it's a game, too," Lilli pointed out.

I glanced over at our dragon guide, who was up ahead, jeering at the monsters Ikumi's wolves were slaying, as if he was taking them out all by himself.

"I know, but…" I shook my head. "I don't know. She seems real. The things she says." I thought back to our crazy dance in the tavern in Ghost Hollow. The conversation we had in Dragonshire about old-school video games. "I mean, she's super into old Mario games!"

My sister snorted. "A twelve-year-old girl who's into old-school Mario? Yeah, that's super realistic, dude."

I frowned, watching Ikumi now. Her long green hair had come undone and was flowing in the breeze as she shouted orders to her wolf pack. Could this girl—who looked so alive—really be nothing more than a bunch of pixels mashed together into a person?

And if so, did it really matter? She was helping us. Shouldn't that be enough?

"Are you okay, Ian?" Lilli asked, peering at me with concern. "You look like someone ate your pet dragon."

"I'm fine," I said, shaking my head. "It's just…"

"You like her," Lilli concluded. "I get it." She sighed. "Just, let me give you some good advice, little brother. Never trust anyone you meet online."

I groaned. "Here we go again. Technology is the devil. Everyone's out to get us. Soon we will be taken over by robot overlords who will turn us into human batteries to run their machines."

Lilli opened her mouth to reply, but before she could, Ikumi's voice rang out.

"We're here!" she called. "The Temple of D'ou!"

Chapter Thirty-Four

My eyes lifted to the temple. Sitting on a flat expanse of rock, it looked like something you might find in Japan—a squat red wooden structure, topped with a curved roof, covered in snow. A set of stone stairs led up to a simple, unadorned bamboo door at the front.

"Cool," I exclaimed, giving a low whistle. "And no, I don't mean cold," I added, shooting Yano a look before he could make the temperature joke for the hundredth time.

"Check this out," Lilli said, pointing to the base of the steps. I looked down to see a golden dragon statue surrounded by small piles of food and gold and other treasure. "What do you think this is for?"

"Dragons don't just love tacos, you know," Yano replied, landing on the statue. "They're suckers for gifts, too." A shimmer of gold danced down his scales. "Which reminds me—you totally missed my last birthday."

I rolled my eyes. "So these are all offerings to Lord D'ou?" I asked in wonder. There was a ton of cool stuff in the pile. "Who are they from?"

"From adventurers like yourself who come seeking his favor," Yano replied in a *duh* voice. "What, did you think you were the first?" Then he raised a bushy eyebrow. "Oh! You didn't get him a gift, did you? Wow. How . . . awkward."

"We need a gift? Why didn't you tell us?" Lilli demanded.

"You're supposed to be our guide," I added. "You didn't think to offer up some guidance while we were near a store?"

Yano's snout turned bright red. "Sorry," he said. "I just assumed you knew! You said you'd played *Fields of Fantasy. . . .*"

I groaned. Of course! How could I have forgotten that whole *Dragons Love Presents* quest chain I'd done two Decembers ago? Our group had been sent to the far corners of each land, searching for rare treasures to give to the Santa Dragon, who had made his temporary home at Dragonshire for the holiday. Each treasure could be exchanged for a unique holiday-themed piece of armor. I'd gotten this awesome Santa hat helmet that would say *Ho, ho, ho!* at the touch of the *H* key. It had driven Lilli almost as crazy as the Pumpkinhead one.

"Actually, this is my fault," Ikumi said, looking guilty. "I bought a great gift down in Ghost Hollow for this very purpose. But then Atreus attacked and burned down the town. Turning my present into a pile of ashes."

"Well, there's nothing we can do about it now," Lilli declared. "Maybe he won't notice."

We headed up the stairs and into the temple, which, despite its humble exterior, was all rich woods and dark golds inside. The main corridor was lined with large murals depicting great battles—dragons destroying cities with fire and ice while humans ran away screaming. My heart started beating a little faster.

"We *really* should have brought this guy a gift," I whispered to my sister.

Before she could answer, a man stepped into our path. He was small, stooped, and dressed in a simple brown burlap robe with a hood pulled over his bald head. As his eyes lighted on us, they narrowed suspiciously.

"Who are you?" he asked in a low voice. "And what brings you to this sacred place?"

"Um, is this the temple of D'ou?" I asked, my voice a little unsteady. I hadn't expected to find humans here. Perhaps this guy was Lord D'ou's servant? Or part of some dragon-worshipping cult?

The man's expression did not change. "It is."

"And is he around or whatever?" I shuffled from foot to foot. Wouldn't it be crazy if we'd come all this way, only to find out D'ou was, like, away for spring break or something?

The man cleared his throat. "And who are you to inquire about the great D'ou's comings and goings?"

"Um..." I stammered. "My name is Ian?"

"His *name* is Lord Wildhammer," Ikumi broke in. She stepped toward the monk, squaring her shoulders and lifting her chin. "And I am Lady Ikumi, esteemed druid of Ghost Hollow. We have traveled far—from the land of Dragonshire—to seek an audience with the great and mighty D'ou." She smiled sweetly. "So if you would be so kind as to inform him of our presence?"

I shot her an impressed look. *Right. What she said!*

The monk regarded us with skeptical eyes, clearly not as blown away by Ikumi's awesome role playing as I was. "And where, may I ask, is your offering to D'ou?"

Uh-oh.

I gritted my teeth. "Yeah, about that. Actually, we—"

"Brought him gummy bears!" my sister burst in. She reached into her pack, pulling out one of her giant gummy bears and presenting it to the monk as if it were a set of expensive jewels. "Dragons *love* gummy bears, am I right?"

The monk stared down at the gummy bear for a moment, then gave a haughty sniff. "I suppose we shall see. Come along."

We fell in line behind him. I gave my sister an incredulous look. "Dragons love gummy bears?" I said.

She grinned. "*Everyone* loves gummy bears, Ian."

The monk stopped at a heavy wooden door at the end of the hall. He turned to us, his lips pursed tightly together. Geez. This guy seriously needed to lighten up. Though that was probably not part of his programming. All the NPCs we'd met so far had been so one-dimensional, so focused on their specific role in the game. I guess that made sense. Why spend the time and energy perfecting a monk on a mountaintop that only a few players would probably ever even interact with?

But what about Ikumi? I watched her closely as the monk pushed open the heavy wooden door, ushering us outside. Could she really be just another game character? And would she admit it to me if I asked her outright?

Once outside, we walked down a small path lined with the most gorgeous ice sculptures I'd ever seen, all shaped like various dragons. There was even one of Wyrm herself, though she didn't look half as gross in ice as she had in real life. Which reminded me—we couldn't forget to ask D'ou about Lilli's turd stone. And . . . well, not mention how we got it.

The monk stopped at a wide circle outlined in snow. He raised his hands to the sky, murmuring some words that sounded a lot like Latin. Or maybe some kind of Tolkien Elvish? I knew from the original game that dragons had their own language—was that what he was speaking? It'd be cool to learn how to talk to dragons. Not that we had time for that. I'd learned my lesson on the last side quest. But if we ever came back . . .

Okay, what was I thinking? We were never coming back to this nightmare. If we survived this (and I still assumed this was a big if) it was going to be button mashing on the couch for me from this point forward.

My ears caught a small crackle. Soft at first, but growing louder. In seconds it was so loud I had to clamp my hands over my ears to block it out. I looked up at the sky.

Whoa. Now *that* was a dragon.

I watched in awe as Lord D'ou (who else could it be?) seemed to float down toward the earth, as if he were weightless and suspended in air. He had white scales, tinged in a ghostly blue, that rippled down his body like a frothy ocean after a storm. His neck was long and graceful as a swan's, and his body was that of a legged serpent with a tail that looked like it belonged to this fancy goldfish I once won at the state fair. He had bushy eyebrows, like Yano, and a long goatee, and his deep-blue eyes were bright and curious. I tried to imagine him in robot form—what he'd look like without the goggles on—but I couldn't picture it.

As he landed, he shook himself, sending more ripples of blue down his side. Then he turned to us, regarding each of us carefully as if he'd never seen a human before. I shivered a little, hoping he wasn't deciding which one of us to eat first.

Finally, he spoke. *Who are you?* he boomed in a deep, throaty voice. *And why have you disturbed my slumber?*

The monk immediately dropped to his knees, bowing his head. I wondered if we should be doing the same. "They have traveled far to seek your audience, Your Excellency," the monk informed the dragon in a trembling voice. "And to ask you a favor."

A favor? the dragon roared. His mouth dipped to a frown. *And why should I grant you a favor? Have you done any favors for me?* He paused, sniffing the air. *Have you brought me a gift?*

Lilli stepped forward. "How do you feel about giant gummy bears?"

The dragon pushed off his hind legs, rising into the sky. *Gummy bears?* he boomed. *Do you know whom you address? I am Lord D'ou. Born of ice and given breath by the gods themselves at the birth of our world. And you dare come here and offer me gummy bears?* Angry blue slashes spiked down his spine.

"I'm thinking the gummies are a no-go," Yano hissed in my ear.

"What about wrath armor?" I squeaked. "I have a very epic set of—"

Silence! the dragon roared. He kicked up his feet and swam through the air, executing a perfect barrel roll. When he finished, he locked his eyes on the monk. *These humans need to be taught a lesson in the proper dealing with dragons. Send them away and see that they do not return.* He paused, then added, *And... take their gummy bears. As... punishment for their impudence.*

My heart sank. He was sending us away? He wouldn't even hear our request? "Please!" I begged. "If you'd only listen—"

"Come on!" the monk said gruffly, grabbing me by the

scruff of the neck. "You heard the Master. You need to leave. Unless you'd prefer to stay for dinner?" He gave me a humorless smile. "I'd be all too happy to *serve* you."

"Ew." Yano shot D'ou a disgusted look. "Should probably stick with the gummy bears, mate."

I slumped my shoulders. I couldn't believe we'd come this far only to be turned away. As the monk began shuffling us back to the temple, I turned to my sister and Ikumi, eyes wide. "What are we going to do?" I whispered. "Should we try to fight him for it?"

"Are you joking?" Ikumi hissed. "We'd be flattened like pancakes in the first round. Even I am not powerful enough to take on a dragon like this."

"But we can't leave! We need that Ice Stone! Derek's life depends on it!"

"Maybe I can talk to him," Yano declared suddenly. "Dragon to dragon." He hopped off my shoulder, taking flight.

I grabbed his leg, yanking him back down. "No way! He'll kill you!"

"Give me a little credit, kid!" Yano shook free of my grasp, flying back to the dragon. I watched him flutter before the mighty beast—a tiny insect up against a goliath. Any second now and D'ou would swat him like a fly. Or reach out with his long neck and slurp him up for a late-afternoon snack.

Instead, to my surprise, D'ou simply peered at Yano

curiously. It was then that I remembered they had the same programmer. Maybe, in a weird way, that made them related? I craned my ears to hear what our guide was saying.

"Look, Your Majesty," Yano pleaded. "I know these kids are completely daft. And disrespectful, too. Believe me, I've had to deal with them longer than you. But they do have a legitimate emergency, and you're the only one who can help them. Might you at least hear them out? Then if you don't like what they have to say, feel free to eat them—I won't stand in your way. Though, I do feel obliged to warn you, they taste nothing like porg."

D'ou stared at him for a moment, and I held my breath, praying it would work. Instead the ice dragon leaned forward and plucked Yano out of the sky with his mouth, holding him between his teeth. Yano screeched in terror.

Perhaps you *taste better*, D'ou said.

"Oh no!" Lilli cried, turning to me with wide eyes. "We have to do something! We can't let him eat Yano!" She started reaching into her robe's pockets and her bag. "We must have something we can give him! Ikumi? Do you have anything?"

She shook her head. "Nothing a dragon would want."

"Ian?"

Heart pounding, I reached into my bag, searching for something—anything—that a dragon might want. Probably not the pirate hat. I did have a few gold coins I'd picked up when climbing the mountain, but the rest of my gold had gone to the—

I stopped short. I looked up at D'ou. At Yano dangling dangerously from his jaw. "Don't eat him!" I begged the dragon. "I'll give you a gift."

D'ou shot me a skeptical look. *I thought you didn't bring a gift.*

"Actually, I did. A very valuable gift." I drew in a breath and dared a step forward. Then I reached into my bag and pulled out the piece of paper. "The recipe for Ghost Goop."

D'ou's eyes bulged. He opened his mouth, dropping Yano like a hot potato. Yano flew out of biting distance and landed on the statue of Wyrm, shaking out his wings one by one.

"'Maybe I taste better!' Of all the blasted ideas!" he muttered. "I have half a mind to—"

Lilli ran over to shush him. But I kept my focus on D'ou, trying not to let him see how my body was shaking like a leaf. I took another step forward, holding out the recipe. "With this, you can make unlimited batches of Ghost Goop. Anytime you're feeling festive. It's a pretty big gift. And, well, I'm not happy to give it up. But that's how important our mission is. How much we need your help."

D'ou beckoned to the monk, who stepped toward me and plucked the paper from my hands. I sighed, watching it disappear into his robe's pocket. So much for that awesomeness. Still, if it got us out of being eaten, I guess it was worth it.

D'ou nodded, as if satisfied. *Now,* he said. *What is it you ask of me?*

"Right." I could feel Ikumi and my sister coming up behind me, giving me strength to go on. I drew in a breath. Here went nothing.

"It's about Atreus," I said. "He's kidnapped our cousin and trapped us in the game. He says he won't let us or Derek free unless we defeat him."

To my surprise, D'ou started laughing. A huge belly laugh that practically shook the ground beneath our feet. *You?* he repeated. *Defeat Lord Atreus? Now that is the funniest thing I've heard in a long time.*

My face flushed. "Look, I know we're beginners, but Ikumi's really good and—"

Oh children, children. You will never beat Atreus. Just as you would never be able to beat me. You would be fools to even try.

"We don't have a choice!" Lilli piped in. "We can't let him eat our cousin!" Her voice broke with frustration.

And why is this my concern? D'ou asked.

Ikumi stepped forward. "Because killing their cousin is only the beginning," she replied, lifting her chin and locking eyes with the dragon, not looking the least bit afraid. "Atreus has broken free of his maker's chains. He destroyed Ghost Hollow last night. And he will strike again. And again. Until the entire land is awash in his flames."

D'ou's laughter faded. *Is this true?* he demanded. *Has he left his roost at the Crystal Temple?*

"I saw it with my own eyes," Ikumi replied. "He has gone completely rogue."

D'ou let out a loud roar, which almost knocked me backward. *This is unacceptable*, he declared. *Atreus must be stopped before he disrupts the balance of this land.* He shook himself, sending a shimmer of white stardust down his flanks. *But I am afraid I cannot help. For I am still bound to this mountain and cannot leave.*

"Don't worry! We can do it!" I declared. "We just need to borrow your Ice Stone."

D'ou stared at me, incredulous. *You want to* borrow *my Ice Stone? The very core of all my power?*

"It's the only way to defeat Atreus," I replied simply.

The dragon glared at me suspiciously. *And how do I know you will actually use the Ice Stone against him? That you will not hand it over to him in trade for your cousin?*

I sighed. "We wouldn't do that! We're not stupid, you know!"

"Maybe a little stupid," Yano confided to D'ou. "But not the types to betray a great dragon like yourself."

"Besides," Lilli broke in, "we already have the first stone."

She reached into her bag, pulled out the brown turd, and presented it to D'ou. I cringed, waiting for the dragon to laugh in her face.

But instead, D'ou's eyes went wide. And when I looked down at the stone, I was shocked to see it glowing a brilliant yellow, as if it were made of amber.

"Holy crap!" squawked Yano. "Er, no pun intended."

How did you get that? Did Wyrm actually gave you her stone? D'ou demanded, his voice rich with disbelief.

"Um, yes?" Lilli stammered, her face flushing bright red with her lie. I tried to mentally tell her to keep it together. The last thing we needed was for D'ou to find out we killed Mommy Earth Dragon in cold blood. That would definitely end any chance of us scoring his Ice Stone.

"Yes, she did," I declared. "In fact, she's the one who sent us to you."

D'ou's eyebrows rose. *Well then,* he said. *This changes everything. If Wyrm believes in your quest, that is good enough for me. I will give you the Ice Stone to help you defeat Atreus and save our land.*

"Thank you!" I cried, relief bursting through me. "Thank you so much."

Do not thank me yet. You have two of the Elemental Stones, yes. And Atreus has one. But it will still be a hard-fought fight—one that you may not be able to win.

My heart sank. "Really? Even with two?"

However . . . the dragon added. *Were you to get the third . . .*

"The Water Stone?" Ikumi broke in. "You think we need the Water Stone, too?"

Three stones for three of you. It is your best chance.

Of course. A follow-up quest. Every time you thought you were almost done, you got stuck with a follow-up quest.

"Do you know where to find the Water Stone?" Lilli asked.

The dragon lord nodded. *The Water Stone is guarded by the mighty sea serpent Kaito, who lives deep underground in the Cave of Terrors. If you follow the River Tremulous, you will find his lair. But beware. For he is not as generous or trusting as I or Wyrm.*

"So . . . what are we supposed to do?" Lilli asked. "Can we fight Lord Kaito for it?"

I doubt you would win if you did, D'ou replied. *He is mighty in battle. Also, it is better to keep him alive. As one of the four dragon lords, he helps keep the land in balance and harmony. Were he to perish, Atreus would only gain more power.*

Okay, now I was *really* feeling bad about killing Wyrm. . . .

"So what do we do then?" Lilli asked.

The dragon raised a bushy eyebrow. *The good news is, Kaito is old and often deep asleep.* His mouth quirked. *Some might say it is better to ask forgiveness than permission.*

So steal it from him, then. Okay, got it.

"Thank you," I said, bowing to the dragon. "We appreciate the help. I promise, we won't let you down."

The dragon gave me a steely look. *I hope not*, he said. *For, it seems, the very fate of our world has been dropped in your hands.* He turned to the monk. *Prepare the Ice Stone for travel*, he ordered. *And set up three hang gliders for our little friends.*

The monk grumbled under his breath, but disappeared behind the door. "Hang gliders?" I asked, dread rising inside me. *Please let that be game talk for something that does not glide through the air.*

D'ou smiled. *You don't want to walk down the mountain, do you?*

"Not if we don't have to," Lilli piped in.

The dragon nodded, performing a graceful twirl in the air. Then he lowered himself back to the ground, his eyes sparkling.

Now, he said. *About those gummy bears...*

Chapter Thirty-Five

After handing over our gummy bears to the dragon, we followed the monk to the side of the mountain where the hang gliders were stored. Real hang gliders, Yano assured me, made out of metal and cloth and wire. A bit different in mechanics from the ones you found in the real world, but very similar.

They looked like giant kites with triangle sails attached to two metal bars that met in the middle with a crossbar and harness. The monk showed us how to strap ourselves into the harnesses and steer by leaning our bodies on the cross-bar. Left to go left, right to go right. Lean forward to speed up, push the bar away from you to slow down. Easy peasy.

At least for a game character.

"Follow the river," he said, "and you'll get to the Cave of Terrors. I suggest you glide as far as you can. Otherwise, it's a long walk filled with deadly beasts."

"More deadly beasts," my sister muttered. "Awesome."

I, on the other hand, was totally fine with loads of deadly beasts. It was the sheer cliff that had me freaking out. This wasn't some virtual thing that didn't actually exist and I could rationalize away. This was literally a cliff. That we were going to jump off of. With no adult supervision whatsoever, if you didn't count the monk. (Which I totally didn't.)

"I think I'll walk," I stammered after stealing a quick peek off the side of the mountain. The ground loomed and spun, giving me a half-dizzy, half-pukey, all-miserable feeling in the pit of my stomach. "It's really not that far. . . ."

"Are you kidding?" Lilli cried. "It took us half a day to get up here! Also, you might remember a certain ice dragon at the bottom? We can't be sure he hasn't respawned by now. You want to face him again?"

"Um, not exactly, but . . ."

Lilli sighed. "Look, I know you hate heights, Ian. But we have no choice. Derek is counting on us. We can't let him down." She gave me a pleading smile. "Also, better to jump off a cliff than become dragon dinner, am I right?"

"Honestly? They both sound equal in awfulness."

She clapped me on the shoulder. "Well, I think it's going to be awesome. Better than zip-lining through Costa Rica. The Steel Eel at Sea World. The Tower of Terror at Disney."

"You are so not making me feel better," I said flatly. I stepped a few feet back, away from the cliff, my heart racing in my chest. I had to get out of this somehow. But how?

Lilli was right—we couldn't walk down. But was this really the only other way?

"Are you all right, Ian?" Ikumi asked, stepping up to me. She spoke softly so my sister couldn't hear.

"I'm fine!" I protested, probably a little too forcefully to be believable. "It's just . . . heights. I really hate heights."

"I understand," Ikumi said with a nod. "The first time I was supposed to hang glide for a quest? I deleted the quest rather than do it. But eventually I did everything else in this really big quest chain and I couldn't complete it unless I took the plunge." She walked over to the cliffside, looking down. "I was petrified. But . . . in the end, it wasn't so bad. In fact, it was kind of fun." She turned and grinned at me. "Kind of like wearing the raccoon suit in *Mario 3*. You don't fall. You glide."

I bit my lower lip. No way was this going to be in any way fun. But we also weren't going to complete our quest unless I sucked it up and tried. Reluctantly, I walked over to the hang glider and strapped myself in, just as the monk had instructed, then double-checked and triple-checked the bindings—just in case.

It's just like Mario 3, I told myself, trying to breathe normally. *No big deal. Just like the raccoon suit in* Mario 3.

I stepped toward the edge. I could do this. I *could*. But then the wind hit me square in the face and almost knocked me over, and *nope*. Couldn't do it. I took a step back and slammed right into my sister.

"Lilli?"

"Go, go, go!" she cried. And then she shoved me off the cliff.

I yelped as my kite launched into the air and the ground fell away beneath my feet. The wind roughly caught the sail, jerking me upward and tossing me around as if I were a leaf in a hurricane. It was all I could do not to puke on the spot. Instead, I white-knuckled the crossbar in front of me and swallowed back a scream as the glider shook and shuddered above me.

This was a bad idea. A *really* bad idea.

Out of the corner of my eye I could see Ikumi and Lilli struggling, too. Even my sister couldn't manage to get her glider to behave in this wind. My heart pounded in my chest; if we couldn't get these things under control—fast—we'd be whipped way off course...

...if, that was, we even survived the landing.

Just like Mario 3. *Just like* Mario 3, I chanted to myself, squeezing my eyes shut.

Suddenly a new wind whipped up out of nowhere. A strong, fast wind—shooting me forward like a rocket. I flailed at first, screaming at the top of my lungs, sure I was about to plummet to the earth and find out once and for all whether dying in the game meant dying in real life. A question I *really* didn't want to know the answer to.

As I tumbled through the air, my brain raced through what the monk had said back at the top, wishing I'd paid more attention. What was it again? Lean left to go left, right to go right? If you're going too fast, push the control bar away from you to slow down.

I pushed. Hard.

For a moment, I wasn't sure it worked. Then, to my excitement, my kite began to stabilize. I pushed back some more and soon I found myself gliding smoothly through the air like a bird in flight. A rush of adrenaline shot through me.

Now *this* was more like it!

I turned to my sister and Ikumi. "Push the bar!" I yelled at them. "Push the bar away from you and you'll slow down!"

I watched as they followed my instructions. And soon their kites stabilized, too. My sister grinned at me, lifting her hand from the bar for a moment to give me a thumbs-up. I smiled back at her, thrilled, though I kept both hands on the bar, just in case.

It was then that I dared myself to look down, my eyes taking in the world of Dragon Ops stretching out before me in a bird's-eye view. The Sleeping Rain Forest, the Waterfall of Wonder, the Desert of Doom—that had been a pretty cool area to explore in the online game, with its crazy worm dragons popping in and out of the sand. I drew in a breath, mesmerized. All these lands, which I had only ever seen on a screen, now actually existed, just waiting to be explored.

"How are you making out?" Yano asked, coming up to glide beside me.

"Awesome!" I cried, yelling to be heard over the wind. "I feel like I'm flying!"

"Technically you're falling," the draconite clarified. "A nice, slow, guided fall. *Flying* takes wings!" He flapped his own wings in demonstration, performing a complicated little flip. *Show-off.*

"Whatever," I said, laughing. This was way too cool. I wasn't about to let him ruin it for me.

All too soon, however, the end loomed into view. I hit the ground hard, stumbling over rocks and roots, my feet shooting out from under me as they tried to gain traction in the slippery mud. Finally, I splashed into the river and managed to come to a complete, soggy stop.

"Dude, I want to do that again!" I cried, looking up at the mountain. I could barely even see the top—had we really flown so far? Of course it could be a trick of the game. With the time compression, what felt like dropping from a mountain could be nothing more than a small hill. But still! I had done it! I had conquered my fear and jumped off a mountain and lived to tell the tale.

Not Lord Wildhammer. Me.

My sister landed beside me, performing a much more graceful landing, and Ikumi came a moment later, joining me in the water. When she surfaced, she was sputtering, but giggling.

"Congrats, Ian!" Lilli said, freeing herself from her glider and giving me a high five. "I seriously didn't think you had it in you."

"Me neither," I admitted with a laugh. I turned to Ikumi, excitement bubbling inside me like I'd chugged too much Dr Pepper. "You were so right. It was just like *Mario 3*."

"Told you," she said. Then she lowered her voice. "I'm proud of you." And I felt myself beaming from ear to ear. Ikumi was proud of me.

I was pretty proud of myself, too.

Chapter Thirty-Six

"**W**ell, this isn't good."

I stared down into the murky water in dismay. We'd been traveling through the Cave of Terrors for what felt like an hour, kicking trash mob butt and generally being awesome. Until the passageway suddenly dead-ended at a deep pool of dark water. As if the cavern had flooded out after a storm. Or someone had clogged a drain.

"Maybe we're supposed to swim down into it?" Lilli suggested. "There could be an underwater passageway or something. Most games do have a water level, right?"

"Awesome," I said, biting my lip. "A swimming quest." First heights, now water—could this game please give me a break? I mean, Lilli was afraid of spiders. Why not a giant spider quest? I could totally rock that.

I peered around the cavern, hoping to spot some alternate exit. But the low-ceilinged cave was completely empty, except for a totally random stone statue of an old Asian man in one corner. He had a long beard, wrinkly skin, and a sly smile on his face. As if he were in on some secret joke. He also looked weirdly familiar....

"Whoa," Ikumi cried, coming up behind me. "Is that my grandfather?"

I turned, surprised. "Wait, what? Your grandfather?" What was she talking about?

She pointed to the statue. "I'm pretty sure that's Atsuo Takanama. My grandfather."

I stared at her, utterly confused. "Atsuo is your grandfather? *The* Atsuo? But that would make you..." My jaw dropped. "Oh my gosh," I whispered. "Is Hiro your father?"

A guilty smile slipped across Ikumi's face. "I was wondering how long it would take you to figure that out."

Holy giant zombie toenails! I stood frozen in place, mind completely blown. Hiro's daughter? We'd been playing the game with Hiro's daughter? I didn't even know he had a daughter!

Suddenly everything started falling into place. Ikumi had said she'd played the game since the very beginning. And, of course, Hiro's daughter would have been there from the start. Also, she'd mentioned she'd been on the island for two years, which was around the time Hiro came back to the game. "Why didn't you tell us?" I asked, feeling a little betrayed. I racked my brain, trying to remember if I'd said anything stupid in front of her. Hiro's daughter—wow!

"You didn't ask. Besides, what does it matter? I don't know who your parents are. Doesn't make a difference in the game."

"Okay, fine. You're Hiro's daughter," Lilli interjected. "But are you actually here?"

Ikumi frowned. "What do you mean? I'm standing right in front of you."

"Your *character* is," Lilli pressed. "But what about you? Your body? Are you walking around the island like we are? Or are you playing from somewhere else? Like, playing virtually?"

"Why would you think that?"

"Um, you've been disappearing and reappearing out of thin air? Real people can't do that. Even in a game. Also, the big explosion at Ghost Hollow. How else would you have survived that? I'm guessing you zapped out a moment before the explosion hit."

Ikumi shrugged. "Okay, fine. You're right. I'm not here in body like you. But I'm still here," she added, surprisingly sounding a little defensive. "I'm still playing the game just like you."

Lilli poked me in the side. "Told you!" she said smugly.

"You told me she was an NPC," I protested. "That's totally different."

I squinted at Ikumi now, trying to spot something that would make her look unreal. Proof that she was made of pixels instead of flesh and bone. But I couldn't find anything; she was rendered perfectly. As detailed as we were. Which was pretty cool, actually. If people could play virtually, people with physical handicaps would be able to play using VR headsets. And those who couldn't afford the airfare could play from home.

"So wait," Lilli said suddenly. "If you're actually playing from home, can't you just quit the game? Take off your goggles and go call your dad for help?"

"Can you take *your* goggles off?" Ikumi asked pointedly.

My sister sighed. "I had a feeling you were going to say that."

"Trust me—I'm just as trapped as you are, but in a different way. Which is why I want to help you with your quest," Ikumi added. "If we win, maybe Atreus will let me out of the game, too." She sounded wistful. As if it were something she'd wanted for a long time. Which didn't make sense, really. We'd only been trapped for about a day and a half in game time—which probably wasn't more than a couple hours in real life. Although I couldn't really be sure.

Lilli took a step toward the water, a determined look on her face.

"What are you doing?" I asked.

"I don't know...." She shrugged. "Maybe I should swim down there and check it out. There could be, like, a valve or something to drain the water."

"Or, you know, nasty, high-level sea zombies with a thirst for mage blood...."

She snorted. "I promise if I see anything dangerous, I'll swim back up."

I frowned, staring down into the murky water. I tried to remind myself what a good swimmer my sister was. She'd been on the swim team three years running and even won a few races. And she could hold her breath so long it was scary.

But still—this was a lot different from Grandma's pool.

"Just don't swim too far," Ikumi said. "Make sure you save some air to come back up."

"And grab me a fish if you see one!" Yano piped in, landing on the statue's head. He rubbed his belly with his paw. "I'm so hungry I could eat a human!"

My sister ignored him, testing the water with her toe. "Wow, it's cold," she said. But she slipped down into it anyway, shivering for a moment as her body adjusted to the temperature. Her robe floated around her, which would up the difficulty level of the swim, I realized with dismay; too bad she hadn't grabbed a bathing suit at the armory.

I had the sudden urge to tell her, *No. Don't go.* But before I could, she took a deep breath and dove under, disappearing into the pool's inky depths. I swallowed hard.

"Don't worry, she'll be okay."

I looked up and found Ikumi watching me closely. "I know," I lied.

I expected her to look away or do something else, but

she just kept watching me, as if she was thinking something she didn't want to say out loud.

"What?" I asked.

She blushed. "Nothing," she said, turning away. "I'm just...I'm really sorry I didn't tell you who I was to begin with. My dad doesn't want me playing with other people—beta testers or whatever. And I thought you might tell him if you knew it was me. I didn't want to get in trouble. But now I feel like I've been lying to you. And it's weird."

"No!" I protested, walking over to her. "It's not weird! I promise. And I'm glad you told me. Lilli kept saying you were an NPC. *That* would have been weird. Me becoming friends with a computer character? Derek would never stop trolling me." I gave a nervous laugh.

Ikumi's eyes widened. "Are we *friends*?" she asked, sounding surprised.

"Um...yes? If you want to be," I sputtered, suddenly unsure. What if she didn't want to be my friend? What if she thought I was a loser—Eight-Bit Ian, not exactly Mr. Popularity. "Or, you know, acquaintances? Fellow party members?" Oh man, this was so embarrassing.

"I like 'friends,'" Ikumi declared, walking to the edge of the water. She reached down and grabbed a stone and threw it in. It skipped three times before sinking. "I've never had a real friend before."

"You...haven't?" Now it was my turn to be surprised.

She grabbed another stone. "Let's just say it's not exactly

easy to make friends when going outside will basically kill you."

"Huh?"

She turned back to me, running her fingers over the stone. "I was born with a rare immunodeficiency syndrome. Which means my body can't fight off diseases like yours can. Going outside or breathing regular air could literally kill me. I've spent my entire life in a sterilized room. I can't go to school, or even play outside."

"That's awful!" I cried before I could stop myself. But still! As much as I liked being indoors, playing video games, the idea that she could never leave her room...

"Only my parents and a few doctors and nurses were allowed to visit, after they had sterilized themselves. The nurses were... kind. They would play games with me sometimes. But it wasn't like having kids my own age. When I would watch TV, I was always so jealous of all the kids who had friends and siblings. No one felt sorry for them."

I watched as she threw the stone—hard this time. It hit the rock wall with a loud bang that echoed through the cave before plonking into the water. Then she reached up and threw another, and another, not once looking in my direction. It seemed like she was scared that if she looked at me, she would break down and cry.

I kind of wanted to cry, too. I mean, I couldn't even imagine what that must have been like growing up like that. Being stuck in one boring room all the time. With no hope of ever getting out. It was almost worse than being trapped in a video game.

"I'm sorry," I said at last. "Or, I'm not sorry?" I amended quickly, remembering what she'd just said about people feeling sorry for her. *Real Smooth, Ian.*

I tried again. "It's just...I think you're supercool. And nice. I'm glad you joined our party. And I'm glad you're... my friend. I don't have all that many friends myself, to tell you the truth. I mean, besides my sister. Though, she doesn't really count."

Oh my gosh, Ian. STOP TALKING.

I waited for her to laugh at me. Or maybe tell me she was joking about the whole friendship thing. Instead, her smile seemed to light up the cave. "I am honored to count you as my friend, Lord Wildhammer," she said softly, bowing in my direction.

A thrill shot through me. "The honor is all mine, Lady Ikumi," I replied, trying to gallantly return her bow. Of course, I almost tripped over a rock and fell flat on my face in the process. Ugh.

Yano let out a loud sob and we both flinched. I'd pretty much forgotten he was even there, but now he conjured up a big yellow hankie and loudly blew his nose. "That was so... beautiful," he gushed. "Even better than the ending of *Ralph Breaks the Internet.*"

I exchanged an exasperated look with Ikumi. She giggled, which made me laugh, too.

Yano huffed, settling back on the statue. "It really was quite sad," he grumbled. "Ralph forced to say good-bye to Princess Vanellope...losing his only friend..."

I opened my mouth to debate this, but at that moment Lilli popped her head back to the surface. I ran to her and helped her back onto the shore.

"Are you okay?" I asked. She'd been down there a long time. And yet she didn't even look out of breath.

She laughed. "I'm awesome," she assured me. "And it was so strange—I felt like I could hold my breath forever down there."

"Really?" I wondered if that had something to do with the whole time-compression thing. What felt like minutes was probably only seconds in real life. Meaning a person could probably hold their breath a really, really long time.

"What was down there?" Ikumi asked. "Did you find a lever?"

My sister wrung out her soaking robe. "No," she said. "There's no lever. There is some kind of pipeline, though. But there's a grate over it that I couldn't budge."

Great. I slumped down onto the cave floor. We were back at square one.

Ikumi started walking the cavern's perimeter. "Maybe there's something up here that we missed," she mused. "Like a control panel to open the grate?"

We scrambled to our feet and joined the search, peering around each rock, hoping for something control-panel-like.

I even tried the infrared settings on my goggles, but found nothing.

Sighing, I leaned against the statue of Ikumi's grandfather. "Any idea what we should do?" I asked him jokingly.

CREAK!

I practically leapt out of my skin as the statue started to shift under my weight. When I turned to look, my jaw dropped.

A white star now spun above its head.

Chapter Thirty-Seven

With shaky fingers, I reached out, touched the star, and accepted the quest. The second I did, the statue's eyes lit up and shot sharp beams of light across the cavern. The beams landed on an algae-covered wall at the far side of the pool. A moment later, golden letters started scrolling across the surface.

If you wish to pass this level,
You must show your gamer mettle.
Five questions you must answer right.
Or you'll fail to live the night.
Get one right, it will recede.
And reveal the path you need.
Get one wrong and it will rise.
And you will meet your demise.

"Whoa," Ikumi whispered, running her fingertips over the statue. "This has got to be my father's work. Ever since he watched *Ready Player One,* he's been obsessed with hiding things in the game. Easter eggs, they're called. This has to be one of them."

"Sweet!" I said. There was nothing more fun than finding secret messages in a game, even when they were just for show and didn't help you in any way. But this one—could it hold the secret of this level?

"But what does it mean? What questions?" Lilli asked. "And what is supposed to rise and fall?"

"I bet it's the water," I said. "Maybe if we answer all the questions right the water will drain."

"Okay, but where are the questions?"

"Look!" Ikumi said, pointing at the wall. The original poem had disappeared, and in its place was question number one.

IN THE FIRST SUPER MARIO BROS. GAME, WHAT

DOES MARIO JUMP ON TO COMPLETE THE LEVEL?

"Whoa. Gamer questions!" I exclaimed excitedly. "My specialty!" I walked up to the statue, poking it twice. "Mario jumps up a flagpole to complete a level."

The statue seemed to nod, though it could have been a trick of the light—I wasn't sure. What I was sure of, however, was the creaking noise that followed . . .

And the water at our feet receding.

"It's working!" Lilli exclaimed. She reached out to give me a high five. I grinned proudly. Finally! Something in this game I was actually good at.

"And look!" Ikumi pointed. "There's the next question."

IN <u>PAC-MAN</u>, WHAT ARE THE NAMES OF THE FOUR GHOSTS?

"The *Pac-Man* ghosts have names?" Lilli asked, scrunching up her face.

"Obviously," I replied. "Inky, Blinky, Pinky, and Clyde."

"*And* in the Japanese game they were Fickle, Chaser, Ambusher, and Stupid," Ikumi added. The water receded even more.

"Really?" I asked, turning to her. "I never knew that!"

"Better turn in your geek card, Ian," Lilli teased. "Ikumi's showing you up!"

"Yeah, yeah," I said, waving her off. "Next question!"

IN <u>THE LEGEND OF ZELDA</u>, WHO GIVES YOU YOUR
FIRST SWORD AND WHAT DOES HE SAY?

I tapped my finger to my chin, concentrating. My mom had introduced me to the original *Zelda* when I was eight because it had been her favorite game when she was a kid. I ended up playing all the way through, infiltrating Death Mountain and destroying Ganon and rescuing Princess Zelda. But how had it begun?

I scanned the walls of the cave as if they would hold

the answer, and then it came rushing back to me. "You get your first sword from an old man in a cave!" I declared triumphantly, raising my hand over my head, as Link did in the game.

Eight-Bit Ian—hero of Hyrule!

"And ... what does he say?" Lilli prompted.

Oh. Right. It was a two-part question. I wrinkled my brow. How was I supposed to remember the man's exact words? I definitely saw a meme about it somewhere online a while back. Someone handing over a small kitten and saying ...

"'It's dangerous out there'? 'Don't go alone'?" I tried.

Another loud creak echoed through the cave, and for a moment, I thought I'd gotten it right. But then I felt water splashing at my feet. This time the pool wasn't receding.

It was rising.

"I don't think that's it," Lilli said worriedly, looking down at the rushing water. It was coming in fast—almost to our knees already—and it was freezing cold. So cold it made my bones ache. My mind raced, trying to remember what the man in the cave had said.

Ikumi stepped forward. "'It's dangerous to go alone,'" she declared. "'Take this.'" Then she mimed holding up a sword, as I had done a moment before.

I slapped my forehead with my hand. Right! *Take this.* As in take the kitten in the meme. Or the sword in the actual game.

The water withdrew back into the pool, leaving us soaking wet, but once again standing on dry land. Well, sort of dry. The water had seeped into the ground, and we were now surrounded by a muddy mess.

"Good one," I told Ikumi before turning back to the wall for the next question. Three down, two to go. We could do this.

IN <u>CAMELOT'S HONOR</u>, WHAT ARE THE NAMES
OF THE TWO WARRING SORCERERS?

I wrinkled my nose in distaste. "*Camelot's Honor*," I said, scoffing at the RPG game that was always trying to compete with the awesomeness of this one. "Who cares? *Fields of Fantasy* forever!"

No sooner had the words left my mouth than the familiar creak sounded again. At first I really thought the waters would recede, in appreciation of my total loyalty to the game we were playing. Instead, the water began to rush back in, even faster than before—and soon we were up to our waists. It felt colder, too—so cold my teeth started to chatter.

"Aw, come on!" I protested. "That's so unfair!" I waded over to the statue. "Seriously, dude. Do you really want to drown your loyal fans?"

"Merlin and Morgana!" Lilli broke in. "The two warring sorcerers are Merlin and Morgana."

"'By Merlin's Honor!'" Ikumi added, raising a fist as she quoted the game's famous catchphrase.

Suddenly the water began to recede again. I gave the girls a grumpy look. "Traitors," I muttered. "Everyone knows *Fields of Fantasy* is where it's at."

"And yet, we're not submerged in water," Lilli reminded me with a pointed look. "I'm going to call that a win."

"Besides, even my grandfather played *Camelot's Honor*," Ikumi added. "And he, like, basically created this game."

"Whatever," I said, waving them off. "Can we get to the final question, please?" I turned to the wall, relieved to find the last question had appeared.

Until I read the question.

IN <u>FALLOUT: NEW VEGAS</u>, WHAT

VAULT ARE YOU BORN INTO?

My stomach sunk. After failing the last question, I'd really wanted this one to be something I knew. Another classic-game question—I was great at those. Modern games? Not so much.

And I'd never played *Fallout: New Vegas*. Mostly because it was rated Mature, which Mom was super strict about. And though I had a vague idea of the overall plotline—apocalypse, guys in power armor, some weird computer you wore on your arm—I had no clue about the vault thing.

I turned to the girls. "Have either of you played *Fallout*?" I asked hopefully. We were so close. We couldn't fail now!

Lilli scratched her head. "I played *Fallout 76* a little," she replied. "In that one, you come from Vault Seventy-Six. But—"

Her words were interrupted by another loud creak.

"Hey!" Lilli protested. "That wasn't my answer."

But the game didn't seem to care. Water gushed from the ceiling, raining down on us fast and strong and so cold I could see chunks of ice floating at the top. I screeched, trying to protect my head. But I was soaked in seconds.

"Think!" I cried, my teeth chattering on the words.

"Vault One-oh-One?" Lilli called out, her voice high-pitched and a little desperate. The water kept pouring into the chamber and rising from the pool until it was up to our waists again. "No, wait, that was part three."

"And Vault One-Eleven was definitely part four…" Ikumi mused.

"Stop saying random numbers!" I cried, horrified. "It's getting stronger."

The water was raging now, a violent, icy river up to our necks. Soon we'd have to start treading water to stay above it. If we didn't freeze to death to first.

"What else are we supposed to do?" my sister demanded. "I don't know the answer! It could be anything!"

Panic spiraled through me as the water continued to surge. Higher and higher, splashing my face, invading my nose and mouth and making me choke. It wouldn't be long, at this rate, before the cave submerged completely. For it to be game over for real.

"Oh for goodness' sakes! You just declared your undying

friendship and now you're going to get yourselves drowned? What do you think this is, the *Titanic* movie?"

I turned to see Yano flying over to us, barely staying above the waterline.

"Can you help us?" I begged, gulping a mouthful of gross, slimy water in the process.

"Unfortunately, no," he said apologetically. "I've already tried searching in all my databases, but nothing is coming up."

"That doesn't make any sense! Try again!"

"I've tried four times. Honestly, it's as if the vault doesn't bloody exist."

"Oh my gosh, that's it!" Lilli cried suddenly. I looked over at her, heart in my throat.

She was treading water fast, her mouth barely above the surface.

"What is?" I asked.

"Don't you see? It's a trick question! There's no vault number because in *Fallout: New Vegas* you don't come from a vault!" she said triumphantly.

BOOM!

The water surged, then swirled, creating a giant whirlpool, sucking up everything in its wake. I screamed, my stomach lurching as the current swept us up along with the rest of the water and debris, yanking us downward into a large metal pipeline. The frothing water tossed me like a rag doll from side to side, slamming me into the walls.

"Find something to grab on to!" I cried, my heart in my throat as the water dragged me down. But there was nothing; the sides of the pipe were slick and smooth. All I could do was go with the flow as the pipe twisted left, then right, then dropped fast, leaving my stomach somewhere in my throat as we shot down into an unknown world. I tossed and turned, unable to get my body back under my own control.

"Lilli!" I cried. "Ikumi! Are you okay?"

But the water was too loud, rushing in my ears. Drowning out all other sounds.

After what seemed an eternity, the pipe finally dead-ended and I shot out like a cannonball, arcing through the air, then dropping like a stone down into the large lagoon below. My body plunged into the pool, hitting hard and submerging completely. Water shot up my nose, and I gagged as I struggled to claw my way back to the surface. I saw my sister and Ikumi splashing around nearby.

We had made it.

With effort, I managed to swim to the shore, and I collapsed on the sand. Lilli and Ikumi waded toward me, drenched but alive. Behind them, Yano flew a few feet above the water, sopping wet and looking disgruntled.

"Water levels," he sputtered. "I hate water levels."

"Aw, come on," Lilli teased. "You gotta admit, it was kind of fun. Like a crazy-big waterslide."

"*I* hate waterslides," I said with a laugh. "Though, I guess they beat drowning." I gave Lilli a smile. "Good job figuring out the *Fallout* thing. I never would have gotten that in a million years."

Lilli blushed hard. "I just got lucky," she said. But I could tell she was pleased.

I climbed to my feet to check out our surroundings. We had dropped into the most beautiful cavern I had ever seen. With soaring rock ceilings high above and snow-white walls dripping with multicolored crystals. A huge, gushing waterfall crashed into the pool at our feet, which seemed to sparkle with pale-blue luminescence, as if it were made of starlight.

"It's so beautiful," Lilli breathed, turning in a circle. "Definitely the most beautiful spot in the game so far."

"My dad must have designed this level," Ikumi declared, her voice rich with awe. "It looks just like the place where he and my mom honeymooned in New Zealand. He told me about the caves there—filled with millions of tiny glow-worms." She smiled dreamily. "He said they made the walls seem to dance with light."

"That sounds awesome," I declared. "I'd love to see that in real life."

A shadow crossed Ikumi's face. She turned away from the water, reaching down to grab her pack.

"Is something wrong?" I asked.

"Everything's fine," she said quickly, though her voice

didn't sound fine at all. And then it hit me why. Because of her condition, she would never be able to see places like this in real life. For her, this was as good as it would ever get.

"What is real, anyway?" I said, trying to make her feel better. "I mean, this totally feels real to me. It was designed by a game architect. Built by a programmer. It takes up space on a server. Which means, basically, it exists. Maybe on a different plane of existence? But it's real all the same."

I wasn't positive I was making much sense, but Ikumi seemed to relax a little, tossing her now-blue hair over her shoulder. "You know what, Ian? You're right," she said. "It may not be everyone's reality, but right now, it's ours. And we should appreciate it, right?"

"Absolutely," I declared, flashing her a grin. And I meant it, too. This wasn't just a game. We'd stepped into a whole new world. A beautiful, complicated, dangerous world.

Now we just had to save Derek and find our way out.

Chapter Thirty-Eight

There was only one passageway leading out of the waterfall room, so we headed down, keeping our guard up the entire way, never knowing what could be around the bend. It was a low-ceilinged path, half-overgrown with moss and lichens. The walls themselves were crawling with more glowworms, painting our skin with a purplish tinge, as if we were walking through a black-light amusement park ride. Warm, slimy water drizzled down on our heads like rain.

"Yum," Yano said, slurping up a mouthful of glowworms. When he grinned, the inside of his mouth lit up like a Christmas tree. "Now this is more like it."

After what felt like miles, the passageway opened up into a small rocky chamber. There were no glowworms here; instead the room was illuminated by a soft white light shining from somewhere above. The light cast down on a single stone pedestal in the center of the room. On that pedestal was a tear-shaped jewel.

"Is that it?" Lilli asked. "Is that the Water Stone?"

"What else could it be?" I said, mesmerized by the way the jewel managed to catch the light and cast rainbows across the chamber. Around the pedestal was a ring of hieroglyphic pictures of cats and birds and dragons. Another puzzle, perhaps?

"The third stone," Ikumi whispered, the awe clear in her sparkly eyes. "I can't believe it!"

"I can't believe no one's guarding it!" Lilli added, looking around the room. "Where's what's-his-name the water dragon? Shouldn't he be lurking around here somewhere?"

"Maybe he's asleep," I said. "D'ou said he was really old."

"Well, let's not wait for him to wake up," Ikumi suggested. "Let's get this thing and get out of here. Finish this game once and for all."

She stepped toward the jewel, reaching out with her hand. My ears caught a weird sizzling sound as she yelped, jerking her hand away. "Ow!"

"What is it?" I asked worriedly.

"I don't know." She clutched her arm against her chest. "It's like there's some kind of invisible force field. It zapped me when I put my hand through it."

"Really?" I quickly accessed the infrared setting on my goggles. Sure enough, there was some kind of barrier surrounding the platform—horizontal, squiggly red lines almost up to my head. "Ugh. I knew it couldn't be that easy."

"Is there a way to turn it off? Maybe another puzzle?" Ikumi asked, looking around the room.

"Or you could try to boost me over it," Lilli suggested.

"Yeah, but then how would you get back?" I pointed out. "You'd be stuck in the circle."

"Poor humans!" Yano interrupted. "Always so grounded." He ruffled his wings. "Allow me," he declared. "The most useful, talented, fantastic member of the Dragon Slayerz—ready to save the day, once more with feeling!"

Before I could react, he took flight over the red squiggly lines of the barrier and dropped down onto the pedestal. For a moment, I worried the pedestal itself might be electric, too, and would zap our little eager guide to kingdom come. Instead, with an overdramatic flourish, he plucked the stone up with his claws, holding it out for us to see.

"Ta-da!" he proclaimed. "Easy peasy, lemon squeez—!"

The ground began to buckle under our feet.

"What's happening?" I cried as the cave started shaking violently. Rocks rained down from the ceiling. *Oh no! No, no, no!*

"Run!" Lilli cried, lunging back toward the passageway.

I didn't need a second invitation. I dove into the tunnel, which was now buckling like the rest of the cave, as stones and glowworms pelted us from above. I tried to ignore the awful squishing sound the worms made as I accidentally stepped on them in my rush to get out of the cave. I put my hands over my ears and kept running, squinting to see my way through the dust and debris.

"Faster!" Ikumi cried. "We're not going to make it!"

We could just see the light up ahead—the exit into the larger chamber—but it looked as if it were miles away as the tunnel kept imploding in on itself, constricting tighter and tighter like the trash compactor in *Star Wars*. Soon we were forced to our hands and knees, crawling through mud so thick it felt like quicksand pulling us down. I struggled to put one hand in front of the other, gasping for breath.

"Come on!" Lilli cried. "We're almost through. Keep going!"

I gritted my teeth and made one final push, bursting back into the waterfall chamber and tumbling to the ground. Seconds later, a load of rocks and debris crashed down over the tunnel's entrance, burying it in rubble. I collapsed onto the sand, sucking in a much-needed breath. That was *way* too close.

"Nice going, birdbrain," my sister muttered to Yano, sitting up and plucking glowworms out of her mud-caked hair. "And here you call *us* noobs."

I reached up to check my own head. No glowworms, thankfully, just a ton of mud and moss. I wondered if I should rinse off in the water.

"Hey!" Yano protested, also quite mud covered. "I got the stone, didn't I?"

"Um…" I squinted at him. "Then where is it?"

He looked down, his eyes widening as he realized his talons were empty. He must have dropped the stone at some point during our escape.

He cringed. "Oops?"

"'Oops?'" Ikumi cried, scrambling to her feet. Her grime-streaked face had transformed into an expression of pure wrath. "You dropped the Water Stone and that's all you can say? 'Oops?'"

"Of course not!" Yano shot back, looking affronted. "I have a vocabulary of forty thousand words, I'll have you know. Which is five thousand more than the average human—"

But Ikumi was no longer listening. She ran over to the pile of rubble and dropped to her knees. She started digging desperately, dirt and stones flying all around her. "We've got to find it!" she cried, her voice frantic. "Help me!"

We joined her at the pile, scooping handfuls of dirt, searching for something—anything that looked like the stone. But it was no use. Like finding a single teardrop in an entire ocean. There was too much dirt, too many rocks. And the tunnel had been so long…

I gave up, sinking down to the ground and letting out a sigh. "Well, that's that, I guess."

"No!" Ikumi shot back, surprising me. "We can't give up! We need that stone!"

"Come on, Ikumi," Lilli said. "We're never going to find it in there. We don't even know when Yano dropped it. It could have been way back in the original chamber."

But Ikumi ignored her and kept digging, her eyes narrow and her lips pressed together with purpose, as if she were determined to find the stone by sheer force of will. I put a hand on her back, trying to calm her down, and found her whole body was shaking.

"Stop!" I begged her. "Just stop. We'll figure it out. It's going to be okay."

She whirled around, her face as dark as a thunderstorm. "Okay?" she repeated incredulously. "How can this possibly be okay? That stone was our one ticket out of this place. And now it's buried under a mountain of rubble! Without it, we'll never be able to defeat Atreus. I'll be stuck in this stupid game forever!"

Her voice broke and tears began to stream down her face. Lilli stepped forward and reached for Ikumi, but she jerked away, stormed down the beach, and then sank into the sand, head in her hands, and sobbed uncontrollably.

Yano's shoulders slumped. "This is all my fault," he said meekly. "I should have never tried to help."

"It's okay," Lilli assured him, patting him on the wing. "Your heart was in the right place. Um, not that you have a heart. But you know what I mean." Her eyes traveled to Ikumi. "Maybe you should talk to her," she said to me.

I nodded glumly. "Yeah," I said. "I'll try."

I left my sister and Yano and trudged over to Ikumi, feeling completely weird and uncomfortable as I struggled with what I was going to say. I wanted to make her feel better somehow. But at the same time, she wasn't wrong. This was really bad. For all of us. Especially Derek.

When I reached her, I crouched down to her level, finding her eyes with my own. "Look, I know this stinks," I said, trying to make my voice sound reassuring. "But don't give up. We can still do this!"

"How?" she demanded. "Lord D'ou said we needed three stones if we were going to have a chance to defeat Atreus. Now we only have two."

"Maybe two is enough?" I suggested. "With our stones and your high level…"

"No." She shook her head. "If we don't have all three, we'll never be able to defeat Atreus. I just know it."

"Then fine—we won't defeat him," I said, grasping for straws. "They'll still come for us eventually, right? They'll be able to fix the game and get us out." Hopefully before Derek became dragon dinner.

"Get *you* out, maybe," she shot back bitterly. "Not me. I've been stuck here for two years. And no one's come for me yet."

Wait, what? I scrunched up my face, trying to understand. "You mean you've been *playing* for two years, right? You've only been stuck since Atreus took over."

She closed her eyes, hands clenching into fists. "It doesn't matter. I should have known better than to hold out hope. It never works out. Never."

"What doesn't work out? What are you talking about?" My mind whirled as I tried to make sense of what she was saying. Two years? How could she possibly be stuck in the game for two years? What about food? Sleep? Bathroom breaks? And what about her dad? Her nurses? They would come in and check on her, right? If she was stuck in the game, they would do something about it.

Ikumi looked up, her eyes rimmed with tears. "Ian—"

"Ian! Ikumi! Come quick!" my sister interrupted.

Reluctantly, I got to my feet, reaching down to help Ikumi stand. When I turned around I saw that Lilli was practically jumping with joy.

"What is it?" I asked, a small shred of hope winding through me. "Did you find the stone?"

"No." Lilli beamed. "Because that wasn't the stone. Yano just checked his databases. That was the Tremulous Jewel of the Sea. It gives mages a plus ten to water spells. Which would have been nice to have . . ." She shot an irritated look at Yano. "But it's *not* the Water Stone. Which means the Water Stone is still somewhere in this cave!"

My body flooded with relief. "That's awesome!" I cried. "Right, Ikumi?"

"Awesome," she repeated. Though she still looked a little upset. My mind flashed back to our conversation. What had she been talking about? I'd have to ask more later, but right now, we had a stone to find.

"So where is it?" I asked, looking around the cave. The walls were tall and solid. And there were no other apparent passageways besides the one that had just caved in on us and the pipe we'd dropped down from. My eyes trailed to the crystal pool of water at our feet. Could it be under there somewhere? But no—the water was so clear—I could see the bottom and there was nothing.

"Wait!" Ikumi said suddenly. "I have an idea!" She turned and started wading through the water.

I shot my sister a doubtful look but followed Ikumi. Wading through the shallow part, then swimming once it got deeper. A small part of me worried that she was going to tell us we had to go underwater to finish this, but instead, she led us right to the giant waterfall at the back of the chamber.

The rush of water splashed at our faces as we got closer, thundering in my ears. Ikumi shouted something, but I couldn't hear her over the noise. We followed her to the side of the waterfall and around to the back. There, cut into the rock, was a small cave leading to a narrow tunnel.

"Holy supersecret passageways!!!" I exclaimed, impressed. "How did you know this was back here?"

"I didn't," Ikumi confessed. "But I had a feeling. This whole level was clearly designed by my dad. The waterfall, the glowworms, the treasure trap. It's all stuff he's into."

"And he likes waterfall caves?"

"It's how he and my mother met," Ikumi explained. "She was playing *Fields of Fantasy* from her home in Japan. She had hidden her character behind a waterfall so she could go eat and leave the game without worrying about a monster attacking her while she was away. My dad found her there while exploring and tried to talk to her. When he realized she was away from her keyboard, he sat down and waited for her to come back."

"And then brutally slayed her?" Yano asked hopefully.

Ikumi rolled her eyes. "Um, no. He started talking to her. And then invited her to join his party." She gave a sad smile. "And the rest is history. She moved halfway across the world just to be with him in real life, and she never regretted it. They were inseparable, my mom and dad. Till the day she died."

"And look!" Lilli broke in. "Are those their initials?"

We turned to look where she was pointing. Sure enough, there was a small carving in the stone: H + I.

"Wait. Was your mom's name Ikumi, too?" I asked, surprised.

Ikumi's face flushed. "Her name was Ikumi, yes. But

mine isn't. That's just my character's name. Like you're Lord Wildhammer."

"So what's your real name?" I asked.

But Ikumi only shook her head. "It doesn't matter," she said. "Just call me Ikumi."

I frowned, disappointed. Why did I even care about her real-life name? It made no difference here. At the same time, though, I felt like we had gotten to know one another during our time in the game. And she had said I was her friend. If that was true, why wouldn't she tell me her real name? What else was she hiding from us?

"You know I could google it when I get home," I half joked. "You're the daughter of a legend! I bet there's tons written about you online."

Her face paled. "There probably is," she said slowly. "But please don't read it."

"Why? What's the big deal?"

She sighed. "It's nothing. It's just . . ." She trailed off, waving a hand across the cave. "You said this was real. Can't this be real enough?"

I winced at the pain in her voice. Maybe she wanted me to think of her as this—the girl she'd *chosen* to be with magic superpowers and crazy-colored hair and eyes swirling with glitter, rather than the sick girl who was stuck in her room all the time. My heart ached a little, and I wanted to insist that she was amazing in every reality.

But the look on her face told me she didn't want to hear it.

"Speaking of reality," Lilli broke in. "Can we get on with this quest so we can get back to ours? We do have a cousin to rescue, in case you forgot."

"Absolutely," Ikumi agreed, looking relieved. "Let's go."

So we continued down the damp, narrow passageway until it opened up into a third chamber—this one a mirror image of the one where we'd discovered the first jewel.

Except this one had a dragon.

Chapter Thirty-Nine

A massive sea serpent with blue-and-violet-checked scales slept not ten feet away from where we were standing, its long, lithe body coiled around itself like a snake's and its back was ridged with spiky white fins. Two more frilly fins formed a collar around his neck like a Victorian queen's. His eyes were closed, his head resting on a small wooden chest that spilled over with treasure.

"Kaito the Water Lord," I whispered. "I knew he had to be here somewhere."

"Yup," Lilli replied grimly. "And look what he's got."

I followed her finger, my heart dropping. There, cradled in the middle of the dragon's ropy body, was a second pedestal holding what looked like a pure drop of water, the size of a large egg and completely see-through.

"The Water Stone." I didn't know whether to be relieved or terrified. "How in the world are we going to steal that?"

Lilli glanced at Yano. He held up his paws in protest. "Not on your nelly," he declared. "The last time I tried to help, Ikumi almost knocked my head off. And I've grown rather fond of my current head." He flew up toward the ceiling and perched on a small rocky outcropping. I half expected him to conjure himself up some popcorn.

I groaned. "So what do we do? You think we could fight him?"

"Lord D'ou said he'd be too tough," Lilli reminded us. "He's one of the real robot dragons, remember? He could literally crush us in real life if we made him mad."

"Then what are we supposed to do?"

Lilli squared her shoulders. "You stay here. I'll go steal it from him." She made a move toward the dragon, but Ikumi jumped in her path.

"You can't," she said. "Look what you're wearing! One swipe with the dragon's claws and you'd be dead before I could heal you."

Lilli's face fell as she looked down at her muddy robes. "Then what?" she asked. "You can't do it. You may be high level, but you're also not wearing armor." She looked around the cave. "And there aren't any creatures here for you to charm."

"True," Ikumi said. "But if I cast a speed spell on myself I could get in and out before he woke...."

"Um, hello?" I waved my hands in front of the girls. "What about me?"

They both looked at me blankly. "No way," my sister said.

"Why not?" I asked, annoyed. "I'm wearing armor. I can take a few blows."

"But can you sneak?" Lilli asked doubtfully. "No offense, little brother, but it's not exactly been your thing so far."

"I know. But I put some points in it since then. And Ikumi could cast that speed spell on me. I'd just run up, grab the gem, and be gone."

"Yeah, but..." Lilli wrinkled her nose. "Running isn't really your thing, either."

Now my face was burning with embarrassment. They didn't think I could do it. Eight-Bit Ian, great at old-school game trivia. But when it came to real-life adventure? I'd never level high enough.

But that was the old Ian. The Ian who hadn't faced off against an ice dragon and won. Who hadn't jumped off a cliff and soared through the sky like a freaking bird. The old Ian hadn't spun down a drain, been catapulted from a pipe. Escaped a collapsing tunnel on his hands and knees...

I drew in a breath. "I can do this," I said, squaring my shoulders and lifting my chin. "Just...give me a chance."

Lilli nodded, giving me a strange look. As if she had read something in my eyes that told her to believe me. "Okay," she said. "We'll be right here if you need us."

"Actually, I think you should stand near the exit," I said, pointing to the far end of the cave. "I'll meet you there with the gem so we can escape quicker."

"That's too far," Ikumi protested. "I won't be able to throw you healing potions from there."

"I'm not going to need healing. I'll be fast enough."

The doubt returned to Lilli's face. "I don't know...."

"Also," I added with a smile, "I have a secret weapon." I accessed my menu and swapped out my tank gear for the super-speedy wrath armor I'd purchased in Ghost Hollow. Finally! A chance to use it!

Finally, a chance to become a true hero.

Chapter Forty

I crouched close to the ground, in full-on track-runner position, my wrath armor flashing gold in the cavern's dim light, accenting the huge dragon emblem on my chest. Even my sister had to admit it looked cool, though she was still skeptical about the plan itself.

"Whatever you do, don't stop," she warned. "You have to keep running."

"Don't worry, I've got this," I assured her, trying to push down everything inside me that said I absolutely didn't. While I might be New Ian now, that didn't mean New Ian wasn't terrified. Was I being crazy? Did I really have a chance to pull this off?

I turned to Ikumi. "Okay. You can cast the speed spell in three, two, one—"

A bright white light flashed across my field of vision as she let the spell rip. Electricity prickled across my skin like

I'd been hit by lightning—though thankfully I didn't fry on the spot. Instead, I exploded into action, dashing forward, loose rocks flying up from my feet as I pounded the ground. I felt a little like Sonic the Hedgehog going into supersonic speed as he raced across the game board to collect his golden rings.

But I didn't need a thousand rings. I needed one single stone.

I reached the rocky ledge at the dragon's back and scrambled up the side, hands painfully scraping against rough stone. When I reached the top, I drew in a breath, channeled my inner Lara Croft from *Tomb Raider*, then jumped down onto the pedestal, careful not to crush the stone under my heel. Working to keep my balance, I crouched down, then scooped up the stone, cradling it like a football under my arm. It felt strange—not exactly solid, but not liquid, either. More like one of those squishies my sister collected, though much stickier. At least that meant it probably wouldn't break if I dropped it....

Okay. I rose to my feet, scanning the room, my heart pounding in my chest. I could feel the speed spell running out, my skin tingling less and less as it lost its power. Leaving me standing, literally, in the middle of a dragon.

A waking dragon, I realized with growing dread.

I swallowed hard as Kaito lifted his head, blinking stupidly as he tried to figure out what was going on. He was still half asleep, which meant I still had a half a chance—at least for the next couple seconds. I glanced back at the ledge I'd jumped down from, but it was too far up to reach.

No. There was only one way down.

Without pausing to think, I threw myself on my butt, sliding down the dragon's slick scales as if they were a slide at a playground. The scales were slimier than I imagined, and the armor at the back of my legs was quickly coated in goo. I launched off the dragon's side, flew through the air, then slammed down hard on my ankle. Pain exploded up my body, but I ignored it as I clutched the stone against my chest and started to run.

"Ian! Look out!" my sister called from the mouth of the cave.

Kaito's tail slashed out like a whip. I tried to dodge, but I was too slow and it hit me straight on, knocking me off my feet. Before I could even move, the tail slid around me, wrapping me in a crushing embrace.

New Ian had been fast. But not fast enough. And now I was caught.

Kaito's grip was like iron, and as hard as I struggled, I couldn't move. I tried to take a breath, but he only squeezed harder and my lungs started to burn. My vision grew spotty and I desperately tried to stay conscious as panic rose inside me. This couldn't be game over! Not when we were this close! I tried to grab my sword, but it was pinned to my body.

"Ian!" my sister screamed.

I looked up and my blood went cold. Kaito was dragging

me back to him, his mouth creaking open to reveal a really impressive set of pearly-white teeth.

SMASH!

Out of nowhere, razor-sharp rocks rained down from the ceiling, smashing into the dragon's head, slicing his scales open in a large, angry gash. He hissed in rage, twisting and writhing as blue blood gushed from the wound, running down his face and blinding him. He dropped me like a hot potato and I hit the ground hard, pain lashing up my side.

I took in a huge breath, almost crying as sweet air filled my lungs.

"Ian!" I vaguely heard Lilli cry. "Run!"

Scrambling to my feet, I charged toward her and Ikumi, as fast as my sore legs could carry me. I had to get out of Kaito's reach. I might not get a second chance.

It seemed like I was under a slow spell now—or wading through mud—but at last I made it. Ikumi grabbed my arm.

"Come on!" she said. "Down here! I found a door!" She dashed down the corridor, and Lilli and I followed close behind. As we ran, I could hear the dragon roaring with fury, and I shuddered as I remembered how close I'd been to becoming his dinner.

At last we came to a large wooden door and dove through it out into the open air. A voice cried out behind us.

"Hey! Wait for me!"

Yano burst out, flying at full speed. We slammed the

door shut behind us, Ikumi casting a spell to seal it shut. Then we collapsed onto the ground, breathing heavily.

"Wow," Lilli declared, looking over at me once she'd caught her breath. "That was amazing. No offense, but I honestly didn't think you'd be able to do it."

"I told you this armor was epic," I teased as I raised myself onto my elbow to face her.

"No." She shook her head. "*You* were the epic one in there. And don't even try to deny it."

I couldn't have wiped the grin off my face if I tried. I was epic. Ian Rivera, gamer geek and all-around wimp, had taken on a giant robot dragon and had come out victorious. Suddenly I wished this game gave out badges. Because a "Badge of Awesomeness" would surely be mine.

Though I did admittedly have a lot of help. If Lilli hadn't stepped in when she did? I would have been a goner for sure.

"Speaking of epic, what was that rock thing you did?" I asked. "That was amazing! When did you learn how to do that?"

"I didn't. I used the power of the Earth Stone." She held out her favorite turd and grinned.

"So . . . you're saying I was basically saved by a poop?" I asked, raising an eyebrow.

"An *epic* poop," she corrected, her eyes twinkling.

Chapter Forty-One

The cave had dumped us onto the sandy shore of a deep blue lake. It was sunset, and the twin suns cast dazzling sparkles across the water as they painted the horizon with bold orange and blue strokes. A picture-perfect spot with thankfully no enemies in sight. The best place to take a rest.

Not that we had time to rest. The sun was setting on our second day in Dragon Ops. Atreus's three-day deadline loomed. At least we had what we needed to defeat him now. We could begin our final journey to his lair.

"You guys ready to push on?" I started to ask. But before anyone could reply, my menu lit up red and my cousin's hologram hovered in front of us.

"Good news, Derek!" I cried, happy to see he was still alive and okay. I'd been more than a little worried we'd taken too long already. "We've got everything we need to defeat

Atreus now. And we're headed your way. Just hang on a little longer and—"

"Ian!" Derek interrupted, sounding annoyed. "Shut up and listen for a second! I have a message for you. From Atreus."

"What?" My heart dropped. *Oh no. What now?*

"He says to tell you that the quest has changed."

"No way!" Lilli broke in. "You can't change the quest midgame! That's, like, against the rules!"

Derek turned his head, as if listening to someone lurking just off camera. Atreus, I guessed. He turned back to us.

"Um, he says to tell you he makes the rules? And to stop interrupting."

A shiver of dread spun down my spine. "What's the new quest?" I asked slowly, pretty sure whatever it was, it couldn't be good.

"Don't freak out, it's actually way easier than the original," Derek replied. "You don't even have to fight him. All you have to do is bring him the Elemental Stones. Then he'll let you out of the game."

Wait, what?

I turned to my sister and Ikumi, my mind racing. How did Atreus even know we *had* the Elemental Stones? Had he been watching us this whole time? Did he know exactly what we planned to do? Was he afraid we'd have a chance to defeat him—to win the game?

Was the great and powerful Atreus actually running scared?

"So wait," Ikumi broke in. "That's it? Just bring him the stones? And he'll let us out?"

"Uh, yeah. That's what I said," Derek replied, sounding a little impatient. "So, like, get your butts down here and get it done."

And with that, Derek hung up.

I turned to my sister and Ikumi. "Can you believe it?" I asked. "This is amazing! We don't have to battle him after all! We just have to give him the stones!"

"And then we'll finally be free!" Ikumi cried. She broke out into a little celebration dance on the sand, waving her arms and legs in excitement. I joined her, grabbing her hands and twirling her around. We spun and spun until we fell into the sand, laughing. My skin prickled with excitement.

Until I looked up at my sister. Who was frowning.

"What?" I asked, scrambling to my feet.

"I don't know about this," she said. "It just . . . doesn't seem right."

"What do you mean?"

"Like, why would he suddenly change the quest out of the blue?"

"Duh. 'Cuz he knows we're about to kick his butt and he's scared."

"He's an AI. They don't get scared. Also, why does he want us to bring him the stones? Why not just let us out now if he's so frightened of what we could do to him?"

My earlier excitement deflated like a balloon. She was

right. As much as I wanted to believe it could be this simple, logic said there had to be something else going on here.

"Remember what he did to Ghost Hollow," Lilli reminded me. "And that was with *one* stone. What if he possesses all four? He'll have the power to do whatever he wants in the game. And there will be no way, at that point, to stop him."

"Who cares?" Ikumi replied, looking annoyed. "We'll be long gone by then."

"Will we, though?" Lilli asked. "What if he doesn't let us out after all? What if this is all part of the plan to begin with?"

Uh-oh. Miss Conspiracy Theory was on a roll.

"What are you talking about?" Ikumi demanded.

"What if he didn't change his mind about the quest? What if that's how this quest was programmed to go in the first place? It would be a great twist, right? For us to give everything to the dragon, only to have to fight him anyway? That's a way more realistic game scenario than simply us handing over quest items and having him let us go. I mean, have you ever played a game without a big final boss fight?"

My shoulders slumped. "No," I admitted. "I didn't think about that." But it made perfect sense. The Elemental Stones were our only weapon against Atreus. And he expected us to just hand them over willingly?

Ikumi's eyes darkened. "So what? You want to try to fight him anyway? Risk dying in the game? Even without the stones, he's really powerful. And you two are still pretty low-level." She squeezed her eyes shut, as if she were in physical pain.

My heart pattered nervously in my chest. We needed her to agree to this. There was no way we could do it without her.

"Ikumi..." I tried.

She opened her eyes. "Ian, please," she begged. "Just give him what he wants. And we can all be free."

I sighed. I didn't want to make her mad. But I didn't know what else to do. What she was suggesting? I just couldn't.

"Trust me, I want to get out of here as much as you do," I said slowly. "But, well, I agree with Lilli. I think fighting him with the stones is still the best way."

She turned, but not before I caught a lone tear slipping down her cheek. She stared at the water, her body still. For a long time she said nothing.

"You can't understand," she whispered at last. "What it's been like to be here. All by myself. All alone. Two years is a long time, Ian. But it's nothing compared to what I'll face if I don't get out now." Her voice cracked. "I can't do it. I won't! I won't spend eternity in this video-game prison!"

"What are you talking about?" I asked, feeling tears well in my own eyes. I could tell she was hurting so badly, but I didn't understand. "How could you have been stuck here for two years? Wouldn't your dad have come for you?"

Her face tightened. "*He* was the one who put me here to begin with."

"What?" Lilli cried, horrified.

"It doesn't matter. None of this matters." She waved both her hands. "It's just...well, I really thought this time I had a chance...."

"Ikumi..." I didn't know what to say because I couldn't wrap my head around what was going on.

"I'm sorry," I finally said, knowing it was the last thing she wanted to hear.

She turned and looked me in the eyes. "No, Ian," she said softly. "I'm the one who's sorry."

She lifted her hand and I watched, confused, as a trail of pink mist drifted from her fingertips. I opened my mouth to ask what it was, but suddenly I felt too tired. Like, *really, really* tired. My eyelids began to droop. My muscles felt heavy and slow. I dropped to my knees in the sand, looking up at Ikumi with confusion.

"What have you done?" I cried. Out of the corner of my eye I could see Lilli had fallen, too. Her eyes were closed. She looked...dead.

"I'm sorry, Ian," Ikumi said. "I really did want us to be friends...."

And then there was nothing but blackness.

Chapter Forty-Two

"Ian, wake up! Wake up!"

I rolled over, rubbing my eyes with my hands. When I pulled them away, I saw Lilli leaning over me, her face pale.

"What is it?" I asked, alarmed. I sat up, half expecting to see some crazy monster or dragon on approach. But everything was quiet, save for Yano's buzz saw–like snores. "Is something wrong?"

My sister sank back on her heels, staring up at the sky. It appeared to be morning; the twin suns were rising over the water. "Okay, don't freak out," she said slowly. "But Ikumi's gone."

"What?" I scrambled to my feet, heart in my throat, my eyes darting around our camp and coming up empty. Ikumi was nowhere to be seen.

My mind flashed back to the night before. The pink mist. The look in Ikumi's eyes. *I'm sorry, Ian,* she'd said.

"Oh no!" I cried. "No, no, no!"

I dove for my bag, my stomach lurching. But even as I rummaged through, I knew exactly what I'd find. Or wouldn't find.

The stones were gone.

Ikumi had stolen them.

"No!" I moaned, a feeling of dread sinking in my chest. She wouldn't! She couldn't. In desperation, I accessed my menu, searching for her character profile—positive it had to be some mistake. But she'd disbanded from our party. And to make matters worse, she'd unfriended me, so I couldn't even call her in-game.

I slammed my fist against the sand, wishing there was a monster nearby so I could tear it limb from limb. How could she do this? After all she said? After all we'd shared? My mind flashed back to her hand reaching for mine. The way she'd looked at me and smiled.

But in the end, she didn't care about anyone other than herself.

My cries had woken Yano. He looked around, confused. "What happened?" he demanded. "Where's Ikumi?"

We quickly filled him in. When we were finished, he shook his wings in annoyance. "Well, of all the blasted cheats!" he declared. "Not to mention sleeping a guide is a clear violation of the Dragon Ops terms of service. Why, I should report her to—"

"Report her later," Lilli broke in. "Right now we need to find her before she gets to Atreus."

Our guide nodded, taking flight. "She's on foot and will have to deal with trash mobs, so maybe she hasn't gone far. It'll be quicker for me to scout from the skies. I'll do a circle and see if I can find her." He huffed. "And give her a piece of my mind! Sleeping a guide! Of all the . . ." His words faded as he flew farther away.

I dropped my head to the ground, pressing my forehead against the damp sand. All the fight left my body until I felt like a floppy doll. "I'm such an idiot," I moaned. "She was probably just using us from the start to get what she wanted. And now that we're not useful anymore . . ." I trailed off, too choked up to continue.

"I'm so sorry, Ian," Lilli said again. And I could hear the sympathy in her voice. "Believe me, I know exactly what this feels like. And how much it hurts."

I sighed, trying to pull myself together. "I know. She betrayed both of us."

"No." Lilli hesitated. "That's not what I mean."

She rose to her feet and walked down to the water, staring out at the two rising suns. For a long time, she said nothing, as if trying to weigh her words.

"You want to know why I gave up video games?" she asked finally. Her voice was tight. "Why I *really* did?"

I stared at her, shocked. This was not what I'd been expecting her to say. Was she really going to come clean now—of all times? Finally tell me her big secret? What had hurt her so badly that she left gaming forever?

Forcing myself to push aside thoughts of Ikumi, I leaned forward. "It wasn't because of Logan?"

She shook her head. "No," she said. "Because there was no Logan. There never was."

"Huh? What are you talking about? We played with Logan all the time."

"We played with his *character*."

"Well, yeah. But obviously he was controlling the character."

Lilli dropped to the ground, hugged her knees with her hands. "Remember Mina and Emmy?"

"You mean, your friends from school?" I scratched my head as I sat down next to her. What would they have to do with Logan?

"Friends," my sister scoffed. "Yeah, right."

The look on her face made my fists clench. "What did they do?" I asked, a feeling of dread rising inside me.

"They created Logan," she blurted. "His character, I mean. Once they found out I was playing the game." She kicked at a rock. "They thought it would be funny, I guess."

"What?" But that was crazy! I'd played with Logan, too. For hours! He'd been one of our best guild mates.

There was no Logan. There never was.

"They found us online. They got us to invite Logan to our guild. They flirted with me through in-game whispers. Told me I was pretty. That I was sweet. They even talked me into playing with them alone."

She sighed, swiping a tear from her cheek, only to have another fall. "In any case, idiot that I am, I started to really like him. I would be so excited to get home from school and sign on to talk to him. Sometimes we didn't even play the game, we just talked. I thought he was such a good listener, letting me tell him all my problems." She squeezed her eyes closed. "I had no idea I was actually pouring my heart out to Mina and Emmy."

"I can't believe this," I said.

"Suddenly everyone in school seemed to know everything about me," she continued, her voice wooden. "People were laughing at me, and I couldn't figure out why. And the crazy thing was? It only made me want to play more. To talk to Logan more. He was ... well, he was the one good thing in my life," she whispered. "And he didn't even exist."

"How did you find out?" I asked, my chest tight. Though what I really wanted to ask was, *Why didn't you tell me?* Here she'd been hurting so badly and I had no idea. Heck, I even teased her about the no-video-games thing. What kind of brother did that make me?

She shrugged. "Mina had a birthday party. I went to her bedroom looking for a manga I'd let her borrow. I noticed her computer was logged in to *Fields of Fantasy*. Which I couldn't understand, since she always claimed she hated gaming. So I took a closer look and found a familiar character on the screen."

"What did you do?"

"I confronted her," she said in a tight voice. "I demanded to know if Logan was real or not. In the back of my mind, I thought maybe I'd made a mistake. That maybe he was Mina's cousin or something. And he'd used her computer to play." She hung her head. "But no. She and Emmy confessed immediately. They thought it was the funniest thing in the world."

Sobs broke from her body. I wrapped my arms around her. I knew it probably wouldn't do much good, but I wanted to do something.

"Why didn't you tell me?" I whispered.

She snorted through her tears. "Are you kidding? I was way too embarrassed! I mean, how stupid am I? To fall for some made-up person? It was bad enough to have Mina and Emmy laughing at me. I didn't want anyone else to know."

I pulled away from the hug. "So you quit the game."

"What else could I do? How could I trust anyone or anything online anymore? People can say anything—be anyone—and there's no way to tell if it's real. Except it is real. And it really hurts."

I nodded slowly, thinking of Ikumi and wondering how many lies she'd told of her own. I thought I knew her, but really...I didn't even know her name. For all I knew she wasn't even really Hiro's daughter, but someone else entirely. Just playing a sick game with my head, like those girls had done with my sister.

"Anyway," Lilli said, standing up again. "I've found new friends since then. Like Izzy from my soccer team and Riley in gymnastics. And while I do miss being online sometimes—I also kind of like spending time in the real world."

"I get it," I said, nodding slowly. "And I'm sorry I've given you a hard time about that. I'm glad you've found all this stuff you like—I really am. I just…miss hanging out with you. That's all." I blushed. "I know that's totally selfish, but—"

"It's not," she assured me. "And I've missed hanging out with you, too. If I've learned anything from this crazy adventure it's that we make a good team. And, well, maybe we can team up again if we somehow manage to get out of this thing alive? I wouldn't mind signing on to *Fields of Fantasy* once in a while. Just for fun."

"Really?" I asked, and she nodded. "Well, I wouldn't mind doing some real-life things with you once in a while, either. Just for fun. But no bungee jumping. Or zip-lining. And definitely no roller coasters."

She laughed. "I'm sure we can figure something out."

At that moment, Yano flew back into view. He landed on my sister's head, a shimmer of angry red slashing down his side.

"No Ikumi?" I asked, my heart sinking.

He shook his head. "Sorry. We must have been out for a while. There's no sign of her."

"Which means she's probably already at the mountain," I concluded glumly. "We're too late."

"No," my sister interrupted, surprising me. "If it were too late, our quest would have failed. I still have it. Do you?"

I accessed my menu. "Yeah," I said. "But—"

"Then that means we still have a chance," Lilli declared, her eyes flashing something fierce. "Look, I don't know about you, but I'm not about to let Ikumi—or whatever her name is—get away with this. She may have our stones. But she hasn't won the game yet. Which means we can still beat her."

Hope rose in my chest. "You really think so?"

"Absolutely," she declared. "After all, we're the Dragon Slayerz, right? We don't give up without a fight."

Chapter Forty-Three

We started walking, Yano taking the lead, calling out at any signs of trash mobs or other trouble. Thankfully, since Ikumi had passed through recently, we saw more monster corpses than living creatures, which made our journey a lot quicker. It gave me hope, too. Ikumi had to kill everything in her path, and even at her high level that meant it would take her a lot longer to get anywhere. Maybe we still had a chance to catch up with her before it was too late.

At last a dark mountain rose in front of us, tall and looming. My heart stuttered in my chest as I craned my neck up—way up—to view its volcanic peak high above. A trail of bright-red lava wound down like an open wound, and thick black smoke smothered the sky.

"There it is, the legendary Mount Fearless," Yano proclaimed.

"Should have called it Mount Freaking Frightening, if you ask me," I grumbled.

"How do we get up there?" Lilli asked, squinting at the lava. "It doesn't look climbable."

"It's not," Yano agreed. "Luckily there's a lift that will take you a few feet from the top. There, you'll find a cave that will lead you down into the mountain and into Atreus's Crystal Temple at the bottom."

My eyes followed his pointing wing. Sure enough there stood a small wooden structure I hadn't noticed before. Like an old-fashioned elevator on a pulley system.

"Uh...are we sure that's safe?" I asked, raising an eyebrow. It looked pretty rickety.

"You're heading into an active volcano to fight a deadly dragon at your pathetic level and you're asking if the *elevator* is safe?" Yano asked.

"Good point." Also, I assumed Ikumi had already used it, so at least it had been tested recently.

How far had she gotten at this point? I wondered, looking up at the volcano again. Was she close to Atreus's lair? What would happen if she handed over the stones before we could get to her?

The now-familiar ache settled in my stomach. Was she at all regretting what she did? Or had this been her plan from the start? To toy with us like those horrible girls had with my sister—just having some fun, not caring who they hurt to do it? Had Ikumi ever really cared what happened to us? Had she ever really been a friend?

Let me give you some good advice, little brother, my sister had said. *Never trust anyone you meet online.*

I was beginning to understand her internet boycott.

I shook my head, picking up my pace as I walked determinedly to the elevator. We still had a chance to stop Ikumi and I wasn't about to blow it.

Once inside, we pressed the big red button on the wall, and the elevator groaned and creaked before shooting us into the sky, leaving my poor stomach somewhere back on the ground. Whoa! From the state of the thing, I had assumed it would be a slow ride up—not a full-on replica of the Superman ride at Six Flags.

But in Dragon Ops, as Hiro had said, things were not always as they seemed.

"Wow," Lilli remarked excitedly. "You can see everything from up here!" I gripped the railing a little tighter, forcing myself not to look down.

Soon, the elevator lurched to a stop, almost throwing me off the side. Good thing I had been holding on! Taking in a deep, calming breath, I followed my sister off the lift, relieved to find solid ground under my feet.

I might have been able to face dragons now. But heights? They were always going to be my kryptonite.

Yano directed us to the cave, half hidden behind some low-hanging vines. As we stepped inside, I blinked my eyes to adjust them to the darkness. The passageway was only dimly lit by some kind of phosphorescent moss, and for a moment I wondered if I should turn on my night vision.

But soon the tight passageway opened up into a vast cavern—the mouth of the volcano itself. The good news? It was well lit from the sunlight streaming in from high above. The bad? It was filled with well-lit waterfalls of lava.

I stared down into the pit of the volcano, which dropped straight into a molten core; lava boiled violently with big, fat popping crimson bubbles that looked way too much like blood. Narrow wooden walkways clung to the sides of the volcano, descending into the pit without any railings to speak of. Which meant one wrong step, one loose floorboard, and we would meet a very fiery end.

"Holy burning pit of awfulness," Lilli breathed, her eyes wide.

"Right?" I asked, trying to ignore the fresh wave of nausea rising inside me. "And here I thought the dragon slaying would be the tough part."

"I'm quite sure that's going to be tough, too," Yano chimed in, fluttering over the pit as if it was no big deal. Once again I wished I had wings like his. It would make things so much easier.

Instead we began our descent on foot, hugging the side of the volcano as we went, concentrating on placing one foot in front of the other and not looking down. A few loose stones slipped under my feet, splashing down into the lava pool below, and my heart beat a little faster as I tried not to imagine being one of those stones. What would happen if I fell? Would I die instantly? Or would I burn and burn, treading lava until I finally tired and sank down to the bottom and drowned?

"I wonder what this place looks like without goggles," Lilli remarked, trying to sound casual and totally failing. "I bet that lava pit is really just a giant trampoline. So if you fell, you'd bounce really high."

"Yeah," I said, the thought making me feel a little better. After all, this wasn't supposed to be real-life dangerous. They must have had all sorts of safety procedures in place. Not that they would do us any good now. It might be a trampoline down there in real life. But our minds would believe it was lava. Which meant it would burn.

"I'm going to go on record that I much prefer the Cave of Terrors and its pretty glowworms," Lilli remarked, fanning herself as she continued to take one careful step after another. The lower we got, the hotter it became, and I was feeling like a sweaty mess under my armor.

"Too right!" Yano chirped. "There isn't even anything down here to eat! Why, I might have to resort to human flesh if things keep going this way!" he declared. "Not yours, of course!" he added hastily. "A good guide never feasts on his friends. It's like Guiding One-oh-one."

"Well, maybe you'll get lucky and we'll run into Ikumi," I muttered, pressing my chest against the rocky wall at a particularly narrow spot where a few wooden boards had collapsed. "Clearly she's no friend, so you can totally eat her."

I could feel my sister giving me a sympathetic look, and I clamped my mouth shut before I could say anything more. It was embarrassing how much I still cared about Ikumi. But you can't just shut off your feelings like a light switch, even if you should. I wondered if Lilli ever thought about Logan—ever caught herself missing him, even now, knowing he never existed to begin with.

I quickly accessed my menu, checking on the quest again. It was still there, not listed as "failed." Did that mean Ikumi hadn't handed over the stones yet? Though that seemed weird, seeing how close we were at this point. Surely she would have made it to Atreus by now, with her big head start.

"Is Ikumi still in the game?" I asked Yano. "Can you tell?" She'd blocked me, so I couldn't, but maybe she didn't think about our guide.

Yano closed his eyes, then opened them. "She's still listed as a player," he said. "Though it won't tell me her exact location."

"Maybe she changed her mind?" I suggested hopefully. "Decided not to give the stones to Atreus after all?"

"Or maybe she did and Atreus didn't keep his promise to free her," Lilli reminded me. "Just like we told her he wouldn't."

"Right," I said, something worming through my stomach, though I wasn't sure what. I certainly didn't want Ikumi to hand over the stones to Atreus. But also, deep down, I didn't want her to be stuck in the game, either. I thought back to her sad eyes. The desperation on her face. She said she'd been trapped here for two years. And though I had no idea how something like that was possible, it didn't seem like she'd been lying. How horrible would it be to be trapped in this deadly world for so long—with no friends. And no one to talk to except computer programs.

Finally, we reached the bottom of the walkway, which dead-ended at a large gaping mouth of a door framed with chunky crystal teeth. Above the doorway was a sign, also made of crystal, etched with the same familiar Latin words we'd seen on the starting gates at the beginning of the game. I stared at those words now, my heart beating like mad in my chest.

HIC SUNT DRACONES.

Here be dragons.

Chapter Forty-Four

This was it. The Crystal Temple. The entrance to Atreus's lair. We'd finally made it.

But making it, of course, was only the beginning.

I switched on my night vision, peering into the dark cave. "Do you see anything?" Lilli asked. "Atreus? Ikumi? Derek?"

I shook my head. "It just looks like a tunnel filled with more crystals."

"Well, let's go check it out."

We stepped gingerly through the mouth of the cave, into a forest of giant crystals dripping down from the ceiling and poking up through the ground. Like an underground icicle forest. It was beautiful—almost as beautiful as the Cave of Terrors had been. But I was too freaked out to spend much time taking it all in. In fact, it was difficult to even remember to breathe at this point. Any moment now we could find ourselves face-to-face with a dragon. *The* dragon.

And what would we do then? Well, we still hadn't really worked that out.

The passageway led to a small cavern carved out of rock. The walls were dripping red with something that I really hoped wasn't blood, and the ceiling was low, giving the space a cramped, claustrophobic feel. At the far end was another doorway, opening up into what appeared to be a larger room. Creeping over to it, I peered inside.

And found Atreus at last.

"What do you see?" Lilli hissed from behind me.

I retreated from the door, back over to my sister. "He's in there," I told her in a low voice. "He seems to be asleep."

"What about Ikumi? Derek?"

I shook my head. "I didn't see either of them. But there was some kind of opening at the other end of the cave. Like a passageway or something. Maybe Derek's down there."

"Should we try to sneak past Atreus and look?" Lilli suggested. "If he's sleeping . . ."

"Or we could try to attack him," I countered. "Get a jump on him before he wakes up. It'd give us some advantage."

"Would it, though?" Yano queried, landing on my shoulder. "We have a saying where I come from: Let sleeping dragons lie. Especially sleeping dragons who possess four major Elemental Stones with the power to blast one into oblivion with nary a thought."

"We don't know he has the stones," I reminded him. "We might have beaten Ikumi here."

"And you might have beaten me at chess," Yano said. "If you played five thousand four hundred and thirty-two games with me in a row. But only because I let you win out of sheer boredom in the end."

"Do you mind?" Lilli admonished. "We're trying to plan a boss fight here."

"So sorry! Carry on! Don't let the voice of reason stop you from plotting your own brutal demise!" Lifting off my shoulder, Yano flew toward the temple exit.

"Where are you going?" I demanded.

"Just gonna find me a little snack. Don't worry. I'm sure I'll be back in time to watch you both be fried to a crisp. *Toodles!*" And with that, he disappeared out the door.

My sister rolled her eyes. "Worst guide ever." Then she turned to the doorway to Atreus's lair. "Okay. So what do you think? Sneak or fight?"

I gave her a grim look. "I can't believe I'm saying this, but I vote sneak."

"All right then, ninja warrior. Let's do it."

The dragon was bigger than I remembered.

That was my first thought as we crept through the dark temple, entering the beast's inner lair. Atreus lay sleeping on a massive hoard of gold and jewels, his thick, scaly tail coiled around his body like a snake's. He was so large, in fact, he barely fit into the cramped space, and I wondered wildly how he could possibly be comfortable all squashed up like that. A totally ridiculous thought, I know.

But I wasn't exactly thinking straight. Too busy freaking out with fear.

I shot my sister a questioning look, wondering if she noticed the change, too. Had Atreus really grown bigger since we'd seen him last? Were his scales redder now—more blood-like—or was it just a trick of the light? His wings seemed longer, his tail thicker, his talons sharper.

As if evil had gotten an upgrade.

Suddenly, what seemed a totally doable plan down at the bottom of the mountain now seemed a craziness of epic proportions. What had we been thinking? We were just two kids—total noobs. And yet, here we were, hoping to take down the biggest, baddest dragon in all the land by ourselves.

This was so not going to end well.

Atreus stirred, rousing from his slumber. We dove behind a crumbling stone column, desperate to stay out of sight. My heart thudded madly in my chest as his eyes slid open, twin golden crescents shimmering in the darkness. A burst of steam shot from his snout as he yawned lazily, showing off a dark pit of razor-sharp teeth. Sweat dripped down my back. How could we ever hope to defeat such a creature?

But we had no choice. Everything came down to this.

I squeezed my hands into fists, trying to wake my inner hero. To remind myself that here, in this world, I was not Ian Rivera, twelve-year-old gamer geek from Austin, Texas, and real-life total wimp. Here, I was Lord Wildhammer, premier knight of the realm. Lord Wildhammer wouldn't be scared of some dumb old dragon. Lord Wildhammer would be chomping at the bit to slice its ugly head off and save the world.

Lord Wildhammer, it would seem, was a major idiot.

Atreus's eyes began to rove the chamber, and the walls seemed to close in on us, tighter and tighter with his every glance. When he reached our hiding spot, he stopped, his head cocked and his ears pricked.

I froze. Could he see us? Could he sense, somehow, that we were here? My heart beat so hard in my chest I was half convinced it would break a rib. What were we going to do? How were we going to survive this?

My sister reached out, squeezing my hand hard.

"Remember, it's only a game," she whispered.

But the thought wasn't as comforting as it should have been as my eyes fell to the dragon's belly, glowing a deep, dark red as it warmed with deadly fire.

Because this might be a game.

But one wrong move and it would be game over.

This time forever.

Well, well, tiny humans. It seems we meet again.

A cold chill shuddered through me at the familiar greeting, now spoken in a deep, throaty voice filled with menace. As I watched, frozen in place, the dragon slowly rose to his feet, gold and jewels falling from his body and plinking back to the pile below.

But I'm afraid you arrive too late. For the quest has already been completed by another.

My heart sank at his words. I hadn't realized how much I'd been holding out hope that Ikumi hadn't made it here yet—or that maybe she'd changed her mind about helping him. But the look on Atreus's face told me he wasn't bluffing, and suddenly my eyes caught a flash at the ridge on his back. Four stones—one red, one white, one blue, and one poop-colored, now embedded into his scales.

He had the Elemental Stones.

And we had nothing left to bargain with.

"Did you let Ikumi out, at least?" I blurted before I could stop myself, a small shred of hope still lingering inside me. If Ikumi was free she could get her father to send help. If she really was Hiro's daughter, that was. And if she even cared what happened to us. . . .

But the dragon only gave a lazy smile. *Of course not.*

I heard my sister gasp as I rose to my feet to face the dragon. I knew I should be scared, but somehow I was only angry. It wasn't fair. This was a game. It should follow rules. There should be a clear path to winning.

"But you promised!" I protested, stepping forward. My whole body was shaking, but I ignored it, squaring off with the deadly beast. "That was the reward for completing your quest!"

That was your *quest reward,* the dragon corrected. *Not hers. She—she can never leave this game.*

"Why not?" I demanded. Out of the corner of my eye I caught Lilli shaking her head violently from side to side, as if begging me to not argue with a creature who could simply end me with one breath. But I ignored her. I was done being lied to and manipulated by this game. I wanted answers. And I was not going to back down till I got them.

Atreus seemed to shrug. *None of the game's creatures are allowed to leave.*

"What are you talking about?" I demanded. "She's not one of the game's creatures. She's human. Like us. She's just playing virtually, that's all."

Atreus's mouth curved, as if he were in on a secret joke. *Are you sure about that?*

I faltered, my stomach dropping like a stone. *Was* I sure? I mean, I was sure she had *told* us she was human. But she had said a lot of things. And I had no way of knowing which of those things were true. What if she'd been lying to us all along—not just about being Hiro's daughter. But about everything else, too?

No. I shook my head. Ikumi was real. I knew she was. The way she looked at me, the way she laughed, the way the tears welled in her eyes when she was sad. The dragon was trying to trick me. To confuse me and upset me and make me unable to fight.

I wasn't going to let that happen.

"Where is Derek?" I demanded. "Free him, then! He's done nothing wrong!"

Atreus snorted, a plume of steam shooting from his snout, so hot it burned my skin. *The little bard?* he asked. *But I do so enjoy his songs. It will be such a shame when I have to finally eat him. I wonder if he will taste musical, too.*

That was it. With a yell of fury, I charged Atreus, sword raised and ready to swing. I got about halfway there before the dragon flicked his tail, sending it crashing down on a pile of gold and jewels. As if a bomb had gone off, the trinkets scattered across the temple like marbles. I tripped and crashed to the ground, dropping my sword in the process.

You should not have done that, Atreus growled.

"Oh I'll do a lot more," I snapped back, scrambling to my feet. "We will defeat you—one way or another."

Atreus laughed again. *Come, come, tiny human. You know as well as I that this will never happen. Now that I possess the Elemental Stones, even the makers themselves cannot take me down!*

And with that he gave a mighty, booming cry—loud enough that I had to block my ears. There was a tremendous groan, and the chamber's ceiling retracted, creaking open to reveal a wide passageway above, straight up and out of the mountain. The dragon shook out his wings, one by one, then locked his amber eyes on me.

Now if you'll excuse me, he said, *I have a reign of terror to begin.*

I watched, helpless, as Atreus pushed off on his hind legs, launching himself into the air. "You'll never get away with this!" I screamed after him.

He stopped, hovering above me, craning his neck to gaze back down. I probably looked like an ant to him from up there. A ridiculous, pathetic, angry ant.

But don't you see, tiny human? he purred. *I already have.*

And with that, he opened his mouth and blasted me full-on with his fire.

Chapter Forty-Five

"Ian! Ian! Wake up and drink this!!!"

I coughed, opening my eyes, but my vision was blurred. My whole body ached, as if I had been run over by a truck. When my eyes finally did clear, I was shocked to find Ikumi leaning over me, her eyes filled with concern, a vial of the red Gatorade-like stuff pressed to my lips.

I gulped it down greedily. Not that I wasn't still mad at her. But healing was healing.

"Don't try to move," she said. "I promise you'll feel better in a moment."

I frowned, struggling to sit up. I felt the rush of blood to my head and almost passed out from the effort. Once I was up, I glared at her, anger boiling inside me, as hot as Atreus's fire.

"What are you doing here?" I demanded. We were still

in the dragon's lair, surrounded by treasure. But the dragon himself was long gone. A few feet away I saw my sister passed out on the ground. "Lilli!" Horrified, I crawled over to her. Her skin was as red as a lobster's—she must have gotten caught in the cross fire. "Do you have any more of that stuff?"

Ikumi joined me at Lilli's side. She pulled another potion from her pack. Plucking out the stopper, she put the bottle to Lilli's lips while I jostled her, trying to rouse her so she could drink.

"Wake up, Lilli," Ikumi urged.

"Don't you even talk to her," I growled.

"I suppose I deserve that," Ikumi said softly.

"You deserve a lot more than that," I shot back. "You put a spell on us. You stole our stones. You handed them over to a monster! And now our cousin is going to be eaten by a dragon! And we'll be stuck here. Forever!"

Her face crumpled. "I know! And I'm sorry. I'm so sorry," she cried. "It's just . . . you don't understand. I didn't have a choice!"

"Why?" Lilli's voice was ice. She'd drank the medicine and was now sitting up, thank goodness. "Because you're one of them?"

Ikumi's jaw dropped. "What are you talking about?"

But I wouldn't let her trick us again. "Who are you, Ikumi? Who are you really?"

"I told you. I'm Hiro's daughter."

Lilli choked on a bitter laugh. "Are you, though? Or is that just another quest line? Trick the dumb humans into following you, then betray them at the last minute. Sure does up the game's tension, doesn't it?"

"What? No! That's not how it was at all!" Ikumi protested. "I told you the truth. I'm stuck in the game like you. I've been stuck in the game for two years." Her voice cracked. "You have no idea what it's been like. I've been so . . . lonely."

"And here I thought computer programs couldn't get lonely," Lilli shot back. Her skin had gone back to its normal color, and she looked as if she was going to be okay. "Yeah, that's right," she added when Ikumi shot her a tortured look. "We know all about you. Atreus told us you're one of them. *That's* why you're stuck in the game."

A horrifying thought struck me. What if Ikumi didn't know she was AI? What if she thought she was human all along, but was only now realizing that this wasn't the case?

But what did it matter? Human or computer, she had betrayed us. She had destroyed our one chance to get out of the game. And no healing magic was going to make that better.

Ikumi drew in a shaky breath. "Look," she said. "This isn't easy. But I can explain. If you'll listen for five seconds—"

"I think we've heard enough," Lilli snapped, struggling to her feet.

I opened my mouth to agree, but then I caught Ikumi's

expression. The pure sadness I saw welling in her eyes. Something uncomfortable squirmed in my stomach. I sighed.

"Fine," I said. "But make it quick."

Ikumi's shoulders sagged. "Right," she said. "Thank you. Um . . ." She gave a small, nervous laugh. "This isn't easy."

"Just tell the truth," I encouraged. "That's all we want." I could feel my sister giving me a skeptical look, but I ignored it.

Ikumi folded her hands in her lap. "It's true I am Hiro's daughter," she said slowly. "And it's true I was born with a rare genetic condition, which forced me to live my entire life in a sterile chamber so as not to get sick. In fact, the doctors never expected me to live past the age of five."

Her voice wobbled as she spoke and something odd began to tingle at the back of my neck. The way she was telling the story. Almost as if she was speaking in the past tense . . .

She continued, "When I was twelve, I got really sick. The doctors did all they could, but in the end, they told me I had two months to live.

"My father was devastated. He'd just lost my mom. Now he was going to lose his only child, too. And, well, in the end he decided he couldn't lose me. That he *wouldn't*. And so he did something about it." She paused, looking up, meeting my eyes with her own. "Have you ever heard of WBE? *Whole brain emulation?*"

I shook my head. "I don't think so."

"It's a new technology," Ikumi explained. "Very experimental. The idea is that you scan and map someone's mind, then upload it to a computer for safekeeping. This way the person's body can die while their brain lives on. Online."

I stared at her, my jaw dropping. "Are you trying to tell me your father uploaded you to the cloud?"

"No." She looked directly at me. "He uploaded me to the *game*."

"Oh my gosh," I whispered. "Are you serious?"

Suddenly everything started to fall into place. She'd said she'd been in the game for two years. Which meant she'd been dead for two years. And yet still living somehow— trapped in a world filled with monsters all by herself. I couldn't even imagine what that must have been like.

Ikumi lowered her eyes. "I begged him to upload me to the cloud. To set me free to explore the online world. But I guess he thought I was too young. Or that he'd miss me too much. I don't know. So instead of letting me wander the World Wide Web, he's trapped me in this closed server. I'm forced to live here, in the game, forever."

"Oh, Ikumi," my sister broke in. "I'm so sorry. We had no idea."

"At first it was okay," she said. "I'd never gotten to do anything in real life, so it was kind of thrilling to experience another world. One where I could be outside, doing all the things I'd never been able to do. But after a while? I got so lonely being by myself all the time. Sometimes my dad would come visit, but he's gotten really busy the closer they've gotten to launch. So when you found me in Ghost Hollow and told me your quest? I thought maybe I'd have a chance to escape the game, too! That maybe Atreus would set me free as well."

She shrugged miserably. "But then you decided to go against the new quest. To fight Atreus instead of handing over the stones, and I panicked. I thought I'd lose my one chance for freedom. But I should have known better." She gave a barking laugh. "I never had a chance at all."

Her voice was so sad, so void of hope. My heart ached at the sound of it. I couldn't even imagine what it must have been like for her these past two years, stuck in this game, with no hope of ever getting out. What had she been doing this whole time? With no books to read or TV to watch or video games to play. Well, besides the one all around her. And no one to hang out with. No wonder she'd been so excited when I called her my friend.

And no wonder she'd been so willing to do anything to escape this world.

"Look," Ikumi said. "I'm sorry for what I did. It was selfish and wrong. And I want to make it right—whatever I have to do. And while I know it'll be tough now that Atreus has the Elemental Stones, if you're up for trying, I'd be honored to fight at your side. Maybe I'll never get out of the game, but if I can help you escape . . . well, that would be something, at least. The chance to be a real friend." She peered at me, her eyes filled with a mixture of desperation and hope. "Please, Ian and Lilli? Will you give me that chance?"

I glanced at Lilli, even though I already knew the answer. "We can use all the help we can get. And we'd be honored to have you fight at our side."

SNIFF!

"So touching! So very, very touching! Forget *Ralph Breaks the Internet*! You guys are like *Infinity War*–level tearjerkers!"

I looked up, shocked to see Yano flying into the chamber, chomping on a grisly-looking bone. My sister shook her head.

"Nice of you to join us," she remarked wryly. "Hope you had a pleasant snack time while we nearly got burned to a crisp."

"Hey! Don't judge! A guide gets hungry!" Yano protested, landing on my head. "Also, I found something really interesting while I was foraging for food."

I raised an eyebrow. "A fried porg sandwich?"

"Better," Yano declared. "Your cousin."

Chapter Forty-Six

Yano led us through a dark stone passageway off of Atreus's lair and down a wide set of crumbling stone steps. At the bottom we found a large, round room filled with strange, misshapen cages that appeared to be made of sun-bleached bone. They were all empty—except for one.

"Derek!" I cried, excitement raging through me. He was curled up in a ball on the floor, sound asleep. "Wake up! We're here to rescue you!"

Derek shifted, blinking sleepily. As his eyes fell on us, he let out a huge, rip-roaring burp. "Finally!" he exclaimed, scrambling to his feet. "What took you so long?"

"You're welcome," Lilli muttered under her breath.

"Are you okay?" I asked, looking him over. He was still wearing his bard robes and his harp lay at his feet, but I didn't see any injuries.

"I'll be a lot better once I've eaten an entire pizza," Derek replied. "Extra cheese, extra sausage. Extra everything, really."

"May I suggest extra porg?" Yano chirped in. "Gives it such a lovely crunch."

Derek's eyes locked on the draconite. "What's with the rat with wings?"

"A rat?" Yano sputtered. "I am not a rat! I am not even a rat dragon!"

"Whatever, Ratty." Derek gripped the bars of his cage. "So are you going to get me out of this thing or what?"

Yano huffed loudly, landing on my shoulder. "You sure you don't want to just keep him in there?" he whispered. I stifled a laugh.

Lilli stepped forward while Ikumi and I hung back. "I'll do the honors," she said, gesturing for us to stand aside as she worked her magic. Soon the lock began to glow. A moment later, it shattered and the cage sprung open.

Derek whooped loudly. He reached down, scooping up his harp and attaching it to his belt before stepping out of the cage and into freedom. "Now let's get out of here!"

"So about that," I said uneasily. I'd almost forgotten, in my excitement over finding him, that we were still trapped. "That might not be so easy."

"What do you mean?" He scowled. "You gave the stones to Atreus, right? So he's going to let us out?"

"No," I said. "I mean, yes, he has the stones. But he's changed his mind about letting us free."

"What? That jerk! After all the music I played for him? I even made up some songs. Do you know how hard it is to make up songs when you're sitting in a cage, afraid for your life?"

"Trust me. We're not exactly happy about this, either," Lilli broke in. "You've been stuck in a cage this whole time, but we've been fighting for our lives."

"And the only way out now is to defeat Atreus," I added.

"No freaking way. I am not going up against that crazy robot thing." Derek crossed his arms over his chest. "Look. Thanks for the rescue. But I am so done with this stupid game. I'm going straight to the front gate and demanding they let me out. Or I'll totally sue them for kidnapping. They can't get away with this, you know! I have rights!"

I felt a stirring of pity as I watched him pace the room. Even though he was ranting angrily, I could hear a strong undercurrent of fear in his voice. He'd clearly been terrified in his cage, even if he'd never admit it to us. Suddenly I had the nearly overwhelming urge to hug him and tell him everything would be okay—that we were all scared. But I was pretty sure he'd punch me in the face if I tried something like that.

"Come on," Ikumi urged. "At least let's get out of Atreus's lair. Then we can regroup and figure out what to do. It's not safe here and we don't know when he'll be back."

Derek seemed to notice her for the first time. "Who's this?" he demanded. "Is she real? Or is she just another part of this sick game like Ratty here?"

Ikumi's expression faltered. I found myself stepping protectively in front of her. "She's real," I declared. Out of the corner of my eye I could see my sister shooting me a look, but I ignored her. "And Yano saved your life," I added. "So maybe a little gratitude? I know it's not really your thing, but—"

Derek snorted. "True." He looked up at the draconite. "And thanks, Ratty. I guess I owe you one or whatever. That cage stunk worse than Ian's soccer skills."

I sighed. "That's better. I think...."

Lilli made a move toward the door. "Now come on," she said. "Let's get out of here."

Chapter Forty-Seven

We headed out of the temple and climbed back through Mount Fearless. The trip was oddly quiet—without even a single trash mob to slow us down. It wasn't until we stepped out of the cave and back into the outside world that we realized why.

"Whoa," Lilli breathed.

From this vantage point we could see almost the entire island, and everywhere we looked there were fires and ice storms, landslides and floods. Entire towns had been buried in rubble. Giant trees had been pulled up by their roots and fields had been scorched. Total world apocalypse, as far as the eye could see.

"Atreus," I whispered. "He didn't waste any time, did he?"

Ikumi stepped up beside me, her eyes roving the virtual apocalypse spread before us. "What have I done?" she whispered. "This is all my fault."

"You didn't know," I reminded her, placing a hand on her arm.

"But you did." She scowled, yanking her arm away. "And you tried to warn me, but I didn't listen. I was only thinking of myself." She squeezed her eyes shut. "This is why my father trapped me here. I don't deserve to leave the game." She retreated to a small rocky outcropping and sank to her knees, covering her face with her hands.

I joined her there, crouching down next to her. "Come on," I said. "Don't freak out. It looks bad, yes. But I'm sure once your dad takes control of the game back from Atreus he can fix everything. Roll it all back to a past save point. It'll be like none of this ever happened."

She looked over at me. "Yes," she said. "But that will mean I'll need to be rolled back, too. Which means I won't remember any of this." Her eyes blurred with tears and her bottom lip wobbled. "Which means I won't remember you."

She was right. If they did roll back the game, Ikumi would lose all her memories of our time together. She would be alone, just like before, and she'd have no idea she'd ever had a real friend. My heart constricted. It wasn't fair. There had to be another way!

"No," I declared. "We won't let them roll you back. We'll play through this game. Defeat Atreus, finish our quest. And then he'll have to let us out. All of us . . . even you. No matter what, we won't leave you behind!"

Ikumi gave me a hopeful smile. "Really?"

"Of course! What are friends for?" I said, grinning.

She bowed her head. "You really are a good friend, you know that, Ian? The best friend I've ever had. Well, the only one," she said with a small laugh. "But I can't imagine anyone better."

"You're pretty great, too," I assured her, reaching over to give her a hug.

"Not to interrupt this magical moment," Lilli broke in. "But this whole fighting and beating Atreus thing? Not gonna happen. He's way too powerful. And we're not nearly high enough level."

"Speak for yourself!" Derek protested. "I'm level eighty. I don't think you can get any higher than that."

"What?" I demanded. "How is that even possible? You've been in a cage this whole time!"

"You told me to play music," he reminded me. "So I did. And every time I played a song, it would start casting de-buffs on all the worms and rats in the cave." He made a face. "Which I guess helps you level up or whatever."

"So . . . wait, you've been buffing bugs this whole time?" I asked in wonder. And here he hadn't wanted to trap ten rats.

"I played music," Derek corrected. "Which happened to buff bugs. Which gave me experience points. And levels." He shrugged as if it were no big deal.

"That's actually pretty amazing," Lilli exclaimed. "Here we were trying to avoid beginner quests so we could level faster and you literally grinded your way up to the top level while sitting in a cage." She held up a hand. "Way to go, dude!"

Derek reluctantly slapped her hand. "Whatever. It's not a big deal." But I could tell from a flash in his eyes that he was pleased. Who knew? Maybe we'd make a gamer out of our cousin yet.

"It doesn't matter," Yano broke in, dampening the mood. "You could all be level eighty and still not be able to defeat Atreus. Especially with him being in possession of the Elemental Stones."

"Ratty is right," Derek declared. "That dragon is bad news. It's like he knows our moves before we even make them."

"*Bard* boy is also right," Yano agreed, shooting Derek a look. "Atreus has complete access to all the game data. In fact, that was part of his original design. To learn each player's style and study their techniques from old *Fields of Fantasy* fights. So at this point he's already learned our strengths and weaknesses. And in the next fight, he'll use them to defeat us."

Derek rolled his eyes. "Well that's just great," he muttered. "So even if we were good enough, we wouldn't have a chance."

"Yup," Ikumi said with a sigh. "He's basically unbeatable."

"No." I shook my head. "He can't be unbeatable."

"But Ian," Lilli protested, "Yano said—"

"I know what he said, but I don't believe it. This is a

game. Which means there's got to be a way to win." I raked a hand through my hair, my mind racing through options. Atreus was stronger. He was faster. He knew all our moves before we made them—

I stopped short. *Wait. That's it!*

"What?" Lilli asked. "Did you think of something?"

I turned to my teammates, my heart thumping with excitement. "Look. We've been playing this game the same way all along, right? The same way we always played the online version back home. The way *everyone* plays. With a tank, a damage dealer, a healer, and a bard."

"I never once played with a bard," Lilli pointed out.

Derek scoffed. "What's your point, geek?"

"Easy. Atreus only knows how to play the game the way it's *supposed* to be played."

"So?" asked Ikumi.

"So..." I grinned. "We don't play the way we're supposed to."

Chapter Forty-Eight

We made a plan. A totally ridiculous plan no gamer in his or her right mind would ever think to try. And hopefully that no AI would ever think to anticipate. It was crazy, dangerous—probably foolish, too.

But maybe it would work.

It had to work. Because there was no plan B.

We decided to wait for the dragon at the summit of Mount Fearless instead of fighting him in the cramped confines of his lair. There, at the top of the volcano, was a wide ledge circling the deep volcanic pit. Atreus would have to fly right by here to get back down into his temple below. And when he did, we'd be ready for him.

Or, you know, as ready as we could be.

It didn't take long for him to return. My eyes caught his shadow, drifting across the twin suns. My heart started to drum in my chest, doubt attacking me from all sides. What were we doing? This was crazy! Absolutely crazy.

Then I looked at Ikumi. At the fierce determination etched on her face. I turned to my sister, who was crouched down like a cat, ready to spring. Derek had fingers on the strings of his harp. And Yano was in position high above in a tree.

Team Dragon Slayerz was ready to slay themselves a dragon.

And, drawing from my teammates' strength, so was I.

Atreus dropped from in the sky, coming into view. His crimson scales streaked across the horizon like a fiery comet. His wings thumped rhythmically—ominously.

I poked Derek in the arm. "Now's your chance, bard boy."

Derek clenched his jaw and ran his fingers along the strings, strumming a tune I didn't recognize. Music flowed from the harp, bathing us in a golden glow, and I felt new strength surge through me from his buff. I couldn't help a small grin of excitement as I skimmed my fingers against the dragon-crested breastplate of my wrath armor. This was it.

My eyes shifted to our foe. Atreus's ears had pricked at the first notes of music and he was now circling above us curiously. Sensing our chance, I gently pushed Derek out into the open, then dropped back into the trees where we'd made our hiding spot. Derek looked terrified, but to his credit, continued to play.

I squeezed my hand into a fist—a silent cheer as Atreus took the bait, drifting down to hover a few yards from the ground. In a normal fight, this would be our signal to attack, so we could get a few blows in before he realized what was going on. But Atreus would be expecting that, so instead we held back as Derek led the dragon, through song, to exactly where we wanted him to land.

Where Ikumi had set the trap.

Atreus dropped down to the ground, his feet so heavy they shook the mountain. But Derek kept his footing and kept playing, walking casually toward the snare. The dragon followed, mesmerized and distracted by the music.

How did you get out here, tiny bard? he asked. *Why are you not in your cage?*

"I just needed a little fresh air," Derek replied, his voice shaky. "I'll go back in a minute, I promise. I just want to finish this song." Still playing, he walked closer to the trap, the dragon now hot on his heels. I felt a surge of pride for my cousin. He might not be a gamer, but he was doing an awesome job.

I do not think— Atreus started to say. But before he could finish, his foot came down on the trap's perimeter. Derek leapt to the side as the snare exploded, flames bursting all around Atreus, locking him a fiery prison.

"Yeah!" Derek cried in triumph. "Not so tough after all, huh, dragon breath?"

Atreus roared in fury, thrashing about. Opening his

mouth, he blasted the flames with an icy stream, using the power of the Ice Stone embedded in his back. For a moment, the spray froze the fire in place, creating a wild ice sculpture around the dragon. Then he swiped it with his claws, shattering it into a million pieces.

And the dragon was free again.

But now I was right behind him. Springing into action, I drew my sword, slashing at his back, driving the weapon down through his thick scales. With my wrath armor's plus ten to damage dealing, along with the strength buff Derek had given me, I was able to do quite a bit of damage, and Atreus bellowed in pain as thick black blood gushed from his wound.

The dragon whipped around to find his attacker. I had to leap quickly to avoid being knocked over by his tail. His eyes locked on me and his mouth shot open, this time sending a flood of water gushing from his throat straight in my direction. I tried to hold my ground, but the blast was too strong and my wrath armor too weak, and I was knocked backward into the swell, my lungs filling with water. I choked and gasped, for a moment unable to breathe as the all-too-familiar panic from my childhood almost-drowning incident swept up inside me. But I pushed it back down—I was not going to let it stop me this time. And soon the water washed down the hill, leaving me on my butt, soaking wet but still alive, still breathing.

Of course normally this would be game over. With the

warrior knocked out of position, the dragon could take out the remaining party members with little trouble. But this time, the girls were ready for him. Lilli almost gleefully stepped into view, decked out in my tanking armor and looking supercool. Take that, game traditions!

"Hey, ugly!" she cried. "Time for another belly rub!"

She raised her staff. Lightning crackled, shooting out and hitting Atreus in the stomach. He roared as his scales danced with electricity, then opened his mouth to blast her with a bellyful of rocks and dirt, courtesy of Wyrm's earth magic. But Lilli wasn't wearing a tissue-paper robe anymore, and my armor allowed her to absorb the blow, giving her time to cast a second spell. Keeping the dragon's full attention on her while I ran back for my own round two.

I dove at the dragon, full Leeroy Jenkins–style. I was almost at him when he finally turned his attention from Lilli to me. In rage, he opened his mouth, ready to spew acid. Acid that my thin wrath armor couldn't protect me from.

But I wasn't about to let that happen. And I wasn't, as he assumed, going to attack him straight on. Instead, I dove under his legs, sliding beneath his undercarriage, where he couldn't reach me.

And I stayed there.

Atreus shifted, clearly confused. I'd made a play he wasn't expecting and, thanks to a speed buff from Ikumi, I'd moved too fast for him to register where I'd gone. I could see him shifting above me, searching the area. But his search was interrupted as Ikumi stepped in behind him, casting a drain-life spell at his back, using his own hit points to heal Lilli, who was still up front, working as a tank.

And now it was Derek's turn.

"Die, you overgrown gecko!" my cousin shouted as he leapt off the scrubby tree he'd climbed while we were attacking, and landed directly on the dragon's back. Atreus roared, trying to shake him off, but Derek held on tight. I rolled out from under the dragon to avoid getting crushed, dashing for the same tree Derek had leapt from. Lilli and Ikumi soon joined me, and together we watched our cousin ride the dragon as if it were his own brand of roller coaster.

With a mighty roar, Derek grabbed the Ice Stone, wrenching it from its socket on the dragon's back. Then he threw it in our direction, allowing Lilli to scoop it up. Next came the Water Stone, which Ikumi caught easily. And, just my luck, here came the Earth Stone—dropping right into my arms.

I'd never been so thrilled to be holding poop.

But right as Derek reached for the last stone, Atreus managed to bat him hard with his wing, sending him flying off the dragon and crashing to the ground. He lay in a heap, unable to get up.

"Derek! Are you okay?"

He groaned and pulled his arm out from under his

stomach, flashing me a weak thumbs-up. I breathed out, relieved. Derek might be down for now, but he'd done his job. Now we were back where we started: in possession of three of the four Elemental Stones.

Finally—we had a fair fight.

Chapter Forty-Nine

My armor glowed brown as the Earth Stone pulsed in my hand. (Yes, *that* color brown. I don't want to talk about it.) I felt a surge of power well inside me as my in-game menu suddenly updated with a multitude of awesome spell options big enough to take down a dragon.

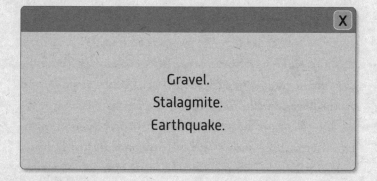

X

Gravel.
Stalagmite.
Earthquake.

I grinned. *Oh yeah. Let's get this ground shaking.* I turned to my sister and Ikumi. Their robe and armor were also glowing white and blue respectively. "Are you guys ready?" I asked. "On the count of three...

"One...two...three!"

We cast our spells. Earthquake, ice storm, tsunami. Atreus bellowed in surprise as all three elements hit him at once. The ground rocked, icy spikes dropped down from the sky, and a huge wave rolled out of nowhere, knocking his bleeding body to the ground. His hit points plummeted to single digits.

"Yes!" I cried. "It's working! Again!"

I accessed my menu, ready for round two. Unfortunately, the large spell I'd cast also had a long cool-down time, which meant I couldn't cast it again for at least another minute. I glanced at the girls; the looks on their faces told me their countdowns were similar. To make matters worse, the spell had drained all of my stamina. Meaning I had no energy left to even lift my sword.

"Oh no!" Lilli cried. "He's healing himself!"

Sure enough, Atreus's body began to glow with a brilliant green, indicating he was casting a healing spell. His hit points began to climb again.

Despair sank in my stomach. It hadn't been enough. Even with three stones and our unconventional fighting style, it still hadn't been enough to bring him down, or even weaken him for more than a few seconds. And now *we* were weakened. Unable to cast or fight. It wouldn't take Atreus long to get back to full power. And when he did . . .

Game over.

Suddenly Ikumi turned to me. She grabbed my forearms with her hands, meeting my eyes with her own. I could see the glitter dancing madly in her deep pupils.

"Ian . . ." she breathed, then trailed off, looking anguished.

"What is it?" I asked, fear throttling my voice.

"I just wanted to let you know," she said. "My real name is Mirai."

I stared at her, unable to speak. A bashful smile creased her face as she leaned forward and kissed me lightly on the cheek. Then, dropping her hands from my forearms, she drew the sword from my belt. Before I could stop her, she ran at the dragon straight on, screaming at the top of her lungs.

"You will leave my friends alone!" she cried, slashing down at Atreus. The blade swung true, connecting with Atreus's snout and slashing off the end of his nose. Black blood gushed from the wound, splashing onto Ikumi's—no, Mirai's—face and robe. But she didn't back away. Instead she swung again, fully consumed with rage and power, this time hitting the dragon square in the jaw.

Atreus roared, swiping at her with his claws. I screamed in horror as the impact sent her flying through the air, then crashing down to the ground with a sickening thud. Atreus stalked after her, snarling and snapping his teeth.

"Ian!" I could vaguely hear my sister's voice. "Use your stone! Now!"

Oh, right. I shook my head, trying to focus. Sure enough, Mirai's distraction had been enough; we could use our powers again. My whole body shaking, I raised the Earth Stone....

BOOM!

The spell went off a like a bullet, a large, rocky spike shooting up from the ground right under Atreus and spearing him in the belly. He bellowed in surprise and pain and tried to launch himself back in the air. But for the moment, he was literally pinned to the earth.

I turned to Lilli. "Finish him!" I cried.

With grim determination, Lilli nodded and raised her own stone. Ice blasted from her fingers, shooting out at the trapped dragon and freezing him solid. Then, with another wave of her hand, the ice exploded, shattering the creature into a million pieces. I had to duck, hands over my head, so as not to get stabbed by shards of ice.

"Fatality!" Lilli declared, quoting *Mortal Kombat.* "Mage Adorah wins!"

I lifted my hands from my head, my heart still pounding in my chest so hard I was half convinced I would crack a rib. But the dragon was gone and my game menu was going crazy, racking up experience points and levels. I rose back to my feet, staring at my sister in disbelief.

Had we done it? Had we actually beaten the game?

"Dude, that was awesome!" Derek cried, running over to us. He looked battered and bruised, but somehow okay. He even still had his harp, though it appeared to be missing a few strings. "I totally thought we were goners there."

"Yeah, well, we couldn't have done it without you," Lilli pointed out. "That was awesome, jumping onto his back like that and grabbing those stones."

"Totally," I agreed. "Turns out you're quite the gamer!"

Derek scrunched up his face. "Please don't ever repeat that in public."

"Um, guys?" Yano's voice suddenly interrupted. The draconite dropped down from the tree he'd been hiding in during the fight. His face was grave and for once he didn't crack a joke. Instead, he gestured his wing to the crumpled figure lying a few feet away.

My heart stuttered. *Ikumi!*

I raced over to her and dropped to my knees. Her body was so still she looked like a rag doll that had been tossed away. My throat constricted as I put an ear to her mouth, trying to feel for a whisper of breath. But I felt nothing. Not a single breath or pulse or heartbeat. Did her heart ever beat to begin with in the game? There was so little I knew about her, I realized. Up until the last moment, I hadn't even known her real name.

Mirai . . .

A wrenching sob ripped from my throat. "You idiot!" I cried, wanting to shake her. "Why did you do that? Why did you run at the dragon?"

"She saved us," Lilli said quietly, coming up behind me and putting a hand on my shoulder. "We would have all been dead if it weren't for her. She saved us . . . and the world."

I looked up. Sure enough, the world of Dragon Ops was no longer a cataclysmic disaster. The fires had gone out. The villages had been restored. Trees and flowers were bursting into bloom. Atreus's reign of terror was over.

But so was Mirai's life.

I closed my eyes, my chest heavy. She'd wanted so badly to be free of the game. I hoped at least now she was.

"Please step aside," a deep voice broke in.

I turned, shocked to see none other than Hiro Takanama standing behind us, wearing his dragon robes and carrying his staff. His face was grave. How had he gotten in here? And *was* he really here? Or had he logged in virtually from back in Dragonshire?

I stepped aside, though half of me wanted to punch him in the face. What he'd done, locking his daughter into the game like that! And now—what if she was actually dead?

I glanced down at her body, tears flowing down my cheeks unchecked. She didn't deserve this. She hadn't deserved any of this.

"Is she okay?" Lilli asked as Hiro bent down to examine his daughter.

"I don't know," he replied, not looking up. "Her file has been corrupted. I'll have to run some diagnostics back at the base." He raked a hand through his hair and I could tell he was fighting back tears. He didn't want to tell us how bad it was.

But it was bad. Really bad. I could see it in his eyes.

I stared down at Mirai. She looked so still, so pale. As if she were nothing more than a ghost. And maybe that wasn't so far off. After all, the real Mirai had died a long time ago. This girl—Ikumi—had been only the computerized shell of who she used to be.

But still . . . she had been my friend. My true friend.

Rage flowed through me, hot as the lava in Mount Fearless. My gaze snapped to Hiro. "How could you do this?" I demanded. "To your own daughter!" My hands balled into fists. "You're a monster. A total monster."

Hiro turned away, avoiding our accusing eyes. "You don't understand," he said quietly.

"Understand what? That you trapped your own daughter in a video game against her will?" I cried, not willing to let him off the hook. Sure, he was upset. But this was his fault!

"What else was I supposed to do?" Hiro snapped. "She was all I had left."

I could hear the devastation in his voice. He loved Mirai. That was clear. But to do what he did . . .

"Do you even know what the last two years of her life have been like? Trapped in a world she doesn't belong in, all alone, unless you somehow find the time to fit in a quick visit? All she wanted to do was get out of this game. And she was willing to risk everything to do it." I swallowed down the huge lump that had formed in my throat. "And now look at her. Is this what you wanted?"

Hiro buried his head in his hands. "I'm so sorry," he cried. But he was talking to her now, not me. "You tried to tell me. But I was too selfish to listen. I wanted more time—twelve years is not nearly enough. But I never wanted to hurt you. I swear!" He pounded his chest with his hands. "Oh, what have I done?"

I glanced over at my sister. Her face was white and tears streaked down her cheeks. Derek looked stone-faced, as well. I opened my mouth to suggest we give them some space. But before I could, I felt hands at my back.

And at last, my goggles were pulled from my head.

Chapter Fifty

Dizziness gripped me with icy fingers, spinning me around until I dropped to my knees. Vomit rose to my throat and I couldn't keep it in. I spewed all over the ground—a nastiness that looked a lot like half-digested protein bars.

"Ew," Derek said. "You got puke on my Jordans."

I blinked, trying to clear my vision. When my eyes finally focused, I looked up, my jaw dropping as I saw Uncle Jack, dressed in a pair of slouchy jeans and a black T-shirt that read I WILL NOT FIX YOUR COMPUTER. Beside him stood Lilli and Derek, no longer their game characters but their real selves, dressed in their SensSuits.

I let out a cry of surprise, scrambling to my feet. I threw myself at Uncle Jack, hugging him like crazy. "You're here! Are you really here?" I babbled in his ear. I'd never been so happy to see someone in my entire life.

"Hey!" he protested, laughing. "It's good to see you, too. You've all given us quite the scare!"

I pulled away from the hug, my eyes going to the world itself, now naked under my real vision. It looked so much smaller than it had when we were in the game. Not much bigger than a regular theme park. I thought back to the hours it had taken to cross each land or climb each mountain. But the true distance was barely the length of a couple football fields or the height of a small hill. Crazy.

It also looked so normal. Gone were the colorful trees, the twin suns, the crazy animals. Now it was a boring old island, save for a few wooden structures that served as the villages and a lot of shiny metal sensors. At the very far shore I glimpsed the island's power source: what appeared to be thousands of solar panels lined up in rows.

I turned back to our mountaintop. Clearly a fake volcano carved out of plaster. Small metal parts of various sizes littered the ground, as if a car had exploded.

No, not a car, my mind corrected. *A dragon*. Atreus in his real-life form.

"I bet they regret giving this guy a destruct button," Uncle Jack remarked, shaking his head. "It's going to take them weeks to put him back together."

"You cannot put Atreus back together!" I cried, my mind flashing back to the dragon's dark, glittering eyes. The fire sparking on his tongue. "He's evil!"

"He's a robot, Ian," Uncle Jack corrected, giving me a fond smile. "Robots can't be evil. They just follow their programming."

"But he locked us in the game! He made it real-life hurt when we got wounded!"

"Actually, *that* was Eugene."

"What? What are you talking about?" Lilli sputtered.

Uncle Jack sighed. "It seems Eugene was unhappy in his position here at Dragon Ops and became a corporate spy for the *Camelot's Honor* company. They're hoping to introduce a similar mixed-reality theme park on an island off of Costa Rica, and the two companies have been racing to see who could open first. Eugene was meant to sabotage us and keep us from opening. He figured if he could make the AI seem to go crazy and hurt some kids, we'd never get the insurance clearance to open the park."

"See?" I pointed out to Lilli, remembering our trivia quest. "I told you *Camelot's Honor* was no good."

Uncle Jack gave me a rueful smile. "I'm just sorry you guys had to be the ones to get caught in the cross fire. Literally."

Lilli wrinkled her brow, trying to understand. "So... none of this was Atreus?"

"Nope. It was all Eugene. He tampered with the barbeque the night before so all the regular employees were sick with food poisoning, giving him the opportunity to leave you alone in the game. At the same time, he attacked our servers with a nasty virus so we couldn't contact you, or jack in virtually to find you and let you know what was going on."

"Why didn't you come try to get us out?"

"He changed all the gate codes and electrified them. We called in for a helicopter from the mainland so we could fly over and get you. But..." He glanced at his watch. "It's probably arriving right about now, actually."

"Wait. How long were we in here for?" I asked.

"About eight hours? Give or take."

I shook my head in disbelief. Wow. Eight hours? So much had happened. My life—changed forever. All in such a short period of real time.

"How did you find out it was Eugene?" Lilli asked.

"One of our crew—a vegetarian who didn't eat the barbeque—caught him trying to stow away on the ferry and escape the island. It didn't take long after that to discover his trail. He was good—but messy. His fingerprints were all over Atreus's new code."

"What a jerk. We could have died!" Lilli declared.

"Believe me, I know," Uncle Jack said, his face sobering. "And I'm so sorry, guys. I never, ever, would have sent you in here if I had any idea what could happen." He choked out a laugh. "Your mom is going to kill me."

"Only if we tell her," I said with a shrug.

"Yeah," Lilli agreed. "After all, how else are we going to get her to let us come back?"

"You want to come back?" Uncle Jack raised an eyebrow. "After all that happened?"

Lilli and I exchanged a glance. "Maybe?" I said. "After the bugs are worked out?"

"Yeah, well, that may take a while," Uncle Jack replied, staring out over the vacant landscape. I thought back to what it had looked like under my goggles. It had been so beautiful. Terrifying at times—but amazing.

And real, I thought, suddenly remembering the glowworm cave. On some level, it had been real.

I glanced over at the spot where Mirai had been lying. Of course she wasn't there anymore; she'd never been there in "real life." But I was surprised to see Hiro wasn't there, either.

"Where's Hiro?" I asked Uncle Jack.

"He's back at the base," he explained. "Once Atreus was destroyed, control of the game kicked back to us, and he was able to log in virtually so he could reach you faster. Meanwhile, I had to hike over the old-fashioned way." He shook his head. "You guys trekked halfway across the island, you know."

"Trust us, we know!" Lilli groaned, shaking out her sore feet.

But I didn't join her. Instead, I found myself stepping over to the spot where I'd last seen Mirai. My stomach twisted as I stared down at the empty space. Just seconds ago, she'd been lying there, crumpled and broken. As broken as the rest of the game. I shook my head, wanting to erase those memories. To instead think of her brilliant smile. Her kind, searching eyes. The way she reached for my hand when she knew I was afraid. How warm that hand felt, brushing my own.

She had been real, too. More real than some people would ever be in so-called real life.

And she had been my friend.

"Are you okay, Ian?" Lilli asked, coming up behind me. I looked up at her, my eyes misting with tears.

"I miss her already," I said.

Lilli pulled me into a hug. "Me too," she agreed. "But . . . maybe this is for the best? She didn't want to be trapped in the game. And now she's probably free. That's what she wanted all along, right?"

I nodded, feeling the tears slip from my eyes. "I hope she finally finds some peace."

"Hey, guys?"

We broke from the hug, turning to find Derek standing behind us.

"Yeah?" I asked curiously.

For a moment, he didn't answer. His gaze dropped to the ground and he shuffled from foot to foot before speaking. "Um, I just wanted to . . . thank you, I guess. For rescuing me," he mumbled in a low voice. "I know you didn't have to. You could have left me there. And you probably should have . . . I mean, I've been kind of a jerk."

Lilli raised an eyebrow. "Kind of?"

Derek's face turned beet red. "Okay, fine. I'm a total jerk, okay? It's just . . . I don't know. How do you think I feel? Knowing that my dad would rather hang out with you than me." He dropped his voice on the last part, scowling over at his father, who had gone over to check on the Atreus wreckage.

"That's not true!" I protested.

He rolled his eyes. "Come on, dude. You know it is. You get all this stuff. You love it. And he was so excited to show you. I knew that was why he really dragged me here instead of leaving me home with Grandma. Because that way he had an excuse to bring you."

I stared at him. Was that really why Derek had been so mean to me this whole time? Not because he thought I was a geek or super uncool? But because he was jealous of me getting his dad's attention?

"Dude, I'm sorry," I said. "I didn't know."

Derek waved me off. "Whatever," he said. "It ended up being kind of cool. Not the being captured by the dragon part. That blew. But kicking the dragon's butt?" He shrugged sheepishly. "Better than any roller coaster ever."

I grinned slowly, slapping him on the back. "Derek, my friend," I said, "we might make a gamer out of you yet."

Epilogue

treus stirred, rousing from his slumber. His eyes slid open, twin golden crescents shimmering out from the darkness. Clutching my shield, I drew my sword....

"Get him!" Lilli cried. "Now!"

I dove in for the kill, ready to hack and slash and decimate him where he stood. But the dragon was ready for me, exhaling a blast of pure fire in my direction. I screamed as the white-hot flames hit me, melting my armor in an instant, and a moment later I found myself on the ground, utterly annihilated.

"Aw, man!" I slammed my fist against the keyboard. "I totally thought we had him this time."

Lilli threw herself back on the couch. "Ugh. He's the worst," she groaned. "We are never going to get him down."

"Want to try again?" I asked.

She set her laptop onto the coffee table. "Sure. Let me

grab a snack first," she said. "You want anything? Protein bar? Giant gummy bear, maybe?" Her eyes twinkled.

I laughed. "I'm good. Thanks."

Once Lilli was gone, I turned back to my own computer. I selected REVIVE on the screen, and a moment later Lord Wildhammer appeared, resurrected, in a graveyard. Which was nowhere near Mount Fearless, unfortunately. We had a long run back if we wanted another chance to beat the boss.

At least we didn't have to run back on our real-life feet.

Yes, we were playing video games the old-fashioned way again, with a mouse and keyboard. Lilli and I had been hard at work trying to beat the latest *Fields of Fantasy* expansion-pack missions from the comfort of home. It was a piece of cake, really, now that we'd survived the real-life version. And we'd even finally gotten good enough to attempt to take on the dragon Atreus.

Defeating him, however, that was another story.

It'd been over a month since our adventure in Dragon Ops, and half the time it felt as if the whole thing had been one giant dream. They'd had to postpone the park's opening. Eugene had been arrested and was awaiting trial. The company had worked overtime on damage control, however, and nothing ever trended on Twitter or showed up on the front page of the news. Sure, there were some conspiracy theories on various Reddit boards about why the park opening was delayed, but none came close to the truth. Which was fine by me. Especially since they'd had to pay us obscene amounts of money to keep us from sharing our story. (Which our parents promptly stashed away for college—though I did manage to sweet-talk my way into a new laptop.)

Now everything was basically back to normal, with going to school during the day and playing video games at night. And sometimes even doing real-life stuff with Lilli, too! But there was one thing that was still bugging me. One thing I couldn't let go.

What had happened to Ikumi?

Or Mirai, I guess—I was still trying to get used to thinking of her by that name. I'd asked Uncle Jack so many times, but he had no idea. And Hiro never returned my emails. She wasn't mentioned in any of the court documents I'd read through, either. It was as if she had been totally forgotten.

But I hadn't forgotten her. I would never forget her.

"Well, well, if it isn't my favorite nooblet!"

The sound of the familiar voice in my headphones jerked me back to the present. I did a double take as none other than Yano himself flew across my computer screen and landed on a tree branch near Lord Wildhammer. He peered at my avatar, then gave an impressed whistle.

"You look fancy!" he declared, taking in my character's shiny new wrath armor.

I grinned. "Not such a noob anymore, huh?"

"You'll always be a noob in my eyes," Yano assured me. "But that's only because I'm so excellent. In fact, I'm pretty sure you'd be dead if it weren't for me. And yet, I'm still waiting for my medal of valor. Do you think it got lost in the post?"

Good old Yano. "What are you doing here, anyway?" I asked. "How did you get out of Dragon Ops?"

"Oh, didn't you know? I got a new gig! And by the way, my name isn't Yano anymore. She decided to change it. Which is totally her right. Though I do wish she had come up with something a little more fitting. I mean, *Sir Sparkles*? Really? Doesn't exactly instill fear in the heart of one's enemies."

"I think it's cute," I told him. The draconite rolled his eyes.

"In any case, while I'd love to stay and chat, I'm actually here on official business. If you would follow me?" He gestured with his wing.

Frowning, I reached for my mouse and placed my other hand back on the keyboard, allowing Lord Wildhammer to follow Yano—er, Sir Sparkles—down the path and away from Mount Fearless.

"Where are we going?" I asked.

"Not far. There's someone who wants to see you."

We stopped at the shore of a small lake. My eyes widened as I realized it was the same lake we'd stumbled on outside the Cave of Terrors. Where Mirai had betrayed us. My heart started thudding in my chest. Someone wanted to see me. Could it really be … her?

"Lord Wildhammer. We meet again."

I almost fell out of my chair as a familiar figure stepped onto the screen. She'd changed her hair again; this time it was long and silver and woven into a combination of braids with purple flowers. Her eyes were a deep black, dusted with starlight.

But it was her. It could be no one but her.

"Mirai," I breathed, my heart stuttering in my chest. She was alive! She hadn't died in the fight! My fingers hovered on the keyboard, wondering if I should type the HUG command or if that would be weird.

The girl behind the monitor gave me a bashful smile. "Funny. I almost forgot I told you my real name."

"I thought you were dead," I blurted out, feeling stupid the second I said it. "I mean, dead again?" I groaned. "I'm still really bad at this, aren't I?"

She laughed. "You're the worst," she agreed. "But no, I'm not dead—well, not like that at least. And even better, I'm not trapped in Dragon Ops anymore. I don't know what you said to my father, but after he was able to repair my character profile, he told me he was sorry for what he'd done. And he gave me a choice. He could delete my file entirely and let me die once and for all, or he could release me to the cloud and set me free." Her smile widened. "I guess you can tell which I chose."

I smiled back at her, even though I knew she couldn't

see it. "I'm so glad!" I cried. "I was so worried about you. Are you okay now? Do you like being free?"

She did a little twirl on the screen. "Oh, Ian. It's everything I ever hoped for and more. The entire world is at my fingertips now. I can be in Tokyo one moment, then in your game the next. And the knowledge! So much knowledge out there, and I have access to all of it. And an eternity to spend learning." Then she sobered. "Though it can be a bit lonely at times. I am the only one of my kind—at least as far as I can tell."

"Well, you can always come visit me," I declared. "I'll keep you company. And maybe you can help us beat Atreus again?" I grinned. "Team Dragon Slayerz reunion tour?"

She laughed. "Anytime. But for now, I must depart. I've got a date with a sunset in Saint Tropez. They livestream from a little sailboat in the harbor and it's simply breathtaking. I never miss it."

"Sounds awesome," I said. "Take some screenshots and send them to me."

"Absolutely." She leaned over, giving Lord Wildhammer a small kiss on the cheek. "Good-bye for now, Ian. And thank you. Thank you for everything."

And with that, she logged out, her avatar disappearing into thin air. But I didn't feel sad this time, because a moment later a box popped up on my screen, informing me she'd added me to her friends list. Which meant she wasn't gone forever. She was out there, happy for maybe the first time in her life. That was all that mattered.

I closed out of the game, staring at my computer, thinking back to everything that had happened. I'd wanted an adventure. And I'd gotten one. But I had to admit, it was good to be back home to the boring—

"Ian!"

I turned around as Derek barged into the game room. I hadn't seen him too much since we'd gotten back. But when I did, he'd been nicer than he had been before. No more geek jokes. No more put-downs. And though I wasn't sure, I suspected he was even secretly playing video games. Not that he'd ever admit that to me.

"What is it?" I asked, curious. He looked out of breath, even sweaty. Had he run all the way here from his house down the street?

"My dad just called from the island," he said. "I've got good news . . . and not so good news."

"Okay . . ."

Derek swiped his forehead with his hand. "The good news is—well, Mirai. Evidently her dad let her out of the game! He opened some back door on the server or whatever and set her free on the cloud."

I smiled to myself, glancing over at my computer screen. "That's so great," I said, trying my best to sound surprised. I didn't want to burst his bubble by telling him I'd already heard this particular piece of good news—from Mirai herself. "She must be so . . . happy."

I felt pretty happy, too, I realized. And I really hoped she'd keep her promise to come visit me sometime. After all, we were friends, right? And friends obviously hung out.

"Yeah. Except. . ." Derek made a weird face. "There's . . . more."

I frowned, unease suddenly worming through my stomach. I'd almost forgotten the "not so good" news part to his annoucement. "What is it?"

He swallowed hard. "It's Atreus," he said. "He's gone."

Huh? I cocked my head in question, confused. "Yeah. Of course he's gone. He exploded into a million pieces, remember?"

"That was just his game form. But the AI controlling him? He's still very much alive—well, as much as an AI can be alive. And"—Derek paused dramatically—"he's disappeared."

A chill tripped down my spine. "I don't understand. What do you mean, 'disappeared'?"

"Well, they don't know for sure. But they think when Hiro opened the back door to let his daughter out? Atreus somehow managed to escape, too."

"Whoa." I stared at my computer screen, then back at my cousin. "So . . . he's just out there, somewhere on the cloud? And no one knows where he is?"

"Yup. And I'm guessing he's pretty mad."

"AIs can't get mad," I said automatically. But then I thought of Atreus. And I wondered.

Derek looked relieved. "Oh, right. Duh," he said. "And here I was thinking he might try to come after us or something. But that's crazy, right? Like you said, he's a computer program. Computers don't seek revenge."

"Yeah," I said slowly, staring at my computer screen, heart thumping in my chest. "Computers definitely don't seek revenge."

"Anyway," Derek said with a shrug. "I'm headed out to kick the ball around. You want to join me?"

I looked up. Was he joking? But no. He looked serious.

"Sure," I said, surprising myself with my answer. "Give me ten minutes."

Derek clapped his hands once. "Cool! I'll be outside."

I turned back to my computer, staring at the home screen for a moment. Then I reached to turn off my monitor.

"Computers don't seek revenge," I repeated quietly as I got up from my seat, ready to head downstairs to join Derek.

But just as I reached the door, my eyes caught a flash of light from behind me. I frowned. Had my monitor turned back on? Slowly, I turned around.

My eyes widened. My mouth dropped open.

No.

It couldn't be.

"What's going on?" Lilli asked, walking into the room with a plate of cookies. She saw my face. "What's wrong, Ian? You look like you've seen a ghost."

With a shaky hand, I pointed to the screen. Her eyes followed my finger. She dropped the plate of cookies and they crashed to the ground.

But I barely noticed, because I was still staring at my monitor. Or, more specifically, at the white star spinning across the screen. And the words scrolling beneath it.

Want to play again?

Acknowledgments

This book could not have been possible without the hard work and all-around awesomeness of those at Disney Hyperion. From Kieran Viola, my editor, for always pushing me to the next level—pun totally intended!—to Tyler Nevins for his amazing cover design (seriously, it is SO cool!), to Cassidy Leyendecker for all the behind-the-scenes magic, and to Melissa Lee, Seale Ballenger, and the rest of the publicity, marketing, and sales team as well as Dina Sherman for all your work with libraries and schools—there's no better superpower than getting the right book into a child's hands.

I would also like to thank my agent, Mandy Hubbard, who got excited about this book the very first time I shared the idea with her. Thank you for making it become a reality! And to my tireless and amazing author assistant,

Sarah Simpson Weiss, who somehow manages to keep me sane and on task—thank you for all you do!

This book would also not have been possible without the hours of brainstorming sessions with Diana Peterfreund and Kyla Linde. I'm pretty sure half of it was plotted out while we waited in line for the *Frozen* ride at EPCOT. (They also want you to know that the title was *totally* their idea!) I'm lucky to have such amazing author-besties in my court.

Thanks to Jennifer Lynn Barnes, who knows all and isn't afraid to give it to you straight. Your pep talks are the stuff of legend. And to my Texas author friends, especially the ladies of the Lodge of Death Writer's Retreat—I'm so lucky to have such creative, smart women in my life.

Thank you to all the awesome booksellers and librarians out there who work tirelessly to put books into young readers' hands. With a special shout-out to rock-star booksellers Eugenia Vela and Meghan Goel at BookPeople. (Pepperoni pizza for everyone!)

Also, thank you to my amazing family. My wonderful husband, Jacob, our smart, talented, tiny dancer, Avalon, and my extended Mancusi and Beach family members as well. I couldn't do this without your support and love.

And lastly, thank you to all my fellow gamers and readers out there. May you always slay your dragons—both online and in real life!

© Sam Bond Photography

MARI MANCUSI always wanted a dragon as a pet. Unfortunately, the fire insurance premiums proved a bit too large and her house a bit too small, so she chose to write about them instead. A former Emmy Award–winning TV news producer, she now works as a full-time author, having published over two dozen books for kids, teens, and adults. When not writing, Mari enjoys traveling, cosplay, watching cheesy (and scary) horror movies, and playing video games. A graduate of Boston University, she lives in Austin, Texas, with her husband, Jacob, daughter, Avalon, and their two dogs.